D1040100

THE NIGHT POLICE

BEYOND THE LINE OF DUTY

CHRIS BERG
PAUL JAMES SMITH

ISBN: 978-1-54399-686-9 (print)
ISBN: 978-1-54399-687-6 (ebook)

Dedication

The Night Police is dedicated to our fathers, James C. Smith, and Gil Berg. They served together in World War II, in the Pacific. Though they never met, they fought on the same islands and faced the same enemy with unimaginable resolve. It is our heartfelt belief that they passed on to us, their grit, piss and vinegar, and perhaps a touch of their courage.

INTRODUCTION

In the 1970s Apple was founded, President Richard Nixon resigned following the Watergate scandal, and Hollywood released *Star Wars*, *The Godfather*, and *The Exorcist*.

In the 80s, Ronald Reagan was elected, John Lennon was gunned down in New York City, and the Black Monday market crash stained the economy.

The decade of the 90s saw the launch of the World Wide Web and the information age. *Seinfeld* and *Friends* shaped a new view of modern relationships, and O.J. Simpson was acquitted of ghastly murders in "the trial of the century."

Law enforcement of the late 20th century bore little resemblance to current policing in America. The customs, the words, and the rhythm of policing was different back then.

The political structures, while annoying as hell, did not pin a target on police officers as they routinely do today. There were even a few instances of political support for the men and women in blue. Albeit, rarely.

The fabric of our nation was a different animal too. It was one that still seemed, for the most part, to embrace the construct of law and order. The media still had a smattering of journalists on the payroll. Political and personal agendas, while still the rule, were more nuanced, less in your face. The educational system, already failing, had not put politics, unions, and aggressive social agendas above schooling our youth.

Social media had not come along yet to give an out-of-context view into the often violent and very human world of policing. We had not yet developed the systems to spew hatred in all of its forms from behind the shield of anonymity.

Some say it was a simpler time, and there's truth in that. It may have been simpler, but policing our streets was still a dangerous endeavor that required uncommon and often extraordinary men and women to pull it off. Just as it does today.

The voice of *The Night Police* is that of these men and women, the ones who rode out the final chapters of the millennia. We have, as faithfully as memory will allow, tried to recreate that voice, to give the reader an inside listen into their conversations. What cops thought about their job, the crooks, and their communities. And we could not tell these stories without attending to the victims. Those who were without a voice, just as they are today.

These are the harsh, honest words that have not been dumbed down for politically correct consumption. The edges have not been ground smooth to avoid abrasive thoughts or suspect tactics.

These men and women who claimed law enforcement as their career were routinely exposed to the unthinkable. Many of them found distance from these experiences and emotions by embracing a new family, in this case, the kinship of the Night Police. This fraternity helped shield them from the intense pressures of urban policing. This is a chronicle of that association and the events, decisions, and risks that forged these law enforcement lives.

Cops then, and we suspect now, lived in a cocoon-world borne of security and brotherhood. A world designed by them to support them and keep them at least at the edge of sanity. Limited success did not indicate their system didn't work.

There is no Bristol City or BCPD. The characters are fictional but were inspired by those who lived and served their communities. The narratives have, in all cases, been adapted to protect the privacy of those involved. No matter how improbable these incidents may seem, all of them are based on true events.

Again, this book is intentionally not politically correct. It's not PC because most cops are not PC. Their stories could not be accurately told if we used political correctness as a filter. And, contrary to conventional wisdom, cops are not particularly racist, homophobic, sexist, or whatever the next 'ist' is. No more so than the community they serve. If you're an asshole, they don't like you, regardless of your skin color, ethnic background, shoe size, etc.

If you are easily offended, this book's not for you.

Every member of this fraternity, either the fictional characters in this book or those still putting their lives on the line each and every day, would cherish an epitaph reading, "Here Lies A Member Of The Night Police."

“People sleep peaceably in their beds at night only because rough men stand ready to do violence on their behalf.” George Orwell

THE NIGHT POLICE

The function of the choir practice, the ancient and culturally appropriate social gathering of brothers in blue, is threefold. First, it provides a place of comfort and social acceptance mitigating the effects of a tough day on the street. A few rounds of drinks never hurt either. Second, it allows detoxification from the stress and brutality of the last ten or more hours of urban battle. Third and almost always, the choir practice devolves into a random recounting of favorite war stories. It doesn't matter if the stories are current or recycled; they are current whenever they are told.

There's always eager anticipation to hear the next tale. Often it leans competitive, each guy jockeying to slip his story into the queue so his voice gets heard. The stories are always true but often deployed in a gray space where total accuracy is not demanded. It's hard to remember the exact details in every retelling, but that's expected by the street-hardened lawmen in attendance.

CHAPTER I

The Li Po Horror Story

Man, it was raining like a cow pissing on a flat rock, water gushing in the gutters. Max Golden was pushing his decaying cruiser through the dark, unnaturally quiet Bristol City streets. Sporadic radio calls broke the sound of rain, but for the most part the denizens of this drab Midwestern city stayed in, out of the deluge. It being 0330 hours accounted for some of it too.

Max was a youngster among his BCPD peers, but was well liked for the most part. Fresh out of the academy, less than a year. Unconventionally, he sported no mustache and his young face belied his aggressiveness. His uniform, crisp, shoes still spit shined, and he was absolutely in his glory.

In his rearview mirror was "Big Mo" as the troopers called the Missouri River Hospital Center, where he'd arrested a badly injured DWI. Happy to be out of the ER zoo, Max trolled the I-64 back en route his beat. Picking out a spot to pull over for a couple of hours of report writing, he yanked his cruiser into a very narrow gravel drive, at the back of a real estate office and a favorite coop. He'd no more than flipped on the dash light, pulled out his paperwork and poured a cup of joe, when the radio crackled to life, pointing him to Unknown Call for Help, "in the neighborhood."

Young, but with enough savvy to understand that a radio call for assistance without even the most basic information should set any cop's radar up and spinning. Obviously it might be anything from some family beef, to an "in progress" rape or stabbing, or hell, anything you could imagine. Little info and potentially high risk.

Out the window went the coffee and Max hammered the accelerator, sending gravel spraying. Within seconds, dispatch squawked, "a second R/P advises an Asian male adult screaming outside of Li Po Restaurant, 28021 Isaiah Ave, cross of West 64th, Fire responding as well." Courtesy and red lights activated, he skipped the siren.

Max knew the location well, situated along I-64 (historically, the locals referred to this stretch of highway as "Highway 40"), the main thoroughfare that was the spine of several cities at the western edge of the state. It was mile after mile of strip malls, auto dealerships, restaurants, and sundry mom and pop businesses, most showing their age.

Li Po, a Chinese joint—and joint was being kind—was known for particularly lousy chow. Cops didn't go there. They'd rather go to Penny's Diner and let the current batch of parolee and gangster chefs piss in their pancakes.

Max's cruiser slid to a stop, two businesses down the street from Li Po. He didn't want to pull right up front, since he hardly understood the circumstances. Fire and his fill unit were probably three to five minutes out.

As he exited his car, he smoothly slipped his nightstick out of the holder and into the ring on his Sam Browne. He could hear screaming and barely made out a shape in the gloom in front of the restaurant. *That's gotta be the guy,* he thought.

As he took stock of the situation, he slapped on the uniform hat he fervently hated. He hated it because it had a checkerboard hat band that made it look like Chicago's idiot looking uniform hat or, for that matter, some taxi driver's lid. He gave in to the more rational argument, after all it was pouring fucking down.

As he cautiously approached, he could better see a very ripened, elderly Chinese man, shrieking and crying. Although drenched in the downpour, Max could make out the dirty white shirt, soiled apron and pants, just the attire you'd expect at a Chinese, greasy spoon.

The only communication going on at that point was from the hysterical restaurant owner who was motioning towards the restaurant with all his might, even trying to push Max towards the front door. Max was totally clueless as to what he might be saying, but he understood clearly the urgency from his wailing.

Max, gently but firmly, guided the grief-stricken man away from the front of the restaurant. He knew his fills were coming, but the circumstances dictated he take action.

He swept his Kel-Lite across the front of Li Po, skimming the roof and adjoining businesses, and then into the darkened front door. He unholstered his .357 and stepped into the inky black interior of the restaurant. Deep inside, a single weak bulb threw a benign light to reveal a general state of clutter.

Max concentrated hard on navigating his way through a tangle of tables and chairs in the cramped space. Listening for a clue, anything to indicate what he was about to uncover, he paused. Other than his own respirations, the only thing he could dial in was an acrid, burnt odor. He slowly stepped around a corner, his weapon leading the way. Max saw the blue glow of a wok still firing. He stepped up and shut it off.

His heartbeat quickened, Max slid along the wall towards the single hanging light bulb. Not wanting to silhouette himself, he reached up and twisted it off. He leaned against the wall and listened. Still not a sound, and he found that a bit unsettling. There was good news; he could hear a couple of arriving patrol cars pulling in out front.

A long, tight hallway was, for all intents and purposes, a dead end until his Kel-Lite caught a doorway at the very far end. Max moved toward the doorway with purpose, all of his senses dialed in. The door at the far end was open, but just a crack. The odors of a fouled bathroom seeped into the hallway. He took a breath, paused, swung the door open with the barrel of his .357. It was black as fuck as he slipped inside; there was something almost metallic in the dank, moist air.

As he swung his light in the cramped space, Max was more than startled by the sight of an elderly Asian woman seated on the toilet. In what felt like slow motion, he surveyed the scene, having difficulty making sense of what he was seeing. As his eyes adjusted in the dim light, he noted her head, leaning backwards against the wall, eyes staring at the ceiling. In a blink, he took in the multiple deep hesitation cuts on the right side of her face. Her throat was slit ear to ear and was gaping wide open. A terribly bloody Chinese cleaver was in her lap, as if she'd just placed it there. One arm was draped across her fully clothed leg, a stalactite of mucusy blood from her fingertip to the floor. Her flesh, yellow like a faded wax pepper, probably indicated she'd bled out. But that was above Max's pay grade.

Max's brain sizzled in response to the gruesome stimuli. Standing in the intense darkness, he could hear water dripping in an ancient sink. The single narrow beam of his Kel-Lite gaudily illuminated the victim. He was assaulted by the gore, the rancid funk, and the very, very odd feeling percolating within him. A chill ran up his spine. He swung the light slowly down towards his feet. The grimy linoleum floor was deep in coagulating blood, and Max slowly recognized the source of his unease...cool, thick blood was over his shoe tops and seeping into his socks.

To a veteran cop, one who'd seen a lot, Max's next move likely would not have happened. The young lawman ignored the revulsion of his clammy, sodden feet, and stepped to the toilet where he pressed his index and middle fingers into the neck of the late Mrs. Chiu. Max winced at the obscene sound gushing from her ruptured trachea.

Twenty or thirty minutes later, the rain finally let up, and Max and Lt. Quinn wrapped up final details at the side of their squad cars. The widower Chiu at the curb was draped in a yellow disposable blanket, awaiting relatives. "C" shift, Fire Engine 45, was idling in the street, and the fire guys were talking with an ambulance crew that just pulled in to see what all the fun was about.

Quinn seemed to sense Max was a bit shaken and talked him down... enough. He made the generous offer to have Max head for the barn, so he could clean up; he'd assign someone else to wait for the coroner.

Sleep did not come quickly for the young trooper that night.

Kramden had heard the Li Po story many times before. It was the stuff of nightmares. Tonight these hard men shared in what was about to evolve into a landmark reunion of best friends. He pondered how they all ended up where they did. Bristol City…

Max Golden stood in front of the mirror in his hotel room at the Seneca working on his hair. The Seneca Hotel had been there for over a hundred years and was one of those old classic places that could offer up charm and hospitality in ways that the modern chains couldn't imagine, let alone duplicate.

Recently grown out from a buzz cut, Max was having trouble remembering what to do with a civilian hairstyle. He was taking his time and sipping on a whiskey to bolster his nerves for the meeting tonight. He allowed himself a smile as he thought, Why am I nervous? I've sure as hell been in tougher places than this over the last few years!

Of course he would be the junior of the group. The rook again. He had been hired last and had left Bristol City PD first. Good ol' Maximum Golden, always going Mach 2 with his hair on fire. Always searching for something new, always searching anyway. The shit was getting old. He added some more gel to his hand and worked it into his hair. Taking inventory, he didn't look too bad. His face was tan. It looked even more so now since his hair had gone prematurely white. His blue eyes inherited from his German father were very sharp and clear these days. But for the prominent nose, he could have been downright good-looking. He always referred to it as his "Hebe" nose, though he was not Jewish at all.

He took another sip of the whiskey and slipped into his suit coat. It was new from Hart Schaffner Marx and custom-tailored to his current physique. No Men's Wearhouse for Maximum Golden. He had put on a good 20 pounds of muscle since he had last seen any of the boys. He carefully folded his top coat over his arm and headed downstairs to the concierge. Hopefully the Seneca's stately old Cadillac would be available to give him a lift over to the Tav.

Bristol City was a disheveled, comfortless township of 900,000 somewhere not too far west of the Mississippi. For some, it's home; for most, it was a placeholder, a moment suspended in the course of a lifetime. More actively fled Bristol City than ever ventured there on purpose. Still, almost a million souls lived there, most in differing degrees of disquiet and hardship. A rawboned example of what the Midwest can be when it's not at its best.

The primary employers in Bristol City's past were big steel and heavy equipment manufacturing. Generations of blue-collar workers made excellent wages and tolerated the belching smokestacks and mill tailings that wept decades of toxic tears. Like many similar US cities, as the mandate for an improved environment advanced, decades of decline and ever increasing unemployment took hold until it settled into its current squalid equilibrium. Scarfing machines, sintering plants, and coke quenching may not be the primary topics of conversation in the watering holes of today, but its legacy is still clear.

Nobody strolls in Bristol City, but if they did, it would be down the ubiquitous, ruptured sidewalks, most sloping as if about to slide into the avenue. Telephone poles, each heavily draped in wires traversing the streets, sidestepped ancient street lamps to complete an aerial web. Pale, grimy, two- and three-story apartments, offices, delis, and laundromats, all circa 1900, littered the avenues. Most wore geriatric awnings in different states of fatigue. This was the shoddy flavor of what was not so affectionately known as the Stock-town Borough.

Mid-block, at 28-09 23rd Ave., a weathered foot-wide bottle cap ("Schaefer Beer On Tap") affixed to a metal door, confirmed the location of Solly's. Its single window looked out to the intersection, a pendant stoplight, alternating green, yellow, and red, faintly glowing in the spitting rain.

At this time of the year, the days meandered on, one after the other, in that early winter gray, the kind that drapes itself to the ground. Not bone chilling, but it's damp, and it makes you want to slip inside, into the familiar warmth that comforts and consoles. For the Night Police, reassurance and seclusion was most often found at Solly's. Technically, it was Solly's Tavern, but the puny, neon sign in the window only read Solly's Tav; "ern" long ago having burned out. Hence, "Tav" or Solly's...you pick.

CHAPTER 2

"Is It Like This Every Night?"

RJ recalled when he had passed all the tests to be a Bristol City policeman, but the academy and a steady paycheck were still a couple of months off. Lieutenant James Hart was one of the Training Lieutenants for Bristol City PD. Hart told his recruits that they should get some exposure to police work, so he set it up for them to ride with a Bristol City PD officer for up to one eight-hour shift per week, a "swing shift" or a "graveyard shift." Lieutenant Hart made sure that they paired with what he termed "one of my Street Monsters." A Street Monster being a policeman who had between five and fifteen years on the street and who dominated their beat. They knew all there was to know about policing, knew all the offenders on their beat, knew where the action would be before it even happened. After RJ's first shift with Street Monster Wendell Kahn, RJ would have done the eight-hour shifts 7 days a week if he could.

That first ride in a police car had never faded from memory. It was a Saturday night graveyard shift, and after a brief introduction from Lieutenant Hart, they allowed RJ to sit through the squad briefing. When the sergeant concluded passing information and making assignments, which included assigning RJ to Officer Kahn, chairs scraped back and cops started filing out. Officer Kahn hung back and offered a beefy paw to RJ. "I'm Kahn. Guess you're riding with me." RJ followed the bald Kahn out the door to the rear lot of the police station. Kahn was over 6 feet tall and looked as though his chest and arms would burst out of the uniform shirt. Out back dozens of cops were loading or unloading police cruisers. Kahn walked up to another cop that was unloading gear from a cruiser to what RJ assumed was his personal vehicle. Kahn inquired how the cruiser was running and seemed satisfied with the response. When the other cop finished unloading, Kahn told RJ to hop in and they drove through the parking lot to his personal car to load up. The interior of the cop car impressed RJ with its rack of electronics separating the passenger and driver. A short-barreled shotgun was clamped into this affair. The smell was part electronics, part nicotine, and some other nuances that RJ couldn't place. In a few months, he would realize all police cars have the same unique aroma.

After placing a couple of boxes of gear and a helmet in the patrol car's trunk, Kahn began a methodical examination of everything about the police car. He explained each step as he went along. RJ soon found out that Kahn was a field training officer, one who takes rookies fresh out of the academy and instructs them to where they can operate on their own. Kahn first pulled the bottom cushion of the rear seat out and searched behind it with his flashlight. The backseat was behind a metal screen, and was used for prisoner transportation. Prisoners, though handcuffed, would try to dump contraband, including weapons, behind the seat. By checking the area carefully, Kahn performed two critical tasks: he knew there were no weapons available behind the seat, and by checking after every prisoner was placed there, any contraband found was charged to that specific prisoner.

Next Kahn triggered some electric solenoid that released the pump shotgun from its locked upright position between the driver and passenger. He methodically unloaded all the shells, inspecting each one before placing them on the hood of the patrol car. Kahn then disassembled the shotgun and dug in his pocket for a penny. He placed the penny over the firing pin and pulled the trigger. He pointed out the dent in the copper penny to RJ. "That's as close as you can get to making sure that this thing works without firing a round," he explained.

He reassembled the shotgun, reloaded it, and replaced it in the rack. The red, blue, and amber lights of the cruiser had been flashing during the entire vehicle check. Satisfied that these worked, Kahn shut them down and did one final walk around the vehicle. "Lights all work. You look pretty stupid to the public if you are driving around with a headlight out."

That made sense to RJ. Kahn slid behind the wheel and made some notations on his clipboard. He reached over and switched off a miniature gooseneck lamp that illuminated just the small area where he had been writing. He buckled his seat belt and suggested that RJ do the same, then he guided the big four-door Dodge out onto the main drag. RJ couldn't wait to see what came next. Kahn grabbed the radio microphone from its hook for the first time. "B12 is 10-8 with a RA."

A remote voice responded through a speaker located somewhere in the maze of electronics, "10-4 B12."

Kahn had a simple set of rules for RJ. "If I tell you to stay in the car, stay in the car. Otherwise it's okay to follow along. If something happens to me, get on the radio and tell someone. Just say it in plain English, they'll know what to do." Sounded simple and ominous. RJ watched Officer Kahn in profile as he adjusted the volume on the radio. He had it down low. The stream of radio traffic was steady and an unintelligible series of code words and numbers. Kahn used the cigarette lighter to light a cheroot and visibly relaxed behind the wheel. "You must have a million questions. Feel free to ask away."

RJ did in fact have a lot of questions and was thankful for the invitation, it was just a matter of trying not to sound too stupid. His first question was about the radio traffic; how on earth could he follow it? Officer Kahn chuckled before explaining that you get used to it. "In fact, what I'm doing right now is getting a feel for what's happening in the city, where the other units are and so forth. I like to stay on the main boulevard until I get it sorted out."

RJ was about to ask a follow-up when the radio emitted three sharp beeps. "All units Highway Patrol in pursuit northbound 585. Taking the eastbound ramp for Maxwell. Suspect vehicle yellow Datsun 240Z. 10-99 J3."

At least RJ understood most of that. Khan had turned on the flashing lights and siren while simultaneously rolling up his window and mashing down hard on the accelerator. RJ had no idea that a car could accelerate that fast, or corner so hard. When they got to the intersection with Maxwell, Khan threw the cruiser into a hard left turn that slammed RJ against the doorpost. He didn't think Khan noticed. He was spinning the steering wheel back and forth trying to steady up the big Dodge on its new course. The cheroot clamped in his teeth. He would brake hard as they approached every intersection. It seemed like they were catching nothing but red lights. As soon as he thought the flashing lights and siren were doing their job, he would catapult the cruiser through the cross traffic. They did this several times and RJ was sure he had never experienced this much adrenaline in his life. Now they could see the red lights of the Highway Patrol car approaching in the distance, and Kahn made another 90-degree turn, braking hard, tires shrieking in protest as they crossed the eastbound lanes of Maxwell. Kahn had no sooner crossed Maxell on the cross street before he had the car burning rubber in reverse. He slewed around to face Maxwell again. RJ's heart was pounding, and he couldn't remember how many times he had hit his head or his knees on something. He had a death grip on the barrel of the shotgun. It seemed the only solid thing within his grasp. They were rolling again, and at that instant RJ saw the yellow 240Z flash past the windshield, its headlights off. Kahn was accelerating hard behind the 240Z when the Highway Patrol car rocketed past them, it having the advantage of already being at speed. They were now trailing behind the Highway Patrol, all of them now eastbound on Maxwell. The nose of the Dodge was pulling down hard as Kahn braked again for another intersection. Ditto the Highway Patrol car. You could smell brakes overheating. The Datsun didn't hesitate to run the red light.

At a speed almost too fast to follow, the Datsun T-boned a station wagon. The two cars spun and twisted wildly, the sound of the collision explosive even with the sirens blaring. Khan was talking on the radio, bringing the cruiser to a stop, and flinging open his door all at the same time. The passenger door of the 240Z opened, and a guy started running. A Highway Patrol officer went sprinting after him. Officer Kahn was at the driver's door of the 240Z yanking on it. The collision had rendered the door inoperable. Khan smashed the driver's side window out with his heavy metal flashlight. Seconds later he had the bloodied driver on the ground and was handcuffing him. A second State Patrol officer was at the station wagon peering inside with his flashlight. There was smoke or steam everywhere. Khan hadn't told RJ to stay in the car, so he opened his door and stepped out. RJ found that his legs were trembling from all of the adrenaline, and he had to hang on to the car door to support himself. RJ could hear someone screaming in the station wagon. Other Highway Patrol and Bristol City cruisers were sliding to a stop all around them. In the distance RJ could hear more sirens. An ambulance, he hoped.

RJ lost track of time. Fire trucks and ambulances arrived. Flares were lit and putting off an acrid, sulfurous smoke. It was one of those catastrophic scenes that you are directed past as a motorist. You know it's not right to gawk, but still you want to look. Human nature, RJ supposed. But this was different. He was part of this! He had witnessed this! Maybe he would have to testify in court. The ambulances left, the fire trucks had washed the car fluids and human blood down a storm drain. Tow truck drivers were trying to figure out how to drag the two destroyed automobiles away.

Khan came back to our cruiser. "Hop in, kid! Let's get out of here!" Kahn took a minute to roll his window down and relight the cheroot he had never lost in the excitement. He shut down all the emergency lights as they pulled away from the scene. He grabbed the radio mike. "Bristol City, B12."

"B12."

"B12 is 10-8."

"B12, 10-4, start moving toward El Papagayo. 574 in progress in the back lot. Large crowd gathering. B52 just went 10-23 at the scene. B51 rolling too."

"10-4 Bristol City, B12 en route."

Officer Kahn reached down and activated the emergency lights as he hammered the accelerator again. No siren this time. RJ didn't know why. As they wove in and out of traffic on the main boulevard, Khan was gracious enough to explain what they were doing. "We're headed to one of the Mexican joints. Typical this time of night that there's gonna be a fight. That's what 574 means. Another unit just arrived on scene, and his beat partner is rolling too. We are number three because that many drunk Mexicans are a handful. This is a stay-in-the-car call, kid. Check?"

"Check," RJ replied.

RJ glanced over at the speedometer, and even from his oblique angle he could see the needle was past 80. More hard braking and hard cornering. He was learning how to brace himself. He hadn't learned how to keep his heart from pounding. Down an alley they flew, and then they were skidding to a stop across a parking lot. It looked like there were at least 50 or 60 men, most wearing dress cowboy clothes, boots, and hats, all carrying long-neck beer bottles. As Kahn was exiting the car, he grabbed his nightstick from a holder in his driver's door. RJ could hear him talking on his handheld radio as he jogged toward the melee, "Bristol City, B12, send more units! I can't see B51 or 52."

"B12 roger." Beep! Beep! Beep! "ALL UNITS, 10-38, OFFICERS NEED ASSISTANCE EL PAPAGAYO!"

RJ could hear what sounded like a roll call of units answering on the radio. He felt useless as he saw the crowd close in around Khan. Soon RJ could see him making short swings with the nightstick. Khan was a full head higher than most of the surrounding Mexicans. RJ could hear sirens in the distance again, getting closer. C'mon, hurry, guys!

Four or five more squad cars swarmed into the lot, and Mexican cowboys ran in all directions. A knot of 15 or so remained near the back door of the bar, but the blue suits seemed to have gained control.

The radio squawks. "Bristol City, this is 51, send the wagon."

"Roger 51, wagon is en route."

"Bristol City, better start an ambulance code 3, we have one with a stab wound here."

"Roger 51, ambulance is en route."

The wagon turns out to be a milk truck–looking thing painted black and white like the cruisers. It got there ahead of the ambulance, and two officers opened up the back doors. Khan and some other officers lead a string of bloodied combatants to the wagon where individual handcuffs came off and the wagon officers put on cuffs that are part of a long chain. RJ counted eight that got put in the wagon. Khan returned to the cluster of officers and emerged with another bloodied prisoner. This one he led to their car, searched him, and placed him in the rear seat behind the screen. The reek of beer hit RJ's nostrils. Khan climbed in and grabbed the mike.

"Bristol City, B12."

"B12?"

"B12 will be 10-15 J3 with one."

"Roger B12."

The Mexican jabbered in Spanish in back, but Khan talked over him. "We're headed back to the station with 52's prisoner. 52 will stay back and try to get some witness statements for his report. We'll put his guy in a holding cell and get back on the street. We'll stay close to Beat 5 and 51. This could start up again."

RJ nodded as though he comprehended. He couldn't help but notice that Officer Khan did not have a scratch on him. Kahn called dispatch when they pulled up to the sally port. The gate opened electronically and closed behind them when they drove into a small courtyard. The wagon was already there, and the line of bedraggled drunken cowboys were being led into what RJ could only assume was the jail. Kahn walked over to a wall of what looked like safe deposit lockers and secured his sidearm in one of them. He then got the prisoner out of the backseat and escorted him to what looked like a dog kennel, locking him inside.

Back at the cruiser, Kahn pulled out the lower cushion of the backseat. "Kid, you want to come look at this?"

RJ got out of the car and walked around to look over Officer Kahn's shoulder. Laying on the floor pan under the cushion was a moderate-sized folding knife. RJ thought Kahn was a genius. Kahn did not, and was chastising himself for missing it during his search of the suspect. "Must have had it up his ass, is all I can think."

Khan went to the trunk of his car and retrieved a latex surgical glove and a manila envelope. With his gloved hand, he picked up the knife and dropped it in the envelope. "Maybe some blood on it. Who knows, might solve 52's stabbing."

They collected the prisoner from the kennel and got buzzed through a thick steel door.

Being inside the Bristol City PD jail facility was also an education for RJ. He had never seen the inside of a jail before. On a Saturday night just after midnight, it was a full house. Loud and raucous, officers strained to be heard as they filled out paperwork. Body smells; sweat, vomit, urine, combined with an industrial cleaner. He would find out that much like the patrol car, this smell was unique to jails.

After booking 52's prisoner and dropping the knife off at the evidence technician's area, they grabbed a cheap paper cup of station house coffee and headed back to the police cruiser. Kahn found a gas station that was closed and backed up to the building so he could watch the boulevard in front of them. He got a form from his clipboard, switched on the little lamp, and started writing. Kahn explained as he wrote that he has to document finding the knife, and that includes documenting his search of the backseat before starting the shift. "If you don't mind, kid, I'd like to put you down as a witness."

"Sure," RJ replied. "By all means." He gave Officer Kahn his full name and information.

It was after 2 a.m., and the radio had quieted down. Kahn finished the short report and asked if RJ was hungry. He queried dispatch to see if they were clear for a meal break. Dispatch gave their blessing, and they rolled.

"I'm sorry to say that at this hour it limits us to Denny's or Denny's."

The pair have burgers and fries with coffee at Denny's. They learned that they had both been Marines, but at different times. RJ had been at Camp Pendleton, or had floated around in a clean ship on the Mediterranean, whereas Kahn slogged through the rice paddies of Vietnam with 1st Battalion 9th Marines. Still, Kahn was gracious about it, and it formed a small bond between them.

They got back in the cruiser, and Kahn put them 10-8 with dispatch. Compared to the start of the shift, the radio was practically silent. Kahn rolled down his window and lit a fresh cheroot. He offered RJ one, and he lit up as well. They began cruising the industrial areas, looking for potential thieves as Kahn explained it. "We could hit the boulevard and get a DWI, but I don't think you would find that very interesting. I'll try to keep us in service."

They drove and smoked in silence for a while, and then the radio broke into their thoughts.

"B12, Bristol City."

"Go for B12."

"B12, 574 family 1422 Nightingale. Neighbor reports distraught elderly woman."

"Roger Bristol City, B12 en route."

"B42, Bristol City."

"42."

"B42, fill with B12."

"42 Roger, en route."

They left the industrial area and were driving briskly, not burning tires like before, but briskly. Soon they were in an upper-middle-class neighborhood, twisting through a maze of streets. Kahn never looked at a street map. He shut off his headlights, and they coasted to a stop in front of one of many dark houses. Kahn explained that 1422 would be a few houses down. He was guessing it would be the one with the lights on. They silently padded up to 1422 Nightingale on foot. The lights were on inside, and an upset elderly woman sounded like she was pleading with someone not to do something. RJ followed Kahn up to the front porch. Through the window they saw an elderly couple facing each other, the woman still in full voice. Keeping the pair in sight, Kahn rapped on the front door. "POLICE DEPARTMENT!"

RJ would never forget what happened next. He saw the woman move to answer the door. The skinny old man laid down on the floor, put a small revolver to his temple, and fired. Kahn slammed RJ against the wall. "STAY!"

He shouted, "B12 SHOT FIRED!" into his handheld before splintering the door open with his boot.

The screaming woman flew out of the house when Kahn got a hand on her robe and pulled. In two bounds he was inside, kicking the gun from the old man's hand. A huge pool of blood was spreading from the head wound across the linoleum. Kahn back on the radio. "CODE 4, it's CODE 4!" He was panting.

B42's cruiser screeched to a stop in front of the house, and the officer was running toward RJ with his sidearm out. "Where's Kahn?" he demanded of RJ.

RJ pointed inside. A moment later RJ heard, "Oh, Jesus!" from the other cop.

Kahn was back on his handheld now, composure returned, asking dispatch to respond a supervisor, an on-call detective, and the coroner's office. Somehow comforting the elderly woman fell to RJ. As she clung to RJ and sobbed, the story came out. Her husband was terminal with cancer. He wanted to take his own life rather than endure the pain and helplessness ahead. They had been arguing about it for the last 3 hours. She didn't know that he had the gun in his pocket.

There RJ was, almost a policeman, with little idea what to do. His best was to keep patting the old woman on the back and telling her she would be okay. A neighbor came over and took the woman next door. Likely the neighbor who had called the police.

It was almost 5 a.m. by the time Kahn and RJ could leave. A detective and the deputy coroner had the scene. Kahn drove to another of his favorite report writing spots, backed in, and started to write out what had happened. Twice he would ask RJ what he saw, and it made RJ feel like he was part of something. At 10 minutes before 6 a.m., they pulled up to the gas pumps in the back lot of the police station and Kahn topped off the cruiser. As he pumped the gas, RJ asked him, "Is it like this every night?"

Kahn smiled. "Pretty much, kid. Pretty much."

Later they shook hands, and Kahn told RJ that he could ride with him anytime that he didn't have a recruit, then he cautioned him not to fall asleep on the drive back to his home. There was little danger of that.

Bristol City PD was likely no different than any other mid- to large-sized police agency in the country. It had officers of every stripe. To the ordinary citizen, all cops are the same; they have a uniform, badge, gun, and patrol car, end of story. People on the inside of law enforcement recognize that there are many different types of cop with categories going well beyond young or old, eager or lazy. There's all of that, but then there is the stuff that really counts to other cops, and crooks for that matter. In Bristol City, the cops who had what counted were the Night Police, and a super subset of them were the Street Monsters. Other agencies in other parts of the country had different names for them, but in Bristol City that's what they were called. Regular cops breathed a little easier when a Night Policeman or Street Monster showed up at a hairy call. Conversely bad guys got that sinking feeling when they realized they were in the presence of no ordinary cop.

There are officers who work afternoons and into the evening hours, and they deserve their due as being the busiest men and women you will ever meet. In Bristol City and in most places, it's called swing shift, and those cops get lots of calls for service and catch lots of paper. Written reports, that is. The evening commute happens on their watch along with the evening commute car crashes. Car crashes equal written reports. When those weary commuters finally make it home, some come home to a missing stereo, TV, jewelry, and so forth, because while they were out making a living, a skinny hype burglar was busy robbing them blind. And who gets to write that initial theft report? Those coppers on swing shift.

As the swing shift officers come back to the station exhausted and looking forward to another hour or two of report writing, another group of men stand ready to take over the cruisers and load their gear. The best of these are called the Night Police, and they are about to roll. They pay particular attention to checking their shotgun, because they may have to use it. They're not afraid to use it.

In some places, it's called the mid-watch, in others the graveyard shift or midnights. The hours vary, but the Night Police will work through midnight and into the wee hours of the morning when most people are pulling the blanket a little closer, or if they wake to the sound of a distant siren, they see the clock and fall back to slumber, smug knowing that hours of sleep remain.

The Night Police of the late 1970s were very adept at serving up curbside justice in a time before surveillance cameras were on every building and Automatic Teller Machine. Night Policemen of that era would feel sorry for the kids coming out of the academy on to the street in subsequent decades. How would they get the job done? Quite likely coppers from the 50s and 60s felt sorry for the 70s generation. It was a given that those old boys knew how to operate as Night Policemen. This phenomenon had been happening since the first Centurion took to the field; each generation had bragging rights over the ones that followed.

The calls for service on graveyard were less frequent and differed in magnitude. The start of shift could be busy, particularly on Friday and Saturday nights, with revelers and partygoers. Plenty of disturbance calls to roll on. A bar or a party could get out of hand, resulting in "Stick Time." Stick Time was a special period where an asshole got a hickory shampoo. The before midnight calls were just people having too much liquid fun. After that time, when evening ends and morning is officially underway, the police radio quiets down. When a call comes across of "shots fired" or "woman screaming," chances were that something very wrong had just happened. Any accident after midnight was likely to be gory due to increased drug or alcohol use and the resulting increase in speed prior to the crash. A silent alarm going off could be a window or door improperly secured to the wind, or it could be persons unknown inside committing a felony crime. Every vehicle stop on a deserted street or alley after three in the morning portends danger. The FBI or Peace Officers Standards and Training have the statistics about when an officer is most likely to be murdered or assaulted, but absent that most cops will say that the real scary incidents take place on the quiet, darkened streets when no one is around, leaving a team of investigators to piece together some poor cop's last minutes on earth from blood stains and shell casings.

Every cop that had worked those wee hours had a story about nearly shooting, or actually pulling the trigger on a startled cat in an alley, or a life-size cardboard cutout encountered in a lonely building search. Cops often worked by themselves, and it strung nerves taught.

Some guys were assigned to midnights and didn't like it. They either had difficulty sleeping during the daytime, or just found the work too devoid of contact with normal people, or too nerve-wracking. These officers did better on day shift with an Officer Friendly hand raised in a prom queen's salute to the fair citizens of the day world. They became neighborhood resource officers, school officers, or something of similar value.

True Night Police officers had a certain aura and a confident swagger in their step. Uniforms were seldom inspection perfect or even day shift acceptable. Shoes and boots were scuffed and trousers marred from climbing roof access ladders or the occasional roll in the street with some perp whose neck they were desperately trying to get their arm around in a carotid restraint. Never a choke hold, mind you. The outliers were Night Police field training officers. They were parade-ground perfect at all times, as an example to the recruits they trained. FTOs had a lot of spare uniforms in their lockers and spent a lot of time polishing shoes and leather. But FTO or regular Night Policeman, all had a salty look about them with cruiser keys stowed under the big chrome buckle of the Sam Browne belt.

A Night Policeman carried extra gear too. Most had at least one more gun secreted on their person and a serious folding knife, such as the popular Buck Knife. Striking devices were popular, and in addition to a nightstick made of real wood like hickory, lignum vitae, or tiga, a sap or sap gloves were handy and worth having. Police trousers still had sap pockets in the 70s. Incapacitating somebody with a fist works in the movies, but in real life it'll end with a trip to the ER and a hand in a cast. A Night Policeman had a big flashlight made of metal, and it was heavy. If pulled from underneath the non-gun arm where it was tucked while in use, it could easily knock a bad guy unconscious or disable the crook with a broken collarbone. A good Kel-Lite could double as a pry bar to pull out an impinging fender on a car involved in a fender-bender, allowing it to be driven from the scene. No tow truck equaled no report. Crash reports were for traffic cops and those busy cops on swing shift, not the Night Police.

There were other tools in a Night Policeman's kit. In addition to the handcuff key on the keyring, there was a tire valve core removal tool. When investigating prowler and peeping tom calls, a suspect vehicle was often nearby. The sounds of cooling metal and a warm hood were clues to the Night Police; a flat tire ensured that Mr. Peeping Tom Pervert wouldn't drive off while cops were still playing hide and seek with him. In a pinch, they could use the ubiquitous Buck Knife to saw off a valve stem for the same effect. The Buck Knife was used on the sidewall of the tire when the Night Policeman was sure that the vehicle belonged to an asshole, and somehow the asshole had escaped into the night or otherwise clowned the Night Policeman. Never clown a true Night Policeman.

The Night Policeman were hunting machines with eyes and ears seeking criminal quarry. A Night Policeman patrolled the streets with the car window down. Winter or summer, hot or cold, because that had to be done to hear things in the dark: breaking glass, a car starting up and speeding away, a gunshot, or a woman screaming.

The Night Policeman owned a small box for 3 X 5 cards of Field Interview notes and Polaroid pictures of known offenders. A good Night Policeman had a card on every regular evil-doer on his beat. How did these cops locate the denizens of the evening? It wasn't hard. Day Shift policemen said that it was too easy for the Night Police, because the only people out after midnight were good guys, drunks, or criminals. The good guys were driving black cars with white doors and a white roof, so that kind of narrowed the field down. Night Policemen knew that it was a bit more involved. The Night Policeman also knew of all the active arrest warrants, and searchable parolees and probationers on his beat. Probable cause was a good thing; good things led to better things, like Mr. Parolee going back to his room at the state penitentiary.

Public relations wasn't much of a concern after midnight. Considering the clientele, they weren't going to have hurt feelings over being called a bad name by the cops. They had been called bad names all of their lives. On rare occasions, though, a regular citizen would get on the wrong side of a Night Policeman's colorful appellations and take offense, resulting in an angry call to the Watch Commander, but for the most part offensive language was understood by all of the nighttime players.

At the end of a Night Police shift, a fellow had a sense of accomplishment. Maybe a great adrenaline-filled pursuit, by vehicle or on foot, that ended with the catching of a bad guy. Maybe a shift spent developing something into a great felony arrest. Could have been a bar fight or a rowdy party that ended up in a street filled with squad cars and paddy wagons. Ambulances too, for the miscreants that wanted to duel with Night Policemen. No two nights were the same, and there was always action.

Of course there were special choir practice hangouts where Night Policemen could congregate after end-of-watch for a six a.m. red beer, Bloody Mary, or an Irish Coffee to dampen down all that adrenaline before attempting sleep.

CHAPTER 3

The Cherished Chieftain

A common name in County Galway, Quinn, derived from O'Cuinn, meant "wisdom" or "chief." It was perfect for the rumpled, bent-nosed, retired Chief of Detectives that all the boys of the Night Police worked for at one time or another. Described once in court by some idiot defense attorney as "irascible and dyspeptic," he may have had those moments. He was definitely a dichotomy.

The guys that worked for him knew that if you were a solid cop, hardworking and an ass-kicker, Quinn had your back and was there when you needed him. A few needed a gentle boxing of the ears or a remedial update in the ways of the street, and he'd deliver that message. It wasn't always fun when Pat tuned a young copper up, but it always was for his own good. Experience and common cop-sense guided his teachings. It was surprising to none of them when they heard him say, "Don't stoop down to their level. When some miscreant pushes your buttons, be the bigger man. Don't act or say things that are demeaning or wrong, just do your job. The right way. Be proud of what you do."

But, Pat's persona could shift. He was hard-wired with a love for mid-shelf Scotch. He was contented when slopping back a few, but he also could get a bit harsh if provoked. Most of the Night Police knew not to ignite him, but civilians occasionally found out the hard way. Occasionally, a football or baseball game could cause a ruckus amongst competing fans, and Pat was ready to use his gnarled mitts to settle a dispute for his side. Just once in a while, though. Hardly worth mentioning.

Pat also had a habit, one they all recognized and one that just annoyed the living shit out of them as young lawmen. For example, imagine cops summoned to a midnight family dispute. They'd been there before, and it was always the same. Heated words, broken lamps, and dishes, torn clothing, maybe a little blood. When the boys in blue appear at the door, the not-Cleaver family is shrieking and screeching at each other. Likely as not, the missus still has the half-pint of Popov vodka in her hand, and the old man's fists are balled up and threatening. A typical Tuesday evening with the not-Cleaver family.

"Hey, HEY! Knock it the fuck off! Quiet the fuck down." The beat cops diligently begin to de-escalate the situation. They push and pull, coerce or bully if needed, but ultimately separate the two idiots, get the potential and sometimes real weapons out of their hands and away from their reach. The missus, with the oft-seen snot bubbles and trembling chin in the bedroom, the groom of 25 years wedged against the refrigerator, a standard-issue 26-inch hardwood baton skewering him in place. "That cunt. I'll fix her wagon!"

The boys think to themselves, *We're making progress here, we'll get this quieted down, a little mutual combat, no one will have to cut any reports.* They're starting to feel good about it all. This was real progress.

Frankly at this stage, they didn't need the patrol lieutenant; they knew their job and things were coming under control. Now to the part that annoyed the living shit out of them…this patrol lieutenant and future Chief of Detectives was doing his job, what he'd been paid to do. He paid attention to his young boys in blue and what they'd got themselves into. The downside with Quinn was that within about 30 seconds of his arrival on the scene, he'd jacked up refrigerator dick-head and the situation immediately re-escalated. When Quinn saw the elder not-Cleaver missus hawk up a big green lunger and launch it toward his junior officer, the game changed for all of them. The old man roughly shoved into the corner next to the fridge while he struggled to stay out of the cuffs. "Snot bubbles" was on the warpath. Her shrieking intensified as she started her mission to free the man she loved, the man "who didn't do no mother… fucking…thing…you pig bastards!"

Cutting to the chase, what should've been a quick in-and-out, becomes hours of report writing, booking, fingerprinting, mug photos, and transporting to the Allen County lockup. Thank you, Lieutenant Quinn, most appreciated. He knew it'd cost him a few drinks. The boys all bitched and moaned, but they got it and we were fine with it.

The Tav doesn't have a pool table, a shuffle board, or pachinko…it's a drinking man's establishment. Unless invited by the unordained, it doesn't have women either. It's not that women aren't treasured, it's just that Solly's is a man's bar. In today's world, that's frowned upon and possibly grounds for litigation. Too fucking bad.

Behind the battered, black-lacquered plank was a simple tarnished brass plate that identified the birth of Solly's, "estb.1929." Tino was likely there at the grand opening judging by his rickety, tottering shuffle behind the bar. There had been many barmen at Solly's, but Tino was the constant. The keeper of the knowledge, the history, and all things on the quiet. Never did he disclose a secret or give someone up. Ever!

Late autumn shadows puddled on 23rd Avenue, and Solly's was the natural landing spot for five lawmen with an agenda. First up, Pat Quinn. He unbuttoned his flannel overcoat as he stepped down the four steps from street level and pushed open the door into the warmth of the Tav.

Pat nodded to the barkeep, Tino, as he made his way past the bar. He navigated through a small clutch of tables into a warren of passageways, to a darkened nook. The smallish, dim space at the back of Solly's was owned by the Night Police when they were in residence. He pushed open a creaky, ill-hung door. The flip of a switch warmly illuminated walls of dark wood and a pitifully small, but wonderfully old, schooner, pot-bellied stove at center stage. Tino had already done them the pleasure of tossing in a few sticks of fatwood from an old leather bucket and giving it a light. The chill was off, a trace of smoke slipped into the room. A worthy exchange for the subtle, crackling fire and the flickering embers viewed through the open fire door.

Encircling it on three sides were five mismatched and battered old leather club chairs. They scrounged more when needed, but five was a good fit, and perfect for this evening. A bit of stuffing coming out of a couple, but it was a nice match to the antique cast-iron stove. Generally, the least senior of the Night Police got the rat squad chair, the one a bit too close to the heat and a bit lacking in support. No bellyaches, it was a privilege just to be there.

Along one wall was a tall set of what looked to be old-school pharmacy shelves, with nooks and crannies, a few books, some newspapers, and assorted detritus of almost 60 years of residency. Locked behind a scarred cupboard door, the contents of one cubby belonged to the Night Police. Pat dumped his coat on the ancient hat rack and pulled out his keys. With what looked to be a great reverence, he kneeled down (which was becoming harder and harder to do as the years wore on), slipped his key in the burnished lock, and opened the prize. Several bottles of Scotch, all in different stages of consumption, and two handsome wooden humidors fit amongst the muddle of books, mementos, and assorted history within the cabinet. Fronting the adjoining brickwork, where a window once dominated, was a stack of collapsing leather dice cups, filled with multi-colored and dissimilar bones.

Tino showed up long enough to deposit a battered galvanized bucket of ice on the drainboard of the cabinetwork, adding to the tapestry of water stains and rings on the ancient wood relic. The Night Police, almost to a man, required just a hint of water, a few drops to a wee dram, to inspire the Scotch.

Tino mumbled, "All the boys showing?" to which Quinn responded, "Special night, old man. Maxie Golden is coming home. RJ, Kramden, and Rimjob will be here too. It's a damned reunion!"

Quinn threw two ice cubes in one of the heavy tumblers kept in the cabinet and liberally splashed Scotch over it. He pulled a framed photo from the cabinet and stared at it. His mind wandered back…

The photo, taken at night, depicted a group of young men in police uniforms. Quinn himself was in the upper left corner of the photo. Twenty-something years ago he had sported a huge, fierce Fu Manchu mustache.

Bright-eyed, young men at the peak of their youth. Quinn much older than the others, but then he was the boss of the Stock-town Borough midnight shift. Quinn did the mental roll call as he always did when it's late, or when he was into his Scotch: There were two acting sergeants that Quinn had brought over from the FTO squad,

Lazzerini and Brownee. The city too broke or too tight to pay overtime, went along with the acting sergeant concept. The troopers comprised the Johnson boys, Bradley and Ronald, Max Golden, Tim Spin, Jack Gleason, Stevie Rimfro, and so on. They were all still among the living as far as he knew. A good number of that special shift were not. Three washed out. Of the remaining 15, 10 were alive, 5 were dead now. Two by their own hand. If he were looking at a class photo of 1975 Northwestern graduates, he doubted that a third would be dead by now.

Quinn swirled the Scotch in his glass and drank deeply. God how he had connected with those boys! He had been their Pappy Boyington, and they had been his Blacksheep. They had coined the term Night Police to describe themselves. They owned the night back then in the Stock-town Borough.

CHAPTER 4

How Much Does a Brain Weigh?

Right after making lieutenant, but before the Night Police, Pat Quinn had oversight of all the city's field training officers (FTOs). None of the more senior lieutenants wanted the job because it carried a heavy administrative burden. There was a lot of paper, but Quinn enjoyed it.

The FTOs themselves were meticulously selected and were some of the best street cops the department had. Some cops didn't put in for it because they preferred to work alone, and sure as hell didn't want some dumbass rookie in their car. FTOs were regarded as the elite of the patrol force. FTOs ensured that recruits could function on their own. FTOs weeded out recruits that just didn't have what it took. Veteran cops on the department counted on FTOs to fill the ranks with men and women who would back them up in the most dangerous situations.

Lieutenant Quinn chaired the FTO debriefs when recruits were going through their field training. All 24 FTOs and the three FTO sergeants were present as they methodically went through the progress of each recruit for the week. Quinn took copious notes on each recruit, though he seldom interrupted the flow of discussion. By week 5 it was clear that three of the recruits were struggling.

Recruit David Prather. Older than his peers by about 5 years, Prather didn't seem to grasp any aspect of police work, though he averaged 90s throughout the academy, and held a bachelor's degree in engineering. Nothing had jumped out from Prather's test results, or oral interviews other than he lived with his mother in an affluent town nearby and he seemed shy and awkward when talking about his relationships with girls.

Recruit Michael Gonzalez. Youngest of his peers, a gifted athlete, a good student. Quiet. According to his FTO, Gonzales didn't help the FTO when a suspect turned combative. This caused a buzz of muted conversations around the room. Quinn got the distinct impression that recruit Gonzales was on very thin ice.

Recruit Anthony Leggo. He had committed the mortal sin of rationalizing all FTO criticism. Sort of intangible with the FTOs, but much like drill sergeants, FTOs wanted to hear a lot of "Yes, Sir" and "No excuse, Sir." They did not want to hear the recruit whine about his shortcomings and failures after being counseled by the FTO. Leggo had been with two FTOs so far, and both were in agreement that while Leggo seemed to understand and perform the basics, they both wanted to strangle him for his backtalk. Again, all of his test and interview results were within norms, but there was something dislikable about him. He was tall and skinny with a protruding Adam's apple, his whole body sharp angles. Quinn placed a question mark by his name.

Before adjourning the meeting, Lieutenant Quinn asked if anyone had a humorous story to end the week on. He always did this, and it was a hit with the FTOs. Soon a chant was going around the room, "Lazz! Lazz! Lazz!" Quinn held up his hand for silence. "Officer Lazzerini, do you have something to share with the group?"

Lazzerini was a quick-witted young man, small in stature, but fearless. Jet-black hair combed back and bushy mustache to match. They well knew Lazz as a prankster among his peers.

Lazz looked around the room and licked his lips, anticipating the story he was about to tell…

"So this is my second week with that big kid Ron Johnson. He's pretty solid. We're working swing shift. Get a call to an apartment complex about a possible gunshot. We had been to the apartment before on a middle-aged boyfriend-girlfriend fight. This time the apartment is dark, but a neighbor and manager both tell us the female is in there for certain. Her car is in the carport, the dude's pickup is gone. Nobody answers our door knock, so we get the key from the manager. I tell the rookie that it's time to earn that big paycheck. Flashlights and guns come out, and we slide through the open front door. There's a funky smell in the air, and there's a hint of cordite too. We clear the living room and kitchen. No one there. We ease down the hall to the bedrooms. There's something crunching underfoot. The first little bedroom is clear. The master bedroom, if you could call it that, had a crumpled woman on the floor, slumped against the foot of the bed. The shotgun on the floor and the missing top half of her skull tell the story. And this was weird...her brain laid on the bed behind her. We back out of the room, now understanding the crunching underfoot was the top of her skull. It looks like a suicide. There's some kind of note on the dresser, but that's not our call. So I tell Johnson detectives and coroner had to be called on this, and we have to document everything that we had seen and done up to this point. Now I say to myself, it's time for some FTO humor and a little character check. So I make him stay in the bedroom with the corpse to sketch things out. Location of the body, the shotgun, the suicide note, etc. Leaving a rookie in a room full of brains seemed like great fun. At some point while we're waiting for an on-call detective, I yell down the hallway, 'You getting everything?'

"'Yes Sir!'

"'You copy the note verbatim?'

"'Yes, Sir.'

"'Did you weigh the brain yet?'

"'No, Sir. How am I supposed to do that?'

"'Just pick it up and guess. Has to be in the report, you know.'

"By now I suspect that he knows that I'm fucking with him, and this is some gut check, gross-out-the-rookie thing. Like I said, he's solid. So the motherfucker picks the brain up from its place on the bed and brings it out to me!

"Then the motherfucker says, 'I'd say about a pound and a half.'

"The look on my face musta been priceless. 'For chrissakes go put that back! Exactly where you got it, and don't tell nobody you moved it!'

"For chrissakes! Fucking rookies! I just need to get this kid into at least one good fight. If he does okay, I'm going to sign him off for solo patrol. Fucking rookie!"

The room full of seasoned cops were howling with laughter. Lieutenant Quinn was shaking his head back and forth. "I should know better."

A woman's tragic suicide wasn't normally a funny event. Quinn pondered how a bunch of cops could find mirth in something like that. He was familiar with the term gallows humor, and he supposed it took a sense of humor to survive. He wondered, what were the consequences involved when they lost their sense of humor? The question was rhetorical. Quinn knew the answer.

Bristol City PD was different from many agencies in that they did not put a lot of emphasis on their recruits graduating the academy. They did, however, organize a small celebration for those recruits who passed their field training program. Now 21 of the 24 recruits who had graduated the police academy were full-fledged policemen and would join the ranks of patrolmen. The problems identified with Prather, Gonzales, and Leggo continued, and all three were let go.

They held the celebration at the North Bristol City VFW hall. This allowed recruits to mingle with other cops as peers for the first time. They could have a couple of drinks and yet remain supervised and out of the public eye. The recruits and invited guests were all in coats and ties. Department policy proscribed drinking while in uniform.

Deputy Chief Nels Anderson, a born-again Christer, led off with a "welcome to the department" speech. It took a downward turn when he got into his hellfire and brimstone bit, lecturing on the pitfalls of drinking, fast cars, and faster women. "This is a very hard job to get, and a very easy one to lose. Take heed of what I just told you."

The chief tried to bring some levity back, telling everyone to relax and have a good time. There was polite applause, and soon the din of conversation rose around Quinn. Though he knew a great deal about the recruits of 1975, Quinn didn't mingle much. He chose instead to listen while he nursed a bottom-shelf VFW Scotch.

At the moment FTO Wendell Kahn was engaged in a serious conversation with recruit Bradley Johnson. He was illustrating something with his non-beer hand.

Quinn leaned against the bar and took in the exuberant conversations around him. Recruits reliving the intense training period they had just survived.

"...So it's week two on day shift, and I'm driving the car now. I'm riding with Mercer. We get a report of a robbery alarm sounding. Mercer tells me it's a Code 3 call, so I turn on the lights and siren. I think I know where I'm going, but I keep waiting for Mercer to confirm. Finally he reaches over and shuts off the lights and siren. 'Do you know where you're going?' he asks me. Nope. Not really. 'Well, that's what I thought too,' he says, 'cause you've been going Code 3 in the wrong direction. Fuck! That was a 2 outta 7 on the ol' daily eval.'"

In another conversation Quinn hears recruit Ron Johnson telling his peers, "This was funny. So me and Lazz are gonna meet Brownee and his recruit for J4 at El Faro. Connie Brewer is Brownee's recruit. We're all paying up at the register. Connie is flexing his pecs and preening like he always does, when some lady asks him if he is a new policeman. Before he can answer, Brownee says, 'No, Ma'am, he is not a new policeman. He is a mere cardboard cutout of a policeman.' You shoulda seen the look on Connie!"

And on it progressed.

Quinn marveled at their newfound camaraderie and bravado. Welcome to the fraternity, boys.

On 24th Avenue, almost exactly behind Solly's, was the entrance to the 41st Street "El," or elevated train. At street level, spent, cast-iron steps lead out of sight into the heart of the huge stone arch that supports Statey Bridge and launches the El towards South-end Borough in Bristol City's heart.

Next to those steps is the Genona Pork Store, a primitive but seductive tribute to the sausage or, frankly, just about any smoked pork product. Worn wooden floors dressed in uneven drifts of sawdust. Four diminutive, ancient cases, crammed full of sausages, smoked meats of every description, and Italian cheeses. Bianco Sardo, Caciocavallo, and the intense Stelvio. The cheeses of the working man. And the most glorious mortadella's, cappicolas and assorted soppressata's and culatello, hanging from the high tin ceiling. A pork curtain so thick you need to push it aside to place an order at the burnished brass cash register, circa 1930. Along one wall, small shelves bowed with the weight of a carnival of items in tins and jars and tubs. Peppers, capers, anchovies, pickled eggs, oils, bottles of vinegar, and even fresh, orecchiette, fregola, seeded Italian breads. Opening the front door released a pungent, garlicky aroma into the street, a gift to anyone lucky enough to be happening by. Genona's was a survivor, and it was gratifying to see it continue as one of the few real landmarks in the Borough.

Backing out of Genona's front door into the chill, with a gallon tub of pickled sausages wrapped in arms, Stevie Rimfro had parting words. "Hey, Tomino, I got the Indians by two runs. You got…let's see…oh, I know, you ain't got shit." In Bristol City, the double-A, Indians who played at the perennially vacant Packow Ball Yard, dominated the local sports news. They hadn't had a winning season since that idiot Jimmy Carter was in office. From inside Genona's, the counterman laughed, grabbed his package, and bellered in return, "I gotchur Indians, Rimjob. Right here."

They often referred to Rimfro as "the little guh-nomed shaped fellow," and he was an ideal character on which to apply nicknames, monikers, and pseudonyms. Some favored douchebaggy, but Rimjob, Rim, the Rimmer, and Steve-o remained popular amongst the Night Police. Two spectacularly unsuccessful hair implant procedures left Stevie wearing a black wool porkpie hat whenever he was conscious. There was nothing that could cause him to pull that Popeye Doyle chapeau from his big round head. 40-something, shortish, and leaning portly, this seasoned lawman was spectacularly well-liked by the boys in the Night Police.

In Rimjob's long and spectacular career, he worked in most of the Street Monster jobs. Vice, Robbery Detective, Narcotics, and Motorcycles (where he had to have those sexy black knee-high boots custom-built because of his fat calves installed on stubby little legs), and he did his patrol time as part of the tightly knit and exclusive Night Police. Though you wouldn't expect it to look at him, he was a great cop and an ass-kicker! He'd do anything for a buddy. Any time.

He did talk a lot, though. A lot. About all things perverse and obscene. Also about today's news, the flight of Chinese nationals in '49, butterflies, and why people prefer tuna salad without onion. Explain again, Rimjob, why hair implants were ever a good idea. Oh, how he'd explain. Ad nauseam. Stories about "the job" just bubbled out of him, like Old Faithful gurgling to life. He could recall details of some case that happened 25 years ago like it was yesterday. Rimjob would regale in graphic detail, the minutiae of the moment, during some pursuit that went wrong. Or right. Oh, how he could talk. Rimjob was funny as hell, and that pretty much was the saving grace that kept those around him from cramming a sock in it!

Shouldering his vinegared pork burden, Rimjob headed for the tight alleyway mid-block. He slid between the three-story brick walls and stepped onto 23rd Avenue, three doors down from Solly's. Thirty seconds later Tino lit up when the Rimmer slid the piquant sausages down the bar. "Thanks, buddy, that saves me a trip. How d'you know to do that?"

"I know things," Rimjob smiled. "And besides, we will need some fat to absorb all the booze tonight."

Quickly shifting gears, "Hey, you know Lyra, that wide-beamed Greek broad at Fat Andy's? The one with the hare lip?" Rimjob questioned.

Tino smiled, the old man knowing where this was headed.

"So I'm having dinner in there two nights ago, you know, those tomato fritters and a gyro. Oh, yeah, there may have been a couple glasses of Savatiano just to set the mood. It happens." Tino nods, the smile still in place.

"So, anyway, just as I sat down, Lyra swishes that fine bucket ass my way. I was so busy monitoring her derriere, I didn't hear her say 'Can I help you?' I continued in my arse-induced fog, but I did most definitely hear her say, 'Rim, are you lithening?'

Both the Rimmer and Tino chuckled at that. "Sorry, what did you say?" Lyra smiled and repeated, "Can I help you?"

Well, she most definitely could, so I reached over and grabbed a breadstick, waggled it her way, and asked, 'Would you mind nibbling on this provocatively?'

Tino, grinning, asks, "And?"

"I got nuttin." Rimjob frowned. "Anybody here?"

Nodding towards the back of the house, Tino says, "Quinn beat you by thirty minutes."

As Rimjob moved to join his old boss, dozens of memories washed over him. He was brimming with anticipation over the night ahead, there was so much catching up to do. No one would be eager to get right at the punchline. Instead, the conversations would meander. It was as though there was a protocol for laying down the old history before new pieces could be added. Rimmer knew that there would be rookie stories, Street Monster tales, and of course the really unique thing that they all shared, the undercover. Undercover work was above and beyond the normal call of duty. Nobody had forced them to do it. Undercover was dangerous, exhilarating, terrifying, and sometimes hysterically funny. Not everyone was good at it, but Rimjob and the men gathering this night were some of the best.

CHAPTER 5

Candyland

As a rookie narcling, the bosses assigned Jack Gleason to work with Teddy Rusing, a seasoned detective that had recently transferred in from a very large PD just north of Bristol City.

Gleason, an inveterate *Honeymooners* TV fan had recently been dubbed Kramden; an affectionate nickname amongst his trooper buddies. Rusing, on the other hand, acquired the not so affectionate, Dickface.

Now, according to Dickface, he'd been around the block. Done stints as a detective in Vice, Narco, Burglary, Robbery, and others. The brass seemed to love the guy and dealt him superb hands at almost every turn.

It didn't take long until the other detectives saw chinks in his armor. As lawmen do, they asked around. In short order, it all painted a picture that was less rosy and more Dickface. In fact, the BCPD boys may have stolen his new moniker from those coppers to the north.

Like many police departments, Bristol City took part in several joint task forces with the county and state Department of Justice. After being promoted from patrol officer to detective, Kramden was in and out of several assignments, from Burglary to Robbery, and he did a fair bit of intel-related engagements. Awaiting assignment to the narco task force, he was in a holding pattern. That's how he ended up working with Dickface; he was supposed to show Kramden the ropes until his assignment came through.

On the day Kramden found out about his new partner, they'd just finished the detective's morning briefing and Detective Paul Abraham pulled him to the side. A lazy eye tagged him fondly with the moniker "Walleye." He and Kramden had different assignments, but they ran in similar off-duty circles. They drank together at Bricks, often to excess.

He'd listen, with rapt attention, as Walleye would recount being a real policeman, "back in the old days." Kramden dripped with envy. Anyway, Walleye and he had an affinity and a deep trust in each other.

Walleye was, to be generous, disheveled, a kind of Peter Falk-Columbo type guy with a stellar rep. Known as a major ass-kicker, he was working Robbery but got pulled into many other "majors" in the bureau because of his huge skill set. If he took you into his confidence, you better fucking pay attention; chances are his advice would be spot on.

In his unkempt, closed-door office, Walleye sat on his desk, and in very precise remarks he schooled Kramden in all things Dickface. He told him to watch his back, not to trust the douchebag, and not to count on him to be there if the shit went down.

Walleye said they had it on good authority that Dickface had not only lied to make the move to Bristol City, but the brass in that very large northern PD even encouraged it. In fact, it looked like they had played him up, forgetting pertinent details to make sure the transfer happened. It was much easier than managing him out of the department. Kramden's novice detective euphoria was becoming a cooling corpse.

Spin this yarn forward about five months. Kramden had had enough of Dickface and was building his own wood on the asshole. In what could've been a career-limiting move, he went to see Pat Quinn, the irascible Chief of Detectives and proceeded to PMS bitch about having to work with Dickface. Kramden told him, he'd rather buy dope by himself than be paired with the duplicitous cocksucker. He didn't trust him, and he wanted out. The good news was that by then Dickface had alienated most everyone around him, including the brass. They'd figured out the prima donna fuck and his prior employer had duped them. Chief Quinn told Kramden to hang in a few weeks so he could pull a few levers to relieve him of his burden.

Three weeks later, it all fell into place. Quinn reassigned Dickface to a full load of check fraud cases, which just tickled the shit out of the rest of the boys in the bureau. Relegated to the crap pile, Kramden knew Dickface would just disappear under mountains of inconsequential paper.

Kramden had his date set to join the narco task force, six weeks out. And, to make his day brighter, they assigned him to share an office with Walleye until the transfer came through.

The CoD told him to game-plan getting cover for his narco cases and he'd leave Kramden alone until he moved to the task force. Quinn added, that since he was going to the state task force he wasn't to play with the city's narco team, he was to stay in his division until the move. The Chief of D's offered, "Walleye's been there and done that, a hundred times over. A narc of mythical proportions, back in the day. Count on him." And that's what Kramden did.

Following the Chief's advice, which Kramden learned to do over time, he arranged with other detectives in his division and in Carthage's drug squad, to cover him on narco deals when they could. It was an acceptable arrangement, but it didn't fill in all the gaps.

Walleye coached him up, and it wasn't long before he was making dope cases without a cover officer. Today that wouldn't happen, and even in his day, it wasn't common. It also wasn't unheard of either. Making a dope case on his own was way the fuck better, and safer, than working one with Dickface.

One of Bristol City's strip clubs, Candy's on the east side of town, was a patrol favorite. If it was on a young trooper's beat, they'd bar check it most nights, and they'd also end up there on calls all the fucking time. It was, as the city fathers liked to whine, "a blight on the city." Of course every now and again you'd see those same city fathers there, in the shadows, nursing a drink with a lovely on their lap.

When the heavy, battered doors slipped open, allowing a slice of daylight to seep into Candy's, you were slapped in the face with a funk of stale beer, cigarettes, sweat, and heavy perfume. Adding to the assault was the incessant throbbing of the classic 80s strip club soundtrack, Rick James' "Super Freak," Mellencamp's "Hurts So Good," and Marvin Gaye's "Sexual Healing."

A half a dozen well-worn pool tables backed the normal crowd at pervert row, the seats around the stage. Two bucks tucked into a pair of panties seemed to feed their fantasies. If they got lucky, they might land a "Stevie," that being when a dancer put the perv's face between her tits... so even Stevie Wonder would know he was in a strip club.

Littered with four tops and cheap red basket candles, Candy's was home to all forms of scoundrels and assorted rascalry. Drugs, cons, swindles, hustles, and most breeds of crooks, perps, hoodlums, dopers, cheaters, fraudsters, and hoods packed Candy's love palace. This was a seedy, spinning disco ball kind of joint. The usual colored floods (the green light was always out), and smoke so thick you could slice it with a Ka-Bar, created its own, odd intimacy.

Not uncommon was the pool cue swinging, broken beer bottle flying, "I'll kick your ass motherfucker" bar fight. Street troopers were more than used to showing up for the festivities.

The young coppers never complained about handling calls at Candy's. Even a bar fight was considered amusing and worthy of the next war story. And, let us not forget most of the girls were smoking hot, at least to the twenty-something-year-old beat cops who were flirting with every one of them. Young lawmen often disappeared into the night with a Crystal, an Amber, or a Jade in tow.

This was also a duck pond for a narcotics detective, and as the rookie in the room, Kramden harvested there often. It was here that he met Shoeford Jackman. His contemporaries (read all the other dope dealers working the joint) knew him as "Shoe." He was a Candy's regular. He was one of those black guys that were eggplant black. What do the Italian guys call them, mulunyan? He had a mouth full of almost perfect white teeth if you didn't count the three in front, snapped off at the gum line. He had the afro-comb buried in about a foot and a half of nappy hair. It was a look. He also had what Kramden imagined was a Southern accent, but it was hard to tell because he talked so fucking fast you couldn't separate the syllables.

Standing at the worn, sticky bar, nursing a beer, Shoe slid in next to Kramden and ordered a Scotch and milk. Well, Scotch and some bad-looking milk. Kramden had already pegged him as a dealer and eyeballed him, looking for an opening. It didn't take long. He'd just ordered another beer from Long Bob when he saw Shoe slip a bindle to the guy standing on his starboard side. When he turned Kramden's way, an eyebrow lifted and a knowing look completed their introduction.

Shoe had that razor-sharp hook in the corner of his big, unkempt pie hole. "You interested in this shit?" he says. And of course, Kramden was.

It was a simple transaction, a gram of coke for $110 bucks. Typical, easy, and now the Shoe was in Kramden's sights. One minor hiccup changed the dynamic. When the lab report came back, the dope Kramden paid 110 city dollars for was bunk. "What the fuck?" Kramden muttered to himself.

He wasn't sure of the best course of action but decided he'd make another buy if he could and see if the Shoe might sell him the real deal. Kramden reasoned he'd rather have a good dope rap against Shoe than a chicken shit "sales in lieu of" case.

Three nights later, Kramden went to Candy's, drank a lot, a lot…and never made sight of the mope. He'd seen him there almost every time he'd been there in the last few months, but not tonight.

It wasn't all for nought. Kramden bought what turned out to be a stolen Taurus .25 caliber auto, a jalopy of a pistol. The parolee who sold it boasted he'd done time for armed robbery. The ass clown even said he was on parole, more of his mating ritual to show Kramden what a badass he was. Turns out not only was he on parole, but he was wanted for a string of parole violations. Oops.

Kramden didn't mind working Candy's. Actually, it was a lot of fun. The new undercover Kramden was becoming a regular, and by now he had the proper credentials at the bar. He didn't have a problem with Snow, the leggy blond of his current infatuation either. While frustrated about not seeing Shoe, Snow eased his pain.

The next time was the charm. When Kramden made his entrance, Shoe was just inside the door, yukking it up with a couple of brothers. Shoe didn't recognize him. He was definitely cracker blind. Kramden went to the bar, and Long Bob dropped a Schaefer in front of him.

He enjoyed his beer and "Centerfold" by the J. Geils Band. Kramden again took notice of Shoe, this time across the room at a tattered pool table, making time with one of the girls. Destiny, a stone junkie, was flaunting her enormous tits, angling for a taste of whatever dope Shoe might have on him.

Kramden made his way toward the dope dealer, and with a nod of his head let Shoe know he wanted his attention. Destiny wanted his dope, and Shoe wanted Kramden's money. There was no competition. Not three minutes later Shoe walked towards the bathroom; Kramden knew enough to follow.

In the grungy pit of a hallway, wedged between discarded cardboard boxes and bags of reeking garbage, the two of them started the dance. "Yeah, I remember you." Shoe didn't. "Sure, another G, no prob. Gonna be $120, this is some primo shit. Right off the rock." Kramden knew he was full of defecate.

The day he got the second analysis report, sitting in his office with Walleye, Kramden was grumbling to himself, "that motherfucking punk dope dealer." He wasn't the least bit concerned Shoe might get plugged by some asshole who took exception to his bunk. This was a personal affront! Again!

Walleye, in his subtle way, "You get burned?" Kramden told him the tale, and Walleye simply said, "You gotta make this right, son. Don't let this dirtbag fuck you. You've got a rep on the street you've got to protect. Get your money back…do what you gotta do. You need help, I'm there for you." There was no way Kramden would ask for help. He had a rep at the PD too.

In a typical, summer downpour, Kramden headed to Candy's. Friday night, about ten o'clock, the joint was jumping, and he assumed the turd, Shoeford, would be there. He'd prepared for his intended summit with Mr. Jackman by secreting two "NarcoSleeve, Narcotic Field Tests" in his boot. He wasn't planning on waiting for the next crime lab analysis. He'd use a presumptive field test to get to an answer tonight.

Shoe and Kramden transacted another gram of who the fuck knows what for the now usual, $120. He finished his beer, shooting the shit with Shoe at the bar, then headed for the bathroom.

As is typical in a strip club, the can was a foul-smelling slum. A tight squeeze between the twin shitters and sinks, Kramden pried open the bent metal door of one of the toilets and wedged his way in, kicking the door shut behind. He pulled the field tester out of his boot, spilled a bit of the whitish powder inside and snapped the reactive capsule. Wait for it. Motherfucker! Fucking Shoe had some pair of balls. What he didn't have was cocaine. Motherfucker.

Kramden went straight for Shoe, but with a smile on his face. "Hey, dude, you got more of that?" Shoe pressed his forefinger to his lips, telling Kramden to hold it down. They stepped to the end of the bar. Kramden told him he was making a trip to Columbus and wanted to pick up a few grams of coke for a long weekend. Long Bob and some fat, hairy fuck wearing a Journey T-shirt and showing about 75 pounds of bare midriff interrupted them. Kramden used this as an opportunity to coax Shoe outside.

They ducked into the downpour and hot-footed it out to Kramden's undercover car, buried deep in the back of the unlit lot. That was by design, as was the backup Smith & Wesson 9mm he'd stashed between the console and his seat. Shoe slid in the passenger side, rain dumping in the slamming door. Kramden turned the car on, and with it "My Sharona" saluted them at this most auspicious of occasions.

Shoe was already into his high-speed marketing spiel when Kramden reached between the seat and console and produced that nasty-looking 9mm. In a blink, it sunk in, and Shoe's line of bullshit just trailed off, his eyes widened, and his jaw dropped. Kramden took advantage of the moment and shoved his pistol in Shoe's mouth as far as he could, pinning his head to the passenger door window. Shoe's hands reflexively shot up, pushing against the headliner. Kramden told him, "Do not move, motherfucker. I will fuck you up." Leaning over the console, he felt for weapons on Shoe's wiry frame, but in the quick search, felt none.

"Now, Shoe, please don't move. I don't intend on killing you unless I have to," Kramden warned. Shoe gagged in the affirmative and did his best to nod in decisive approval of Kramden's plan. "Listen, motherfucker, you've now sold me bunk, three motherfucking times. I'll tell you, I'm not fucking happy about it, and you shouldn't be either." Kramden added, "You're going to slowly, very slowly, empty your pockets. Dig out your cash and your dope. Now!"

Shoe froze in fear. He wanted to comply, but he was sure Kramden was about to splatter him. Kramden nudged the Smith against the back of his throat, and Shoe's hands drifted down towards his filthy jeans. He grubbed in the pockets, and amongst the usual keys and other shit, he produced a wad of bills, and eight or ten bindles Kramden assumed were bunk. Keeping him pinned to the glass, he told him, "Hands back up, motherfucker." Kramden pawed through the cash and retrieved his night's investment. The rest of the cash, he stuffed back into Shoe's shirt pocket.

Shoe was hyperventilating, and Kramden was running a close second. He wasn't the least bit used to committing an armed robbery of some dope fiend to get his city money back. Kramden thought to himself, *Fuck him, he started this bullshit!*

Kramden reached behind Shoe and popped the door. It swung open, and Shoe fell ass over teakettle out the door onto his back, into the muck. As he stretched across the console, still training his pistol at Shoe's forehead, Kramden suggested he might find another place to ply his trade. Shoe was crying, at least Kramden was pretty sure he was crying, it was still raining cats and fat chicks. He threw the rest of the bindles in the mud behind Shoe and suggested he "Get the fuck outta here." Shoe rolled over and bolted into the rain…the last Kramden saw of Shoeford Jackman.

Until he went to jail, of course. And yes, for the chicken shit "sales in lieu of" charges. It turned out, Kramden wasn't the only dupee. Two other agencies had done dope deals with the Shoe over the course of that summer. All of it was bunk.

The next day Kramden motored into the office, drinking a cup of steaming joe, and sat next to his old, battered detective friend. Walleye looked him over. "You take care of business?" Kramden replied he'd gotten his money back. "Anybody die?" Walleye smiled.

Getting the answer he wanted, he got up and grabbed a pack of files from the desk. "Off to court." He patted Kramden on the shoulder and strolled out the door. Kramden knew he approved. Walleye didn't need details and likely didn't want them. He was a smart guy.

Jack Gleason is an affable man. Some might characterize him as mirthful. At six foot and about 250, he's a big son of a bitch. It was only natural that a big guy named Jack Gleason should get tagged Ralph Kramden. Pat Quinn once estimated him at about "18 stone of noble character and enlarged liver." Kramden liked his drink.

Kramden was one of the original Night Police, from before they'd even given themselves the appellation they all so revered. He hadn't been on the PD more than a few months when he was assigned to Lt. Pat Quinn's midnight shift team. The hulking newbie was a particular favorite of Pat's, and Kramden hung on his every word; it was gospel to him. It didn't hurt that while Pat was between marriages, Kramden was a practicing adult male, known to have chased a skirt or two, and the two of them spent an inordinate amount of off-duty time at Brick's. At that point in their careers, Brick's was one of the four iconic cop bars in Bristol City, each catering to a different police district. Brick's had its own unique distinction. It was assigned as the lair of the young bucks. Brick's and Solly's couldn't have been more different.

Third-generation law enforcement, Kramden never gave a thought to doing anything else when he was growing up. He never considered being a doctor or an actor or an accountant. Only a policeman. He was a good policeman too. Uber aggressive, good instincts, and mostly fearless. It sometimes was an issue, and he occasionally crossed a line. It was most apparent as a rookie officer, but Lt. Quinn would educate him, coach him, and often keep his tit out of the ringer. Kramden didn't mind getting, as he would say, "edumacated." He was aware it was part of the process.

He packed a lot into his abbreviated career in law enforcement, including his time pushing a cruiser on graveyard, proud as punch to be part of the Night Police. He was assigned as an evidence technician, a precursor to today's CSI role and served time in the Detective Bureau, mostly as an undercover narcotics detective. He was an adrenaline junkie, like every one of his Night Police brethren. It was, in fact, an unstated requirement of the fraternity.

The fact that his police career was cut short, forced to retire, at eleven years on the job, clung to him like a wet blanket. At first, it smothered him, and he self-medicated. The days and long nights blurred into each other, and the hangover…well, it just remained constant until he drank it away. Again. And again.

Eventually, he gave it up, but he always looked back. He always kept his warrior fellowship in plain view. It might not have been the healthiest approach or mind-set, but he was hard-wired to be the police.

In time he moved on, the best he could. His current incumbency as the lead butcher at Heartland Meat Company did not define him. It did not provide a single molecule of adrenaline rush, but oddly, he'd be the first to admit he liked his job. It paid the bills. It also may have something to do with his not so svelte waistline. It couldn't have been the whiskey.

Tonight he lumbered down the steps of Solly's, a six by sixty, Ashton cigar poking out of his face. His modest limp was evidence of the wreckage that was his surgically repaired hip. It always embarrassed him he wasn't retired in some blistering shootout. It was harder to explain he got the boot from the job after an unfortunate attempt at charming a red-haired court reporter during a cops versus firemen football game. All these years later, the Night Police still find it amusing.

As Kramden slipped past the plank, he paused just long enough to lean over the bar and pull out a battered, cut short, 105 mm howitzer shell casing, his ashtray of choice for the back of Tav's. He slipped a twenty on the bar for Tino and moved into the muddled twilight.

"Hello, boys!" Kramden shouted, causing Rimjob to literally leap from his chair. This tickled Kramden of course. "God damn it, fuck! You're an asshole!" Rimjob bellered. Quinn just grinned. "Good to see you, buddy."

Kramden pulled off his damp overcoat and hoodie and flung them in one of the leather chairs, fireside. An ancient Allman Brothers' Eat A Peach T-shirt, jeans, and heavy work boots completing his ensemble. Even at 43 years of age, Kramden still had an almost boyish, pink-cheeked, Irish look to him. He didn't, however, have a single Irish bone in his body.

"Fuckin' great to see you, boys! I'm in the mood."

"Aren't you always?" Rimjob was happy to reply.

Ron Johnson, sometimes known as Heckle from his patrol pairing with Jeckle, or more commonly RJ because at the time he joined Bristol City PD there were no less than 12 Johnsons on the department, including his academy mate Bradley Johnson. So RJ he became. He had never intended on becoming a Bristol City cop, but when he was home on his terminal leave from the Marines, he saw a job announcement in the paper and applied on a whim. His plan was to return to sunny California and seek his fortune there. However, Bristol City offered him a job, and the rest was history.

RJ took the steps down to Solly's in two long-legged bounds. He was in one of his thinner, athletic phases. When he was drinking steady and not running, he could get a lot thicker. His looks were classic Brit, including the weak chin. Had he not had good American dental care as a kid he would look like a typical snaggle-toothed Liverpool pub-goer. Something worked for him, though, because he always punched way over his weight with women.

He stopped at the bar to make his manners with Tino. "Hey, Tino! Long time no see."

"No shit! How long's it been? Six, seven years? You don't come around much anymore."

"Damn. I guess it's been that long. Time flies, huh, Tino. Who all's here?"

"Quinn, Stevie, and Kramden. Quinn said Maxie's coming. That true?"

"He's over at the Seneca getting spruced up far as I know...you know fucking Maxie...not a hair can be outta place and not a speck can be on whatever thousand-dollar suit he's wearing."

"Shit. Be good to see him."

RJ dropped some bills on the bar for Tino's trouble and followed the cigar smoke to its source.

Back slaps and greetings all around as RJ joined Quinn, Kramden, and Rimjob. He stepped to the sideboard and fixed a drink with a fair amount of ice cubes and water. Best to pace himself on what promised to be a long night of tall tales and booze. Before he sat in one of the two remaining club chairs, he pondered leaving the better chair for Golden but decided not to. Golden was the rookie of the group and always would be regardless of his prodigal son status this evening. Might as well give him the rat squad chair and make him feel right at home, start busting balls upon arrival. In fact, as he tuned in to the conversation, Rimjob was busting his.

"So the big-time feds decide to visit the lowly cops of Bristol. Ya ever notice how these guys always forget where they're from? Forget who raised 'em?"

"Hey, thanks, Rimjob! Good to see you too, ya little wiseass. As you'll recall I was just down here three months ago for Kahn's retirement. And for the record it was Kahn and Quinn that raised me, not you, you little Guh-Nome."

Rimjob ducked the insult like a boxer slipping a punch. He countered by raising his near empty glass toward RJ. "Hey, just this once you think the feds could help a local out? There's probably no press conference in it for you, but I'd be most obliged."

Johnson, in his clipped, dry Brit style suggested Rimjob might bugger off, completely ignoring Rimjob's plea for the bottle of rye sitting about eight inches away on the side-board. Rieger's Monogram Rye Whiskey, a rare treat, had mysteriously appeared for the day's soiree, and Rimjob was most keen on it. Johnson perused the selection of cigars in the two humidors, humming to himself and enjoying what he knew was Rimmer's mild annoyance. "Don't make me come over there," Rimjob good-heartedly warned. Johnson laughed out loud, handing him the bottle. "Let me dig around in here. I'm sure we've got a nipple you can stick on that."

The stories making the evening's cut were always all over the board. In and out of context, often not even tied to whatever was being discussed in the present. Whatever trooper's got the floor, it may go story to story at a gallop or have his current saga clipped mid-sentence by a buddy who's just so God-damned impatient that's he's just gotta tell his. It doesn't matter to any of these guys. They'll get back to it. Or not. Doesn't matter. They are simply enjoying each other and the reminiscence of brothers, brothers they'd give it all for.

CHAPTER 6

G-Men

They were listening to Paul Abraham and Dino Callahan talk about their narco days. Abraham and Callahan were the scariest-looking pair to ever work undercover in the Borough. Abraham had been a fleet champion boxer in the Navy with big hairy arms covered in tattoos when nobody's arms had tattoos. An eye long since detached in some Navy bout wandered wherever it pleased. Callahan was a mountain of a man with heavy silver rings on every finger. Golden had seen him smash the nose right off a perp's face in a bar fight. Add long hair and bristling beards, and common citizens would not even dare eye contact with the pair, Abraham's roaming eyeball notwithstanding.

So Golden and Johnson sat in awe as the one-time narcs spoke in revered tones about going on raids up in Chicago with the DEA and ATF boys. Typical Golden, just a few years on the department and already antsy for something new. He swore that night that he would become a federal agent.

When Golden figured out the process, he cajoled Johnson into taking the written tests with him. DEA had its own test, and there was another test that covered all Treasury agencies, including his first choice, ATF. A year after taking the test, the U.S. Customs Service offered Golden a job. This was primarily because he spoke passable Spanish. It was not ATF or DEA, but Golden knew that Customs worked drug cases too. He quickly made the mental leap to visions of high-speed boat chases in the Caribbean. Anything was an improvement over the depressing environs of Bristol City.

In the 1980s, with the notable exceptions of the FBI, DEA, and the Secret Service, all federal law enforcement officers and investigators began their careers at the Federal Law Enforcement Training Center at Glynco, Georgia. FLETC is a town unto itself, built on an old US Navy auxiliary airfield. It has its own post office and zip code, convenience store, barbershop, security force, and bar. The acronym FLETC is pronounced "Flet-See," or sometimes known by the 2000 some odd students in residence there as "Flea Tech" in honor of the voracious gnats and sand fleas inhabiting the sandy soil of the place.

It was six o'clock a.m. on a steamy Coastal Georgia morning, and Max Golden was walking the half-mile from his dorm unit to the chow hall. The ground was flat, pine trees lined the footpaths, and the sickening smell of the Brunswick pulp mill permeated the heavy humid air. He had been very excited when he passed all the hurdles to become a special agent with the feds; a process that took over a year of testing, interviews, and a full field background leading to a top secret clearance. At the moment, Golden did not feel all that special, attired as he was in a light blue shirt, dark blue trousers of polyester, and running shoes. The FLETC training uniform looked very much like a low buck gas station uniform, known in FLETC parlance as "The Smurf Costume." Despite a shower just 15 minutes prior, sweat was pouring off of Golden. He thought to himself, it would be a long 20 weeks.

Despite the heat and silly costume, Golden was happy to be away from Bristol City and the hellish prison of a home life that he had created for himself. He had met a beautiful Japanese girl, her name was Akiko, while stationed in Japan with the Army, and had subsequently brought her home to the states to marry. Her English skills were minimal, and it embarrassed her to try to socialize in America. Akiko depended on Golden for companionship. He wanted out, but could think of no exit strategy that wouldn't crush the Japanese girl who looked up to him and loved him. Smurf costume and sand fleas be damned! Golden would savor the time away.

The curriculum turned out to be easy, basic police academy stuff, legal instruction on federal law, shooting, and physical training. It was not at all like Army boot camp, or even the police academy that Golden had attended a few years previous where they stood formation in their uniforms, had inspections, and underwent other military-type practices. Max smiled at the thought of the 48 members of CI-85-02 standing formation in their Smurf costumes and tennies. His old DIs would have chewed up the Smurf mob, and it would have been rich for sure! Weeks went by, and everyone settled into the routine. The older guys with prior law enforcement experience, like Golden, quickly struck up friendships and became drinking buddies.

It was a Thursday night, and Max Golden occupied a bar stool at the Gay Bar nursing a PBR. It was the "Gay Bar" because male students outnumbered female students on about a 5 to 1 ratio. The Gay Bar was always good for middle of the week drinking because it was within walking distance of the dorm units, and one could avoid a brush with the FLETC security force for drunk driving. Tomorrow, class CI-85-02 would graduate and it would mark the halfway point at FLETC for Golden. He had done well and would have Distinguished Graduate appended to his graduation certificate for achieving over 95% in academics, PT, and shooting. On Monday, he and a handful of other Customs agents would move on to 10 weeks of Customs specialized training. Golden was missing his old partners, and thought how much more fun it would have been to have had Kramden, Johnson, and Rimjob with him. He still had hopes that Johnson would get picked up.

As he drank his beer, he wondered about his next posting. He hoped it would be big and exciting like New York or San Francisco, or Miami. Max Golden didn't know how Akiko would adjust to a major city. Maybe there would be other Japanese there. Maybe she would meet a nice Japanese man and want a divorce.

After taking Spanish throughout grade school and high school, Ron Johnson could ask for "Two beers please," and "Where is the train station?" In his dealings with Mexicans on the street, he had also perfected some border patrol Spanish. "Put your goddamn manos aqui, pardner." Something, but not enough to get past the government language proficiency test. It took Johnson an additional year to get hired by the feds.

When Ron Johnson got hired by Customs, he was pleased for assignment in the same state where he had been a municipal policeman. The assignment could easily have been to a field office in Sharp Stick, Arkansas, or Elk Nuts, Montana. And then the icing on the cake, getting assigned to the same field office as his old buddy from the police department, Max Golden. During his first few weeks in the office, Johnson had to go through all the administrative burden that accompanies a new job, including unpacking several boxes of printed documents and empty binders. He assembled these into his personal copy of "The Manual," something they expected every agent to have and to keep constantly updated. In one of their first interactions, Golden came by RJ's desk and informed him that no one paid much attention to the manual. Later he tacked a neatly lettered message to RJ's cubicle divider—"The manual is for sheep!"

Johnson's first year on the job was divided between the academy classes held at Glynco, Georgia, and time with his training agent in and around the field office. Johnson's training agent was a talkative former Border Patrolman named Kline. Kline had damn near a photographic memory and wrote some of the best reports ever written. He had thousands of facts and charts on dozens of criminals; problem was, he could never close the deal. He was a talker, a chart maker, but not a case maker. Having been a police detective, Johnson could put cases together and make arrests. Suddenly Kline was making cases. Burchfield, their lanky Texas-born boss, wondered out loud, "Who is training whom?"

Normally new hires stayed with a training agent for 2 years, but Burchfield signed off on Johnson after just 11 months on the job. The agency was expanding, and needed good agents in the field. Max Golden had been cut loose early as well. Both were seasoned cops and didn't need their hands held.

Once Johnson and Golden got clear of having training agents and all the usual rookie constraints, they each in their own way started letting the locals around Capital City know that they had come to play. That they would help them by taking that big federal stick to any of their problem children; any crook that needed a good 10-year stretch in the federal pen, they could arrange that. After a few good cases word got around, and the local cops were steering them onto solid crooks and sharing their informants.

Max invited Johnson to join him checking out a lead up in Jasper County somewhere in the northeast corner of the state. On the road trip to a remote law enforcement outpost near the state border, the two agents had several hours in the car to rekindle their acquaintance. Somewhere on the interstate well north of the state capital, it began something like this…

"Ron, you wanna grab us a couple of road-cokes outta that cooler on the backseat?"

It surprised Johnson to find that the cooler on the backseat did not contain Golden's lunch. It was stuffed full of ice and cans of Heineken. This shouldn't have been a shock, as Golden had always been a go-out-to-lunch guy versus a pack-your-lunch type. As he handed one of the icy cans to Golden, Johnson said, "I take it you are not overly worried about the Highway Patrol?"

"Not so much. Set the cruise for 10 over and stay between the lines usually works. Beyond that the badge does say U.S. on it, kinda like having Master Badge. You gotta quit thinking small, Johnson."

Maxie always had style. Three hours, two piss stops, and 18 Heinekens later, their friendship was re-solidified. The former Bristol City lawmen were riding together again. Neither could have predicted how it would all end.

They met with the Jasper sheriff's sergeant about some suspicious activity on BLM land consistent with a clandestine meth lab. The sergeant had also run several out-of-town vehicles, and one had come back to a notorious Outlaw motorcycle gang member known to be a cook.

Meanwhile, evening had seeped into Solly's. A decided chill, just outside the warmth of friends and fire. The boys were settling in. Golden would show. He always seemed to have a parallel agenda. Sometimes it made him tardy to the party.

Quinn was focused a bit more than the others on trying to square the corners of the AWOL Maxie Golden's life. He nudged RJ. "You think any of this had to do with Maxie's upbringing? I know he was kinda sheltered as a kid."

RJ looked toward the door, expecting Max to appear, then he thought for a minute before trying to put it into words. "Maxie, for all his bravado, was actually a shy kinda guy."

Kramden snorted some of his drink and cigar smoke simultaneously. Not a pretty sight.

"No, really, he was an only child. His mom raised him. She was a Dunkard."

Before RJ could continue, Rimjob seized on the word. "A drunkard…Jesus, no dad and his mom was a drunk?"

Kramden recovered from his previous explosion enough to correct Rimjob. "For fuck sake, Steve-o. Dunkard! Like a Quaker. They were from Germany! There's a bunch of them here in the Midwest."

RJ continued his history. "Kramden's right. The Dunkard Brethren were part of a German religious movement. Maxie's dad came over from Germany about long enough to meet and marry Maxie's mom before he hightailed it back to the Fatherland. The order of Maxie's conception versus the marriage is questionable, which may explain dad's early exit. Maxie was raised among the Dunkards until his momma finally gave it up when he was done with high school. Spent his summers in Germany with dad… don't think that was much fun either. Old man was rich, but strict as hell. Obviously,

Maxie broke away from all of that shit too, in a big way. Maxie knows his Bible though, I'll give him that."

Quinn studied the ash on his cigar and mulled over the new information. "So you think he just went a little crazy when he finally got the chance?"

"A little crazy? That's like calling the Titanic a boating accident!"

"Thank you, Steve-o Rimfro, sarcastic conscience of the room and lead metaphorist." Kramden trying to swat Rimjob down.

"Would you two assholes let RJ finish...please?"

Kramden and Rimjob eyed each other, a truce in the battle of insults…for the moment.

RJ resumed. "Golden went to a small Christian college up north. Worked his way through. Then he enlisted in the Army, enlisted in the Signal Corps… didn't go for the commission, just wanted to be a simple soldier. Did most of his time in garrison over in Japan. Somewhere along the line Army Intel recruited him, probably when they figured out that he spoke Spanish, German, and passable Japanese. Maxie had a real talent for languages, especially if it could get him closer to some pussy." When RJ paused, Quinn served as bartender and primed the storyteller's glass.

Fresh drink in hand, RJ finished the chapter. "The rest of the story you guys pretty much know. He came back home to Missouri and BC hired him. From then on there wasn't a car too fast, a woman too fine, a prank he wouldn't pull, a dare he wouldn't take."

RJ had one final thought. "Oh, you guys probably didn't know this, but his dad died about 5 years ago. Left Maxie millions, however it's all tied up behind legal firewalls somehow. The old kraut didn't want it to go straight to Maxie just to be consumed in the lawsuit." The other three former investigators in the room digested this final piece of the enigma that was Max Golden.

Finally, Rimjob, ever the master of the obvious, "Could of had it all and still fucked it up."

There was a rare silence in the room, every man lost in his own thoughts. Kramden was the first to rouse himself and broke the silence by quoting Hunter Thompson,

"I hate to advocate drugs, alcohol, violence, or insanity to anyone, but they've always worked for me."

"Well, I'll tell you this much, that shit seems to work for 'pert near everybody. Somebody once said that. I can't remember if I heard it in the academy or in some tap room, but there was a lot of truth in it."

The bit about insanity inspired Rimjob, and he's now in the driver's seat. "So the call comes in. Unknown medical problem, blah, blah, blah at The Templeton Manor. When we get there, there's this nut job up on a fourth-floor balcony. Naked as a fucking blue jay and leaning over the railing. I get out the cruiser, and I can hear him. 'This is the time, this is the time, the time.' I try yelling up at him, but it's of no use. He can't hear us, so we hit the stairs.

"On the fourth floor, we're trying to figure out which apartment he's in when some scabbed-up, bad-eye hype starts pointing at one of the apartments on the south side of the hall. Sure as shit, the door's open and in we go.

"It's a dump. Like they all are at the Manor. Nothing special, just your basic hype, shit hole dump. Stinking funk and stacks of crap everywhere. And of course now we can clearly hear this idiot shouting like he's got his dick caught in the car door. As we step into what would normally be called a living room, we can see him on his little shit balcony leaning over, his scrawny bare ass saying 'How do' to us. Me and my recruit look at each other. I motion him to be still, and then I say to whack face, 'Hey, buddy, you okay?'

"Whack face stops his bellering and turns to look at both of us. Surprised. Like, where the fuck did you come from? Just for a blink though. Then I'll be fucked if he didn't turn right around and fling his dumb ass over the balcony. There was, in fact, a splatting sound.

"We hustle back downstairs, and there's whack face splashed on the pavement. Not sure how fortunate it was, but he broke his fall, just a little bit, by bouncing off a bank of apartment mailboxes before he slammed into the asphalt.

"While we waited for the wagon to drag him off 632 to the local loony bin, he's still yapping away. He's bleeding from most everywhere and pretty broken up, but

he's merrily just chattering away. I assume he never stopped, even during his recent, rapid descent.

"Well, what we found out before they bundled him up and took him off to the laughing academy was that he was most concerned about the horns that Beelzebub *had placed on his forehead. I shit you not.* He *also said that he didn't want us to stop him from leaping into the night, because the only way to get rid of the horns was to bail out onto his head and knock them off.* Personally, *I might've given him different advice, but the last time I spoke to him, he leaped off a fucking balcony."*

CHAPTER 7

Schnitzle and Tugjob

With a luminous harvest moon bathing the streets of the 588 Borough, the 2nd District graveyard shift briefing was winding down. The troopers in attendance peeled themselves off the cheap plastic chairs, clipboards and a briefing note or two finding its rightful spot amongst their gear. Slipping nightsticks into their Sam Brownes, they adjusted the armament needed to get them through the shift, if all things went right. The sarcastic jabs that would last through the shift were just beginning.

As a clutch of blue suits moved towards the door, Major Norbert Pinney stopped them in their tracks. Pinney, a slick blowhard who was profoundly enamored of himself, was the ranking police administrator suffering through his graveyard shift assignment. Suffering was the operative word as he was paying penance for stepping on his dick with the wife of one of his detectives.

The Major, or "Hair Hat" as he was lovingly referred to, was easily ignored when not in attendance. His officious bullshit was mocked and eye-rolled at every turn. Topping it off, he had a tedious and galling habit of applying unwanted monikers to his troops. They leaned insulting or abusive. Occasionally even slanderous. It made him feel better about himself.

This day, he'd made his way to the muster room with an agenda, one that wasn't in the best interests of Max Golden or Steve Rimfro. As the lawmen moved back towards their chairs, awaiting his latest nauseam, he scanned the crowd looking for Max and Rimjob. He knew very well who these stellar young night policemen were, but in his own inimitable style, he pointed and bellowed, "Tugjob, Schnitzle. I need your asses in my office at the end of shift. Do not fucking make me wait." And, the snickering began. Both men in blue knew that they'd be Tugjob and Schnitzle for at least the next 10 hours plus. They both hoped it wouldn't stick.

The effects of mental illness are an issue the beat cop deals with every day. One example routinely presented itself during civilian interactions when John Doe has stopped taking his meds, more often than not, lithium. Lithium has a stabilizing effect on the mood, which means that a person taking it will have a more even-keel, balanced mood and will be less likely to experience the highs associated with mania and the lows associated with depression. A cop doesn't know if lithium does all those things, but he knows he takes calls damn near every week, possibly more often, where dodging lithium is a contributing factor.

There is a slightly higher likelihood of violent behavior among people with psychotic illness. Many studies suggest that this may be more the result of abusing drugs or alcohol or having a history of violent behavior independent of the illness. Cops understand this. They've seen all the manifestations. They deal with them every day.

Depression, suicidal thinking…routine for the boys in blue. Some nut job with 16 cats and a tinfoil hat, living in a 2400 square foot, suburban litter box that hasn't been cleaned in three years. Oh, yeah, they live that. Laureen, the 22-year-old cashier at Manny's Meats who hung herself in the meat locker, with of all things, a coat hanger. The Night Police see it all.

There's no doubt some will bitch and moan that their favorite mental disorder hasn't been mentioned or that there's been a mischaracterization of the symptoms or the behaviors of these maladies. Cops are routinely given a minimal amount of instruction on mental illness, including ways to identify and de-escalate or otherwise manage these issues on the street. The goal is to assist the poor soul who's so afflicted. It's also considered convenient not to get anyone gravely injured or killed.

Unfortunately, even a few troopers fall victim to mental disorders, but that normally manifests late in their careers. Or early in their marriages.

Bristol City had several acute psychiatric inpatient facilities, lock-down wards for the very violent. They were privately run and were part of a piss-poor support mechanism for a piss-poor state mental health system.

These locations were the only private facilities in the city that had hard-wired alarm systems that terminated in BCPD's emergency services dispatch center. If they had a patient who malfunctioned in a big way and the staff couldn't handle it, they hit the alarm and dispatch sent in the boys.

This night, about 2 a.m., fledgling Officer Rimfro got tabbed to respond to the Marytyme Facility on Madison and Kenmore on an unknown alarm call. Because of the nature of the alarm, Rimjob hit the lights and siren and hammered the accelerator, pushing his cruiser into the neighboring beat to take the call. As usual, fills were scarce, but this call required one by policy. Max, another young buck with just two years on the job, had to terminate a car stop and divert to Marytyme.

Alarm calls from Marytyme were infrequent, but almost always the real deal. Both squad cars covered ground at a high rate of speed. Max radioed in, "When you free up more units, send them our way."

"A-firm," replied dispatch.

The narrow drive at the front of Marytyme was dark and tight for the two arriving cruisers. Their light bars, a kaleidoscope of color in the cramped space, added to the unfolding drama. As Golden and Rimjob exited their vehicles, the front doors exploded open. Bright fluorescent light spilled on the driveway apron.

Silhouetted in the doorway was a female staffer…young and hot, Officer Rimfro hypothesized (cops and nurses were a thing). The name tag pinned to her blouse read "Alvogado." Holding on to the crash bar and leaning acutely outward, she held open the other door with an outstretched leg. She was obviously in distress and was alternating between hyperventilating and trying to relay information. Max, in his typical straightforward approach, told the orderly, "You need to calm down. NOW! Tell us what's going on."

In between gulps of air, she squeaked out, "In B Unit," desperately trying to catch her breath. "They're fighting. He's really hurt…really hurt, hurry!"

Alvogado was pleading, and Max was encouraging. "Just show us. NOW."

Golden and Rimjob followed into the bright vestibule, one that might have doubled as an admissions area. From the foyer branched two hallways on either side of the building. Both cops noted that the bright lights didn't extend down the almost dark hallways. Alvogado was hurrying into the B wing and made the turn, only late hours' lighting casting some negligible illumination.

There was a tangle of men on the floor at the far end of the hall. Arms and fists swinging, legs twisting, trying to gain leverage on the glossy linoleum. Like a pan of popcorn on the stove, bodies were being launched out of the pile. The bedlam produced a din of cussing, shrieks, bellowing, and bawling. Out of place, in this shit show, was a deep, I guess you'd call it, a howl.

Max bolted down the hall, Rimjob a half step behind. Alvogado didn't move, which was just as well. They passed two male staffers, presumably orderlies. One appeared to be unconscious, the other was on his hands and knees, bleeding badly from the mouth.

The patrol officers waded into the fray, trying to understand who was malfunctioning and who was trying to restrain. Max immediately took an elbow to the temple and went down. Rimjob barked into his radio, "Respond more units." Dispatch knew whose radio was activated by the computer tones generated when the mic was keyed.

Rimjob got an eye on the uniquely named Iggigidio Izarra, and grabbed at a wrist. It was difficult to get a hold, as there was a plethora of body parts in motion, everyone trying to grab at a limb and apply restraint. The young cop was on his belly sinking into the pile of writhing combatants. Izarra was seriously strong and covered in sweat or other bodily fluid. Rimjob got hold of Izarra's wrist, with both hands and tried to get a knee on it. The three other orderly types each had a limb in one degree of restraint or another, for the moment. One poor son of a bitch shrieked in pain as Izarra literally bit through his Achilles tendon…out of the game, without question.

As Max groggily re-applied himself to the pile, two more arriving troopers piled on, a third barreled down the hall towards the throng. It was amazing the profound strength Izarra mustered against all those relatively fit and mostly young men. Someone from the heap yelled out to the observing staff to "get restraints, leather restraints."

The tide was turning, albeit slowly, at least in terms of how time flies when you're fighting your ass off. The orderlies, to a man, were gassed, and there'd been a perceptible transition from a pile of white on Mr. Izarra to a pile of blue. That fucking baleful howl continued, and you could hear leather, batons, and metal rattling off the floor and the walls.

One more unit arrived and settled into the mass, ultimately applying the first set of cuffs behind Izarra's back. He flopped over, and the two officers who'd been attempting to restrain Ibarra's head, and more importantly his snapping incisors, were able to get a towel, or some staffer's shirt, across his open mouth. They pinned his head to the floor with bodyweight applied from each side.

With the balance of the blue suits laying across his whipsaw legs, they were able to get a set of leather restraints around his knees and then his ankles. The action, for all intents and purposes, was thankfully over. Izarra's howling had finally subsided and taken the form of a dripping whimper.

Six patrol officers were sprawled in the hallway darkness on and around Mr. Iggigidio Izarra. There were uniform parts, batons, flashlights, even a badge strewn on the glossy, sweat- and urine-covered floor. Wreckage from a memorable engagement. Max and Rimjob were both on their hands and knees taking huge gulps of air, trying to stabilize and normalize.

At about that moment, fluorescent lights flickered to life, sequentially down the dark hall. When the business end illuminated, Max gasped, "Holy fuck! We knocked his fucking ears off!"

"What?" from somewhere among the panting troops.

"We knocked his fucking ears off!" This did grab the attention of his partners, and sure as fuck, there were two ears laying in the hall about three feet apart.

This was the first time there was enough light and shifted focus to take a gander at Izarra. He was a mass of scar tissue, from his head to his calves. He was the disfigured sculptor, Vincent Price, of the 50s horror film, *House of Wax*.

As a 31-year-old, ex-Marine and recently back from his third tour in Vietnam, E-6, Staff Sergeant Izarra got liquored up on a three-day run. Seated in a broken-down recliner in his girlfriend's garage, he lit a match, but not until he'd drenched himself in the contents of her lawn mower's gas tank. Burned over 60% of his body, most of it third degree.

It was unfortunate for him that he was a miracle of modern medicine. He survived. Sentenced to forever, in wretched physical and mental misery.

Izarra's ears had been burned off in the fire, only smears of scar tissue in their place. The ears on the hallway floor were prostheses. Faux ears. Hand-painted, health-grade silicone ears. Ears that marginally improved his hearing, but they were far from helping with his appearance.

The facility staff moved in to apply more medically approved restraints. They had options at that point. Restraint mitts, chest vests, body blankets, helmets that prevent sense perception, and the ever-popular chemical restraints and seclusion. The cops had none of these.

The patrol officers picked up and reassembled the debris that had been their uniforms just a few minutes before. Together, except for Rimjob who would get the paper, they trudged for the door.

There was still that little issue with Major Hair Hat to clean up. Tugjob and Schnitzle decided he could wait.

Solly's wonderful old potbelly was puffing a little smoke. It needed someone with enough energy and awareness to adjust the draft. Four of this nation's finest, all professional investigators at one point or another in their career and not one noticed a few errant drifts of smoke perfuming the room. Actually it may have been noticed, but not one of them gave a shit. All the boys had had a couple of drinks, and cigars were in play. As was typical, stress was giving way to a general comforting amusement.

Rimjob was mentally still in the last story. He recollected how he and Golden desperately needed some booze and a place where they could relive the odd battle they had fought that night with a lunatic man with rubber ears.

Of the four main cop shops in Bristol City—or for the uninitiated, bars—that policemen frequent, there was one where the rookies, the young bucks tended to gravitate. It should be said that while geography played a part and it was easier to head to a tavern close to home, it was more important to head to a spot that fit you. That fit your crowd. That made you whole, when you were amongst your brethren. Brick's was such a place, and that was where he and "Schnitzle" headed.

CHAPTER 8

A Gin Mill in the 588

Brick's was a Shemp of a joint. Open for business 5 a.m. to 3 a.m., accommodating to all shifts in the 588 Borough. Disheveled. Ragged at the edges. Brick's had a good heart, as far as a bar goes.

Less than a block from headquarters, it drew a crowd that reflected it. Rookies showed often, and for many, it was the first cop shop they'd ever been in. They flocked to it like moths to a flame. A fair number of detectives and admin staff attended because it was close enough for a quick pop or two before heading home to she who must be obeyed. Records clerks, a few beat-wives, and various hangers-on would occasionally show, which is the reason most of the journeyman troopers opted out for other saloons.

Dark in the corners, with cheap red basket candles at each of the five shabby, Naugahyde banquettes, Brick's screamed indifference. An acrid beer funk permeated. Old Styles, Schaefers and dice cups littered the worn Formica slab. And a few singles for the barkeep. The battered Rock-Ola jukebox, with a handful of red quarters laying on the glass, poured out favored standards of the day. The most popular appeared to have been

Hall and Oates' "Private Eyes," which was playing for the third time since "swings" walked in the door.

As she wheeled into the table with another round for the semi-rowdy group, Duffy's piercing green eyes penetrated the gloom. A pleasant enough face, very full lips, and just the right touch of lip gloss. It was a shame her ass was about six ax-handles across, not that that stopped these occasional admirers from trying to slip it to her.

Dark blue, wool uniform pants, blue T's, windbreakers, and for good measure, black tactical boots, appear to be de rigueur for this young trooper crowd. Tight cut hair, and a mix of fresh and seasoned features marked these guys to all but the oblivious as lawmen. To the oblivious, the Model 19, .357 Smith and Wesson surreptitiously bulging at each man's hip was a dead giveaway.

A smear of competing conversation threads. Laughter and the building melody that was "motherfuckers," "douchebags," and the ever-popular "hick'ry shampoo" filled the cracks between the boys. Longneck Schaefers slapped the table and vied for room amongst cocktail napkins, ashtrays, and Marlboros, empty shot glasses, and several pairs of Ray-Bans. A drink spilled, and two of Bristol City's finest leapt to their feet, sending chairs toppling. This didn't even come close to pausing the conversation. Everyone was already on to the next hot ripper.

Life at Brick's was Joe Wambaugh's choir practice. The kind taking place at every end of watch, in every metropolitan city across this country. It was the place these cops went to unwind, to share their shit with each other. And then there was beer and maybe some shots, maybe a few kamikazes.

The vets and the aging detectives in attendance were more likely slamming Dewars or Jack and Coke. Some of these guys were "Cardinals" like Lieutenant Pat Quinn, most of them had taken a run at it. This is the place where liar's dice rolled, ship cap'n crew sailed, and a lot of other maladministrations of the truth took place.

Cops are an interesting strain. They're as different, conflicting, and divergent as any group you might define, but somehow they're more alike than most. They're homologous yet not interchangeable. Somehow they maintain an affinity for working with each other and a certain equilibrium toiling in the trenches.

The boys in blue at Brick's were the usual mix of small, tall, skinny, fat, and the more interesting hulks, the scrawny, and the little Napoleons, all buffed the fuck up. They may have leaned right, but there were plenty of libs amongst them. Some were religious, some were vehemently not. There were the needy, the strong, the leaders and followers.

A lot of the cops were family men, with kids and wives (and ex-wives), including some sitting at Brick's this night. Some were faithful husbands. Most were not. Most of the young bucks had girlfriends, often several. There were plenty that supplemented on-shift by bedding the amenable women in their patrol sector, their beat-wives.

There was a slew of cop groupies to choose from, you know, the holster sniffers and fender lizards. They were usually identified as the ones leaving the newbies cards or flowers on their favorite cop's cruiser. Or perhaps balloons delivered to shift muster or briefing. This activity usually caused the rook embarrassment, a shitload of derisive commentary, and occasionally it became the first stage of an "as yet to be endured" practical joke.

Prejudice and cynicism marked some of this brotherhood. More were just trying to do a good job, knocking the shit out of bad guys, and if the city, the fucking attorneys, and the all-knowing legislature would let them, help put their city in order.

They were just trying to have a good time, do the job, and not get killed. The young guys felt bulletproof and, by far, most of them proved that theory. Most of them. Every one of them took risks every day that the average guy or gal sitting behind a desk at General Motors or selling slacks at Sears and Roebuck would ever come within a cunt hair of experiencing.

If you looked at the typical demographics of a group of young cops (vs. the baggage-ridden, senior lawmen), they'd be off the chart for the number of hilarious motherfuckers per department. There are more laughs per shift hours than in any other profession. There's no data to support that, but cops know it to be true. Anecdotal, blue, dark/gallows/ morbid, deadpan, dry, droll, epigrammatic, farcical, hyperbolic, ironic, sophomoric, parodic, satirical, self-deprecating, situational, slapstick, the professional police officer's favorite—juvenile, and almost routinely at any choir practice—cocktail-fueled stand-up. As Bennett Cerf once said, "laughter is the best medicine." Actually it was a close second to booze.

Booze, broads, and bills were the undoing of many in this profession. They taught that in the academy. Colorfully and repeatedly, they illustrated just how this manifested itself amongst the troops. It was drilled into you—avoid, avoid, avoid! "For fuck's sake, youngster, I'm promising you'll step on your dick if you don't pay attention!" It worked too. For a few. Most of them at Brick's had problems in one of the three aforementioned categories, a couple of them in all three.

Duffy was back with another round, four Old Style's, four shots of schnapps, and a Dewars neat, with a water back. Oddly, Duff appeared to have lost about an ax-handle, maybe more, and in just the last hour and a half.

Brick's was a more typical cop bar than Solly's Tavern, the one the Night Police had cultivated for their exclusive use. And the Night Police liked it just that way.

Solly's is not Brick's. It's not even close. It is most definitely not on the radar of most of BCPD's eleven hundred plus officers. That's exactly why Quinn's crew of Night Policemen adopted it as their own. Conversations could be had in Solly's without obvious risk, without fear that a misplaced word or an unflattering comment about the brass would come back to bite them in the ass.

Surprisingly enough, Solly's had been discovered by Quinn's former wife, Suzanne. A moderately successful deputy district attorney, she was busty, loud, and irreverent. She was also whip fast and unwilling to put up with even a single molecule of male bullshit. Especially male cop bullshit. She could manage Quinn. She could dominate him. She also loved him 'til the day she died at the age of 39. Quinn didn't talk about it, ever, but her death left a gaping hole in his heart. His boys on the job helped fill that void, and he channeled his love in their direction. And Solly's became their watering hole.

Rimjob, about three ryes into the evening, was wrapping up his story of two dismembered corpses they'd scooped out of a 110 gallon yellow, salvage drum, dumped behind the Devonshire Industrial Rubber plant. He offered up that his "janitors in a drum" had to be squeegeed out, "after the little chunks slipped through our fingers."

Kramden suggested that he might've left that job to the body baggers, the professionals.

Rimjob suggested Kramden go fuck himself.

The back and forth tickled Quinn. He took a draft off his cigar, a chipped but serviceable heavy bottomed highball glass with two fingers of Macallan Oak in his fist. If you asked, he'd give you its pedigree, 15 years aging in some farm distillery on an Easter Elchies estate and standing above the Spey near Craigellachie. No one else had any idea what the fuck that meant, but it pleased Quinn to no end to be in the know.

"I'll take your janitors in a drum and raise you a fresh road smear!"

Quinn remembered that being a young policeman was a wet dream. Everyday events happen that are out of the realm of a typical young person's experience or even fantasy, good or bad. A yearling-officer experiences more in those first 12 months on the job than the average Joe will see in a lifetime. A lot more. He recalled one of Golden's formative moments. Seemed like the kid saw a lot of gore in his first year, but hell, hadn't they all?

CHAPTER 9

Alone in the Dark

Max Golden left Fire Engine House 29 a bit after midnight on a cold December night, days before Christmas. He had just re-read one of his favorite Penthouse Forum missives while completing an exquisite dump. Mid-shift and things were feeling downright positive. Somehow you knew that would change.

Max liked the sound of his leather on his Sam Browne, sweetly creaking as he slid into his patrol car. His cruiser, a Chevy Nova 9C1, a single cherry on top, air filter flipped over to make it sound more throaty. Golden was so new on the job, he sometimes got in his patrol car and just looked around, soaking it all in. Cherishing his pressed, intoxicating, dark blue uniform and the lustrous silver star he'd worked so hard to have pinned on him by his ex-wife-to-be.

Max had lots of quick turnaround calls with little paper, at least to that point. The usual family beefs, moms and dads liquored up on spiked eggnog, arguing over little Johnny's decision to desert the Marine Corps and run to Puerto Whothefuckknows in Mexico with that whore girlfriend of his. Only two routine alarm calls (and even to a rook, they can become routine...a dangerous mind-set).

He had to help the paramedics load a drunken bicyclist, excess avoirdupois aplenty, into the wagon or ambulance as some might call it. He'd crashed his bike through a storm drain grate, the front wheel slipping into the slots and flinging him over the handlebars, not unlike a fleshy aerospace pioneer. The poor guy landed bridge of the nose first into the curb, rearranging all of his God-given facial features. Two hundred and sixty pounds of shimmering suet slamming into a concrete curb will do that.

For a rookie, it was hard to beat a shift with lots of action and little paper. They were hard to come by. If you worked swings, you'd get some great calls, but they would stack up as reports to be written and that would surely screw up the last few hours of each shift and often long after.

The night police had it best. Shift start at 2300 hours, the citizenry would routinely already be in its cups. It was a brawling, fast-paced, ass-kicking five or six hours followed by a few very slow hours that were routinely devoted to report writing, just prior to the sun's reappearance. The longer you pushed a patrol car, the more you learned about alternatives to report writing, but that's another story.

As Max drove up Fayette Ave. towards Winterberry, the incessant radio chatter was building momentum. It does that. Most young guys like that radio chatter. It's somehow comforting and connecting. What sounds like gibberish to the uninitiated is a crystal-clear life force for the man or woman behind the wheel. In his mind, he can picture where most of his team is geographically within his sector, or in this case, borough. And how that relates to where he is at any time. He knows the calls they're taking. He's always keeping abreast of breaking hot calls and sincerely hoping the next robbery in progress or man with a gun call is his.

That frigid night, graveyard shift was pitching into a higher gear. Lots of units were asking for fills or some other type of assist, but many were going unanswered.

Bristol City wasn't big on paying overtime, and it seemed they felt just about the same for minimum manning. Beats were consistently short-staffed, never matching the need, based on the calls for service. The city council, the police brass, and the bean counters were very aware of the shortage of manpower and the risk to the men and women in blue. They could articulate a clear and concise staffing strategy to the citizens of Bristol City and probably to the press, but they weren't fooling the city's finest. It's disquieting to radio in you've stopped a suspicious vehicle and the situation requires additional units, only to be told, "No fills available 4S32, will advise." They just carry on and count on good tactics to get them home each night.

Max had cleared the firehouse about four minutes when he heard the two-toned radio alert, indicating a significant event. Dispatch advised Engine 29 and paramedics were being dispatched to a "10-50J2, motorcycle versus auto, Winterberry and Taylor Young Drive." A major injury accident, a 10-50J2 in their radio parlance. These calls always required the dispatch of a fire truck, which carried lifesaving and auto extrication tools, the paramedics for obvious reasons, and a single patrol officer. It was always a call they looked at with a mix of curiosity and dread. They never knew what they'd see upon arrival, often it was more than gruesome. And if they were first on the scene, they'd need to coordinate in terms of lifesaving resources and protecting other drivers on the roadway. Even the idiot ones.

Max knew he had about a three- or four-minute, lights and siren, emergency run to get to this accident. He knew he was ahead of Fire and assumed that the paramedics would take the bronze.

Winterberry at Taylor Young Drive was a typical four-lane, suburban surface street separating commercial from residential areas of the city. Since it wasn't purely residential, the widely separated street lights left long, dark pools between them.

As he pushed the screaming Nova down Winterberry, he could see, materializing out of the dark, a car crossways in the street. You guessed it, it was geographically centered in a spot mostly void of lighting. As he slowed, he flipped off the siren, advised radio he was on scene, and started combing the roadway for the motorcycle or the rider; that mess must've been somewhere off the roadway. As he closed in, Max pulled his cruiser perpendicular in the street, a blocking maneuver to protect the accident scene and emergency personnel from other traffic. At least on one side of the roadway.

Max swung his spotlight onto the accident scene, and about 20 feet in front of him was a smoldering, green Volkswagen bug. It was obviously a grievous crash as the rear half of the vehicle had been torn open, as if you took a giant church key to it. The rear engine compartment was peeled back and was the source of the smoke, and engine fluids draining in the street. Golden noted the cooling engine, pinging.

He bounded from his car, flashlight in hand, and approached the crash. Only at that moment was it clear what had happened to the motorcycle. The bike had hit the VW at such a high rate of speed, it had breached the vehicle, at just about the backseat. The inertia had driven the stolen Suzuki GT 380 almost completely into the passenger compartment. About 83 inches long and almost 400 pounds, the motorcycle was strewn across the backseat with about one-third of the rear tire visible from outside the bug. The motorcycle driver was not visible in the wreckage.

Max could hear a siren off in the distance, probably Fire. When he swept his Kel-Lite into the front seat, he located the driver under the passenger dash. Moaning, and a very faint "help me" came from that part of the car. Two things were immediately clear, the driver was alive and was breathing. Max told him, "Don't move, pal. We've got all kinds of help on the way." There was no response but the sound of labored respirations.

Max still had another issue to sort out; where the fuck was the motorcycle driver? He moved towards the rear of the ruined VW, but in his peripheral vision, he saw a smear of blood at the top of what would be the rear door frame if the bug had back doors. He lit up the roof as he rounded the car and could see a spray of blood over the top. This was making some sense now, and as he got to the passenger side of the car, he turned his light into the street. Maybe 75 feet away and on his back was a body, motionless. "Fuck!" Max said to himself. He took a quick look into the VW's passenger seat and the driver was still breathing and had no sign of any substantial blood loss.

Max sprinted towards the prostrate victim, the second siren, that of the oncoming ambulance, in his ears. In the number two, southbound lane, spread-eagled and face up was a face Max knew. Bobby Capato was a local hood, mostly despised by the Far West boys in blue. He was a burglar, which wasn't so much, but he had a penchant for knocking around women. More on that later.

Max knelt beside Capato's ashen body and instantly noted one of his knees had landed in Bobby's drainage. Fucked up another pair of $85 uniform pants flashed through his mind. Golden made a quick visual assessment, and noted no helmet, a compound fracture of Bobby's upper left leg, and another compound fracture of his left arm, the bone slicing through his cheap leather jacket. His very long, very dirty hair framed his head and face and was soaking up the blood that was literally pouring out of him.

Max tried for a carotid pulse and there was none. It was clear that Capato was not breathing. Knowing that the next step was CPR, he knew he had to tilt the head back, supporting the neck and start mouth to mouth if there was any saving the guy. With his left hand, he reached under Bobby's blood-drenched neck and lifted to support it. Max's right hand instinctively settled onto the crown of Capato's head, and he began to rotate the head backward to create a clear airway for mouth to mouth. Deep in concentration and in what seemed like very, very slow motion, Max could feel his hand slipping through the blood-soaked hair towards the back of Bobby's head. His hand slid into a warm, wet space. A soft, warm wet space, the space that used to be the back of Capato's skull. Just that fast, Max realized he was holding Bobby's brain in his right hand.

You've probably heard of situations that caused one to pause and reevaluate their chosen career path. Well, this wasn't one of those situations, but Max would definitely have a drink or two at shift's end and try to re-balance.

One of the two arriving paramedics and a fireman were now at Max's shoulder asking in unison, "What have we got?"

He told them, "One's alive in the passenger seat of the bug. Think this one's done." That, my friends, was an understatement.

The medics and fire stepped in like they do, and worked on Capato. Max stepped away, in a bit of a daze. He was glad when he looked around and there were lots of emergency lights, a fire crew, an ambulance, and paramedics. His family. When you're alone in the dark, on your knees on the raw, cold pavement and you're cradling some guy's brain in your hand, it's kind of a lonely feeling.

Later that morning, while still writing his crash report, one of the elder Night Policemen schooled Max. "If you had one fucking courteous bone in your dimple-dick rookie body, you would've at least cleaned out the fucking driver's seat of my ride. Fucking blood all over the place." The senior officer was smiling, and Max knew the chastising was in jest.

It was also the opening volley of an overture to Max to join the Night Police for their morning choir practice. Cops take care of their own.

Later, Golden was one of six, huddled around a fire pit, drinking Irish coffees. The recently purchased and highly mortgaged home of Officer Tim Spin, and the camaraderie of men he practically revered, was just what the doctor ordered for young Max.

After it was all pieced together, it appeared Capato, traveling in excess of 80 miles per hour on a stolen Suzuki, with his headlight off, T-boned one Leo B. Lister's 1974 VW bug, breaching the vehicle. Lister got off with five broken vertebrae in his back, a severe concussion, and an eye that had been forced from the socket, but he would recover.

Capato, not so much. When his bike slammed into Lister, it launched him over the handlebars and he struck the back of his head at the roof-line, shearing the skull away and exposing his brain. Skipping across the pavement at 80 miles per hour didn't help all that much either. Capato was likely dead at the moment of impact. The other injuries, what turned out to be five compound fractures, a ruptured spleen, collapsed lungs, both of them, and a severed spine, were merely accessories.

Bobby Capato had brutalized his last woman. "Fuck him!" was the consensus amongst the lawmen. They drank, told stories, laughed their asses off, and broke up a bit before noon.

After a lingering shower, Max Golden shut his blackout blinds and slept really quite well.

Rimjob interrupting, "That piece of shit burglar kicked the shit out of every woman he ever got close to. Fuck's sake, boss, you ever see the pics of when he bounced his old lady down the stairs? A wife, a girlfriend, I can see that, but this cocksucker punched his mother right in the temple, and she was ass over teakettle into the fucking basement. I know she was a cunt, but that was his fucking mother for fuck's sake!"

Kramden, pensive and savoring his drink, kicked a tipping log back into the mouth of the stove. "Usually it's the good guys, the innocents who get the knife in the eye. I'm not losing sleep over this one. Pass me the fire, would you?"

"He had it coming to him. He was a piece of shit." All the boys that night had a visceral dislike of Capato, but Rimjob had the most history with him and had detested the miscreant. "I wouldn't of given him the sweat off my balls if he'd been dying of thirst."

"He always thought very highly of you," Johnson poked.

Thinking about Bobby Capato brought another thought to Kramden. "Didn't Capato run with Artemis Wicks for a while?"

Quinn affirmed it. "They were two peas in a pod! I think they were into rooftop commercial burgs for a while. Capato must have been the brains of the operation because—"

Kramden, in a rare moment, didn't let Quinn finish. "Let me tell you just how stupid Wicks was." Kramden took lead on a tale that had flummoxed him as a rookie undercover cop.

CHAPTER 10

The Injectable Artemis Wicks

Artemis Wicks. Goof. Skinny, hype, burglar, shit head. Curly blond hair, pizza face, cat scratch wisp of a beard. Sticky, baggy jeans hung on his bony hips. The only thing holding them up was the old leather belt with about 16 belt holes exposed. Goof seemed to think a white, filthy, wife-beater and a short-sleeve, Hawaiian shirt unbuttoned to the bottom was an unparalleled look.

He had a propensity for dope. All dope, pretty much. And if taken together, all the better. Coke, crank, heroin, pills, cheap red wine intravenously, you name it, Artemis found a reason he needed to ingest it.

He also had a propensity for burglary. He seemed to adore being a deficient burglar, inadequate in all skills burgle. He was a bungler. A bungler and a burglar. A bungling burglar. And as a result, the cops routinely snatched him up. Artemis couldn't burgle his own wallet without getting arrested. That was fun for the blue-suits. The simple-minded, little hype provided the law enforcement types with hours of family fun, mirth, and merriment.

Now Artemis was an interesting young man, interesting from the perspective that he was still living. If there was ever a dude that should've been toast already, it was Mr. Wicks. Goof made enemies almost every day and on purpose, mostly. He snitched on just about everyone he ever met. Goof was not above ratting out people he'd never met, or ones he'd just fabricated in that vacuous melon of his.

Just an aside, at one time the Night Police had a pool, a fin a piece, on the hood of a squad car about Goof. They forecasted the month and day they'd find him behind the Stanton Sunoco with a significant portion of his head splattered on the bricks. So many enemies and so little time.

Goof wasn't a real bad guy, just a hype, who supported his habit by stealing from others. Oh, and selling dope. Oh, and being a professional rat. Not a bad guy though.

Goof mostly snitched for the patrol guys who were in his shorts for one misdeed or another, just about every day. They'd spot him all over his neighborhood and often at the Landing's Lounge. When out in public, he was fair game.

For the narcs, it was a different scenario. Since Goof and whole crews of like-minded mischief-makers frequented Landing's Lounge, they frequented it too. When they could fit it in their schedule.

Jack Gleason often found the Lounge on his schedule. Assigned to a regional task force, the Landing's was still his town. He used to sign out at the office, "Kramden/the lounge/city biz."

He would often chat Goof up, invest in a beer for the boy, and routinely beat his ass at pool. The unsuspecting hype merrily rolled along. He was always on the hunt for his next fix or his next deal. He was always playing the system. Just like the narcs.

They saw him as a strung-out user, low-level dealer, and a patrol rat. They didn't think of him as a CI material; too much of a stretch. Imagine not having the acumen and savvy to be a confidential informant? Poor Goof couldn't cobble together his primary skill sets of incompetence, ineptitude, and insolvency to get his dumb ass through the day without landing in the clink.

On a beautiful, warm, summer evening, Kramden was driving his undercover Z28 through the Landing's lot, looking for Mark Whalters, a crook he'd been trying to track down for some time. He and others pegged Whalters as good for an Allen County dope robbery. The Sheriff's Office report, forwarded to the narcs, suggested Whalters had spanked one of the local Alter boys for about a half-pound of coke with, per the description, "the biggest fucking gun" the victim had ever seen.

Kramden knew Whalters through some other shit heads he ran with, and he too was unsuspecting of the Kramden's other life. He wanted to spend some time on Whalters and see if he could get enough wood on him to flip him or help the Allen County Sheriff's Office detectives with their case.

Whalters was doing most of his banditry in Kramden's backyard. The shittiest part of his backyard, but still in the same city where he plied his trade. His old partner Ron Johnson used to say, "It's such a shit hole, how could you not love this place?" They were in complete agreement.

So who did Kramden see this fine evening walking down the street with Mr. Whalters? Yup, you guessed it, the Goof. They were both motoring along at a good clip, symptomatic of a couple of deviants obviously up to no good. Kramden pulled his car up alongside their fast-stroll and rolled down the window. Goof was the first to chirp, "Hey, dude, what's up?"

Whalters remained more circumspect. Kramden told Goof he was looking for Snow, "that big titted blonde bitch from Candy's."

Goof, ignoring that all together, pulled in close, stuck his head in the window, and said, "Hey, can you give us a ride?" Kramden was on the cusp of some disrespectful commentary when the ass-clown added, "Hey, we just scored from Lizette. Drop us at my mom's and we'll make it right."

Kramden switched gears, thinking okay, maybe he could make this work. "Sure, hop in," he tells him. The hypes piled in, Goof in the front seat, Whalters in back.

It wasn't optimal or even a desirable practice, to let two known felons, one on the lam for robbing a dude with "the biggest fucking gun" ever seen, into your undercover car. Kramden and other narco buyers made shit like that work, back in the day. They looked at events like this as calculated risks. Kramden knew both the players, knew of their backgrounds, and had a social arrangement with them. Not to mention he had a Model 59, 9mm and a Walther PPKS within reach. He felt reasonably safe.

They hadn't gone five blocks when Artemis pointed. "Mom's is down here. Make the next right."

Whalters finally chimed in. "If she's there, just ignore her. Dumb as a stump." They laughed at that, with Goof lobbing more disparaging comments about the old gal, her way. Apparently, she did not live up to their high expectations.

Hoping to get more engagement from Whalters, Kramden asked, "I thought you were working for the city?" which was a lie he'd heard Whalters tell at the Lounge. Kramden knew he'd been bounced for drug use on the job. Kramden worked for the city and had done his homework, but fuck-face didn't know that. Whalters said he worked for the city, but his boss "was a dick and I told him so." He added, "He fucking fired me, the ass wipe son of a bitch." The fertile mind speaketh.

Goof interrupted, pointing to the house, a flat-top, run-down, hunk of shit amongst hundreds of other flat-top hunks of shit that were the Landing. Knee-deep weeds and overgrown shrubs flanked the house. Clearly, Goof could've spent more time tending to mom's garden.

Out of the car, Whalters hopped up the steps, stopping just short of the door. Goof held back and in a conspiratorial tone told Kramden, "You tie me off, and I'll give you a taste. Right?"

That was not what Kramden was expecting. These guys were planning on injecting some dope, he got that. Why Goof needed him to tie him off was a mystery. Why didn't they just tie each other off?

Just a point of instruction here. It's not uncommon for heroin and other injectable drug users to tie a belt, string, extension cord, you fucking name it, around their arm on the vein between the point of injection and the heart. It restricts blood flow, ensuring a plumped-up vein to make it easier to stick with the needle. That's tying off.

So, conceptually they were all in agreement. Kramden would join the mopes at the elder Wick's place to assist them in injecting some unknown narcotic, non-narcotic, or other unknown substance into their dumb asses. If all went well, they wouldn't immediately fucking perish. That would save Kramden from going to jail and ending up getting boned in the ass and/or moderately almost killed for trying to make the case. Yup, sounded like a smart plan. So in they went.

The screen door screeched and slammed behind them. The living room was orderly and didn't smell all that bad. Done in traditional geriatric, it had the Formica dinette, doilies, and on the coffee table, a few stacks of coupons. Seated on an aging floral couch, with the ubiquitous plastic slipcovers, was Mother Wicks. Her blue hair, half glasses down her nose, and...she's knitting. The quintessential folksy tableau. Almost a Norman Rockwell moment, had he used hypes, low-end gangsters, and suburban decay as subject matter.

Mother Wick's turned on the light next to the couch. Pushing her glasses up, she'd yet to spit out a word when Goof yanked the TV guide from the very unused electric organ and sailed it into her kisser, knocking the glasses from her face. "Shut the fuck up, old woman. I fucking told you, we are not speaking."

Kramden was clueless what that was all about. Mrs. Wicks was crying, and the scrawny hype acted as if he'd just told her he'd picked up her

Metamucil at the SuperValu Pharmacy. Life just ain't all that grand if you're a dope fiend.

With a shit-eating grin on his face, Whalters stepped around Kramden and Goof and headed for the kitchen. "Getting the grape. Getting the grape." *What a fucking moron,* Kramden thought.

Goof motioned for Kramden to follow him down the dark hallway. At what appeared to be a bathroom undergoing a messy remodel, Goof pointed and said, "Wait in there. I'll be right back." Goof continued down the hall, and Kramden pondered his situation. He didn't like the instruction "Wait in there." He didn't like that both bad guys were now at different ends of the house and he didn't have eyes on either of them. Kramden was not enthusiastic about his situation.

Within seconds, Whalters appeared in the tight hallway. He settled in just outside the bathroom door, amidst a pile of construction materials and tools. And, all the while licking a big soup spoon straight out of the jar. He offered Kramden some grape jelly. "Want some?" Fucking moron.

Goof made his way down the hall and squeezed into the cramped space that had been a bathroom just weeks before. He sat on the toilet. Kramden wedged in against the sink. Whalters seemed happy; he had his Welch's.

In one hand, Goof had a small tooled, leather box, about the size of a coffee cup. Kramden was sure the rig was booty from some burglary he'd fashioned to hold his dope tools. It was not Goof's type of accessory.

Whalters spied the rig and took a "Viet Cong in the rice paddy" squat in the doorway. Out came a spoon, some used, wadded-up, cotton-ball-looking shit, a Bic lighter, and a unique (to be kind) hypodermic needle.

Goof was holding the barrel of a pen, the syringe for his purposes, with a needle he'd fashioned at the business end. In place of the plunger was an eyedropper type bulb that would force whatever you were actively killing yourself with, down and through the syringe. Goof used an artificial rubber grape glued in place like an eyedropper bulb. Artificial grapes weren't all that scarce in the 70s and early 80s. You'd often see them as a decor element sharing space with green shag carpeting and the ever so prevalent lava lamp.

Whalters grubbed through his pockets and, sure enough, out came a single, pitiful, little balloon, likely filled with heroin. A gram weighs about the same as a large paper clip. This wasn't half of that. These two mopes were planning on sharing this minuscule score between themselves, and, for sure, Goof hadn't informed Whalters of the sharing plan he had with Kramden.

The two addicts argued about the junk and who would hit it first. Artemis had the rig and that settled that. They wanted to beef, but the prospect of sticking that nail in their arms focused them. As much as two junkies could focus.

During their verbal scrimmage, Goof pulled out a rubber tie that looked like vacuum tubing he'd stripped from some neighbor's engine compartment. He handed it to Kramden who wrapped it around Goof's arm just up from where he was planning to jab himself. Kramden pulled it tight.

Goof bit open the balloon and dumped the contents in the spoon. He cooked the dope with a bit of water over his trusty Bic lighter. He strained the sludge through a very well used cotton ball, up into the barrel of the pen-syringe, ready to jab.

Whalters, sensing a big moment, but with characteristically poor judgment and timing, took a last lick of his spoon. Turning around, he set the jar on the floor just outside the door. Artemis took advantage of the moment and fired the full load up his arm.

Goof told Kramden to "pull it," wanting him to release the tie. It appeared Kramden's job had devolved into that of tie-off-releaser person. Being ever cooperative, however, he pulled the kink out and let the tie drop to the floor. Out of the corner of his eye, Kramden noted an incoming but poorly aimed haymaker. He slipped the punch as did the slumping Goof, the intended punchee.

Whalters was a punk without a single athletic bone in his fuckered up body. He also threw a punch very much like Shirley MacLaine. That did not, however, mean that Kramden would take a poke from the douche-bag, even if he wasn't the intended target.

Kramden knocked him backward, onto the tools and equipment in the tub, ripping down Goof Wicks mother's sunflowered shower curtain. Kramden didn't need to throw more punches, but he drove his knee into the back of Whalters' neck, pinning him face down in the tub. Trying to keep things in a state of relative order, Kramden barked, "Knock it the fuck off, you fucking morons."

Goof was of no use, content, wedged in next to the toilet. A glimpse at him and Kramden could see his lack of awareness and the spreading euphoria pouring across the Saharan wasteland between his ears.

Whalters sputtered and fizzed and coughed a bit before he could articulate coherent words. Words like "cocksucker and motherfucker." Now Kramden was assuming he wasn't talking to him, as he was neither of those things. When Whalters strung together, "You motherfucker, you snatched all that dope, you cocksucker," it became clear that yes, Artemis was the irritant of the moment. If you didn't count his case of knee-neck.

This solved the "tie me off" mystery for Kramden. Goof had no plan at all to share his dope, with him or Whalters. He just needed to protect himself long enough to take the whole load and fuck his buddy over. He was a devious little fucker. Sort of typical for his kind.

Goof had collected his limited thoughts and tried to smooth things out with Whalters. With the shower drain's "Kohler" now imprinted on his face, he wasn't really in the mood. Goof said, "Whoa, wait the fuck up! I'll take care of you, brother. I'll make it right. Don't sweat it." In Kramden's opinion, Whalters was sweating it!

But, he was calming as Goof sweet-talked him. One hype to another.

Kramden told him, "I'll let you up, motherfucker, but you better be fucking cool or we'll do this again." When he let idiot number two up, Whalters' face was tomato red, but he had already shifted his interest to Artemis, fumbling with the rig again.

This is the part wherein Kramden's mind, Goof would add water to his blackened, encrusted spoon and re-cook the filthy cotton ball... then he would have the very diluted remains that Whalters could inject into himself. Kramden had heard of that before, but he'd never seen it. He was dead wrong.

These two boys made this next play as if they'd rehearsed it a dozen times or, sadly, perhaps they'd done it before. Goof inserted the needle back into his abused vein and drew out a syringe of blood. Smiling like Alice's Cheshire cat, he handed it off to Whalters who'd tied himself off and...wait for it...he injected himself with Goof's blood.

To be honest, Kramden thought he'd seen a couple of things at this point in his career, but he was a bit goggle-eyed at that development. There's no way Whalters would get high, except maybe a needle high, or some other mental miscarriage that he was projecting. He might get a lot of things, but high wasn't likely one of them.

Kramden didn't get his taste that night, but he swiped the cotton ball mess and the discarded bindle as evidence. It was unlikely the district attorney would ever file on a no-dope case with these two mooches, but it would be important to have the evidence when they sat Whalters down for a counseling session.

This whole experience had been like an evening of likely success with Christie Brinkley and just as she unbuckles your belt and is sliding the zipper down, she says, "Oops, forgot to feed my cat. Got to go."

The Sheriff's Office eventually popped Whalters for the armed robbery and recovered a .45 caliber Colt Peacemaker that he'd stolen in Carthage. It was one of the biggest fucking handguns Kramden had ever seen too.

Most importantly for the narcs, they flipped Whalters while hanging the dope case over his head. It was a pile-on charge, that just added to his legal burden. It was a tool, and narcs were good with tools.

And yes, Artemis continued as a professional confidential informant. A shitty one.

The assembled group commented all at once about the sickness and perversion surrounding drug users and their fucked up world.

When the talk died down, RJ weighed in. "We dealt with those guys a lot as detectives, and knew they were lowlifes. Thank God we didn't have to hang out with them like you and Rimjob did. What a fucking eye-opener that must have been...I mean, me and Maxie worked a lot of UC with Customs, but it was a higher grade of crook."

The ever thoughtful Kramden was still on the junkie life, "The do-gooders who know nothing at all about the dope world, will always tell you drug crimes are victimless. My ass."

Rimjob was ready for a change of tune, and he chided the boys about forgetting just how much fun you could have running around undercover. "Christ, you two sound like a couple of old dyke social workers. Lighten the fuck up! Did I ever tell you guys about the time me and Red Davis were at the State Narco Association meeting..."

Kramden and RJ smiled and settled back in their seats, knowing that Rimjob was off on a tear.

CHAPTER 11

"Talk to a Real-Life Narc"

The marquee on the Marriott Lafayette Hotel & Convention Center blazed "Welcome State Narcotics Officers Association!" That was the welcoming message for 260 undercover narcotics agents from around the state.

You couldn't have found another group of people who more craved anonymity unless it was the dirtbags the narcs spent their time investigating. Hell, why didn't they just throw up some neon on the freeway for fuck's sake? "Talk to a Real-Life Narc!"

Rimjob's silver Trans Am was sporting a lovely new crease down the driver's side, courtesy of a willful paddle marker that attacked during a narc lane run-up Memorial Drive. The sulky valet at check-in pointed it out. "Fucked up your car, dude."

Bite me, ass face is what Rimmer was thinking. As he drug his chintzy war bag up the steps to check-in, he heard ass face tell his associate, "Bet you money he's a narc." Rimjob just sighed. He couldn't help but think, *There's a fucking sign up there, you nitwit!*

Training sessions for narcotics officers were a blend of information, tactics, and strategies. If there was an underlying theme to this intense educational effort, it was drinking. It wasn't all about the drinking, however. There was also golf.

A typical day might mean taking in afternoon classes, perhaps Asset Forfeiture, and maybe Drug Abuse Recognition. Or perhaps, a Cartel Kidnapping Debrief or certification in Electronic Surveillance Wiretapping. There were classes on every subject relevant to narcotics enforcement. Many of them were well received, but there was a single constant about the coursework. The very moment the boys and girls had gained "all the knowledge," it was cocktail time. Sometimes they'd already have "all the knowledge" they felt they could manage, even prior to class. That was a case that called for red beers and Bloody Marys. After class, all bets were off, as the hotel bar revealed.

It was 4:30 p.m. in Marriott's SkyBar. It didn't matter that it was on the ground floor, or that no one could see the sky unless they had painted it on the ceiling. Blue neon, a slick black bar top, some high-tech plastic, and chrome, lots of gleaming chrome. It was a place narcotics detectives in good standing would never steer to unless they were doing a dope deal.

The natives of the SkyBar comprised two categories, barkeep and waitress. Overworked and underwhelming were the bartenders, Tito, and the boozy Renee. The two cocktail waitresses, both solid, made-over divorcee types, one of whom was sporting a "USDA Prime" tramp stamp, were no more enthusiastic.

There was already a din in the room, cocktails being slung at perhaps not record pace, but with alacrity. Voices were stacking up, and a few of the younger, less chic narcotics agents were starting their adolescent mating rituals. None of the wait staff had yet been tempted, though they were snorting enough coke and slopping back enough Jack Black to narrow profit margins.

And then there were the self-described reprobate, veteran narcs. Sometimes characterized as scruffy, vulgar, or even shameless, in their minds they were professionals and even virtuous. You can't judge a book by its cover. Somebody said that.

They knew they were good too. Being a detective implied you were a top-notch lawman. Being a narc, at least according to this crowd, meant you were a cut above that. There was more ego, testosterone, confidence, and hubris than you could find in just about any of the more manly endeavors. They knew they didn't stack up to Navy Seals, but they had it on almost everybody else. They'd be the first to tell you too.

Rimjob was banging around that day with "Red" Davis, a sergeant from the city that butted up to Bristol City to the South. Red and his team were Rimjob's second narc family, and they worked with each other daily.

Rimjob got some time on the beach behind an internal affairs investigation aimed at Red and his crew. The investigators shared with the BCPD's administration that "Detective Steve Rimfro was not forthcoming" in their internal affairs investigation. If you were to ask Rimjob, they just didn't ask the right questions. Idiots.

Anyway, Red and Rimjob had been at it for most of the day. Guess they'd just had "all the knowledge" they could manage. In fact, before they left the hotel pool, they finished up with some drink that Red remembered as having both an umbrella and a water slide in it. Their judgment continued to improve while practicing at the SkyBar. While they couldn't tell you how many vodka grapefruits they were into that afternoon, they both recognized that "all the knowledge" was leaking out.

Somewhere in this chronology of events, they met a local Highway Patrol trooper, assigned to a narco task force up in Fort Michael. He'd been on board less than two years, but to hear him tell it, he'd been there and done that. He was not lacking ego. The first clue to the contrary should have been his name, Diamante Montañero. Monte was a transplanted surfer from California, somewhere on some sunny beach south of LA. He regaled them with his exploits in the nausea ponds of the US seaboards and Australia. Drink. Drink. Drink. They couldn't say he was boastful, it was high-concept, interesting stuff. Drink. Drink. Drink. He'd surfed them all, and while maybe not what he'd call world-class, he was the real deal, according to him. He fit right in with the Red and Rimmer crowd. Accepted by unanimous acclamation. Drink. Drink. Drink. That's just how it went.

As the evening wore on and they became even more intelligent, music became the subject. They talked about the music they liked and hated. Tunes that put them on their feet, sometimes causing them to break out their Elaine Benes' hokey pokey. They talked about everyone, Zeppelin, Pink Floyd, the Stones. Even George Strait and Austin Texas' outlaw country maestro, Jerry Jeff Walker. It was a well-attended conversation with way more opinions than they were legally entitled to. And, they exhibited no real knowledge on any subject, their lack of temperance and abstinence highlighting the point.

That's when Monte turned to Red and said, "You and your partner want to hear some awesome ADS monitors? Fuckin rock your world!"

Well, what could they say but, "Fuck yeah!"

About 20 minutes later, Red and Rimjob were standing out in front of the hotel. They were both a bit vertically compromised, but their ability to lean seemed without impairment. They were managing. Screeching to the curb, a neon yellow, convertible 'vette with—you guessed it—Monte behind the wheel. A beer between his legs and two more clenched in his right hand. "Climb in, my brothers. A short road trip to my place."

Both Rimjob and Red were 40 regulars, perhaps a 40 short in Rimjob's case, but they were grown men. What they were not, was designed to fit two to a bucket seat. But, then again, they were more flexible than normal. It had been a long time since Rimjob had gone anywhere with a police detective sitting on his lap.

They pulled out the drive and onto the frontage road. Red and Rimjob popped open their beers and were enjoying a very nice summer evening. That lasted 37 seconds. As Monte hit the freeway, he banged the afterburners. Their heads whiplashed rearwards, the vertebrae disjointing in their necks and that jaundiced, yellow 'vette roared! Fifteen to 90 miles per hour in about the time it takes for your sphincter to slam shut. Red and Rimjob glanced at each other, both trying to disguise their terror. Both of them were white-knuckled, grabbing whatever they could hang on to. Blasting through traffic, weaving in and out, up the narc lane or hugging the center divider. Steve McQueen's 68 "Bullitt" Mustang fastback had nothing on Monte! They pinned survivability on the hope and prayer that Highway Patrol Trooper Diamante Montañero was as stated—a professional, high-speed pursuit driver.

When they pulled into a mammoth condo complex, their collective hearts had not oriented their P waves. Rimjob and Red were far from being in sinus rhythm. You couldn't have slipped a hot buttered pin up their asses. There would be more drinking.

Rattled by the experience, Red revealed his inner Clint Eastwood, grumbling, "Wake me up if we crash into the mountain. I wouldn't want to miss that."

Monte popped out of the car, oblivious to their distress. "Second-floor, palies. Follow me." So they followed. As he unlocked the front door, they stepped into a handsome and fashionable space with what appeared to be fine art on the walls. Rimjob guessed it was fine art. It had frames and everything.

As a good host would, the first thing out of Monte's mouth was, "H'bout some margaritas?" He'd already pulled out a blender, a bowl of ice, and some kind of top-shelf tequila. The boys were all in.

As he was throwing together the first round, Rimjob and Red prowled the condo, giving it a once-over. They weren't used to being in a living space so clean you'd expect surgery to break out. There wasn't one fucking thing out of place, and, of all things, it smelled good. Rimjob's place smelled nothing like this.

About that time, Monte stepped in with two professionally built margaritas. "Here you go, boys." And they were fucking great margaritas. Rimjob and Red were already planning rounds two through six when Monte torched off the stereo. It was as indicated, stellar sound. Red was more of a country guy, so the smooth jazz was beyond him. Rimjob couldn't care less. He had his margarita. What the hell, the drinks were free, and it smelled nice.

Rimjob was looking at two surfboards, something called a Gordon and Smith and another, a Lyman. Beautiful surfboards, for sure, and antique it would seem. On the wall next to the fiberglass planks, he noticed a picture of a cherry red 66 Corvette Stingray Coupe, a classic. Monte in a pair of cut-off jeans and no shirt was leaning against it with two other guys, a leggy blonde standing behind. Monte appeared to be quite the Corvette aficionado.

They were shooting the shit about Corvettes and engines and other indices of manly pursuit when Monte walked out of the room. Red stepped to the blender, poured another and shouted to Monte, inquiring if he wanted another. He did. And so did Rimmer.

When Monte returned, he was sporting a pair of short shorts, and a muscle shirt. Red. Bright, fucking red, short shorts, and a red muscle shirt. Oh, and red flip-flops. He started the second batch of margaritas. Both Red and Rimjob gawked incredulously, mouths agape. Though both of them were in shorts and T-shirts, it was a different look. Monte was styling. Not that there's anything wrong with that.

They were working on round two, but Rimjob found himself somehow interested in that Lyman board Monte was all agog about. Rimmer didn't know shit about surfboards. Being born and raised in the middle of the country would do that. Rimjob listened as Monte shared the full pedigree of the board, including its when and where. He seemed to like the fact that Rimmer was interested and listening. He told Rimjob he even had a signed picture of himself with this guy, Jim Lyman. "Wait, I know where the fuck it is," he said, heading towards his bedroom. *What the fuck,* Rimjob thought, *it seemed to make Monte happy, and he's buying.*

Before Monte returned with his artifact, Rimjob caught Red out of the corner of his eye giving him the "look at this shit" eye. He was leafing through an autographed book that had been displayed on the coffee table. Neither of them would remember the title, but Red shared that it was about the openly gay, San Francisco politician, Harvey Milk. The two intoxicated detectives looked at the book, then at each other. Red paused, finger to his upper lip, and said, "Rimmer, this fucking guy's gay…and we're on a date!" What the fuck?

The manner in which Red and Rimjob behaved next would be hard to explain. It just happened. Red slurred, "Follow me, we're outta here." Well, he WAS the sergeant. They slugged back their drinks, but instead of making a B-Line for the front door, Red bolted across the living room, out the open sliding glass door and over the railing on the deck. And, as a lemming might, Rimjob leaped over the railing right behind him.

After a full day and most of a night drinking, it seemed to have slipped their minds they were on the second floor. Fortunately for them, below was a very steep ice-plant-covered slope. They tumbled ass over teakettle, both arriving at the bottom in a heap. After taking inventory, they were relatively sure nothing significant had snapped off. And, then they laughed. Rimmer and Red rolled, tears streaming down their faces, in the ice-plant, bottle caps, and other debris and gutter rubble until they caught their breaths.

They were in a city they didn't know, lost, and didn't have wallets or ID (you don't need them at the pool bar, they'd thought that through. And, at the time, it had seemed very intelligent). It was about four in the morning, and they had nothing. So, as any two resourceful police detectives would do, they commenced wandering.

They'd only gone a short way, made a right, and not two hundred yards down the street was a Sunoco gas station. Perfect, right? The plan was obvious. Head down there, make a call, and be back at the hotel just a tad early for the breakfast buffet. That was incorrect, and this was why: When they got to the Sunoco, it was closed.

There was a phone booth outside, but between them, they didn't have a single dime. Not two nickels or a quarter. Nothing. Fuck.

Surprising the boys, a spindly, graying woman slipped up from behind. She was walking some pitiful excuse for a dog, a patch of fur with a leash. She and Pookie, both with similar wadded-up mugs, made a wide berth of the disheveled police detectives.

Red, sensing an opportunity, staggered her way and asked if she "could spare a dime?" Now maybe two long-haired, booze-breathed, dirt-bag-looking blokes begging at a closed gas station at four in the morning spooked her. You wouldn't know it, though. She just ignored them and shuffled along.

So they sat on a Metro Transit bus bench as the sun started to pinken the sky. What strategies should they use to get themselves down the road? There was little traffic, so hitchhiking was likely out for another hour or two. So they paced and sat and stood and paced. Rimjob, light bulb blinking on, stumbled into the phone booth, stuck his finger in the coin return and damned if there weren't two dimes in it. Bingo!

Rimjob made a call and woke up Momma. Affectionately known as Momma, she was the office manager at the Menome-Carthage Task Force. The keeper of the baby narclings and the glue that held their unit together, she was beloved. If they needed help, she was their go-to. Without hesitation, she said, "I'm on my way." It was 4 a.m., but these were her narclings. She was full speed ahead.

The boys sat back down on the bench and decided that when they got back to the hotel, they'd get some scrapple and eggs and red beers.

Things were looking up. After a retreat the French would be proud of, Red and Rimjob were famished.

It wasn't 10 minutes when a patrol car pulled up in front of the bus stop. Well, hell, that could be worse, at least they were on the same team. That was incorrect, and this was why.

Remember, this was 1981, and Red and Rimmer were both surprised when two split tails stepped out of their cruiser. Women were just starting to show in the ranks of law enforcement, at least in their corner of the country. Two of them pushing a squad car together was unheard of. As they approached, the boys sized them up and, to be sure, had Red and Rimjob been in their high heels, they'd have been suspicious too.

Red and Rimmer both believed women in law enforcement had an attitude, a chip on their collective shoulders. Maybe it was because they believed they had to be tougher than their male counterparts to succeed. Maybe? They thought that was an excuse. It didn't matter. These troopers would prove the point without even asking.

They asked the boys for ID and explained that someone had complained about two panhandlers at the Sunoco. Rimjob explained in his boozy way that they didn't seem to have any ID. They asked where the two of them were going but dismissed their explanation as typical bullshit. That was when, what they took to be the rookie hen, decided she was going to verbally tune them up. The senior hen was quieter but was all hands on the hips, giving them the superior eyebrows akimbo, pinched face treatment. It was rolling downhill.

Red tried to set the record straight. He started by lying to them. He told them they'd only had "a couple of beers," and they were just fine. They were not. Then, settling into his full-throttle truth mode, he explained that they were, in fact, police detectives in town for a training seminar. Eyebrows asked, but, between Rimjob and Red they didn't know a soul on the hen's department that could vouch for them. How could they? They didn't know what city they were in.

Rookie Hen was having none of it and was making her point being dismissive as possible of the two veteran detectives. This caused Red to experience an awakening. He didn't believe there was a place for women in law enforcement, and he especially didn't see a spot for Rookie Hen. And…that's when he told them both how he felt and in some of the most colorful language Rimjob had ever heard him use. It was, perhaps, not Red's best moment.

As Eyebrows moved around the patrol car, she opened the rear passenger door. Rimjob was wrecked, but he recognized jeopardy when he saw it. At that precise moment, Red flipped open the mace holder on Rookie Hen's Sam Browne gun belt. She was not at all happy about being touched and was even less amused when Red said, "I s'pose that's where you keep your tampons?" That was incorrect, and this was why.

First, there wasn't even a single tampon in that pouch and, second, the Rookie Hen was now street trooper pissed. She threw out her meager chest and started on the officious, "First, keep your fucking hands off me and…." She wouldn't even let Red stand up. Actually, that was to his benefit. Though impaired, Rimjob knew this was bad.

By miraculous intervention, a blue Ford Falcon pulled to the curb behind the cruiser. Eyebrows, distracted, retreated to Mama's car, where they engaged in what appeared to be earnest debate. Red and Rimmer, knowing their salvation was just behind that police cruiser, were paying way more attention to that than the Rookie Hen. She wasn't apoplectic they weren't paying attention, but clearly she didn't appreciate their dismissive selves.

Momma was smart enough to have hit their hotel rooms on the way and bring their IDs, and she had all the details the boys couldn't remember about their convention of narcotics agents.

Rimmer and Red were sure that it disappointed Eyebrows and the Rookie Hen when they cut them loose. The ladies more than wanted to yank them in, but when weighed against the paperwork and bullshit that it would take arresting two police detectives, they relented. It also helped that they were about 10 minutes from going 10-42, End of Shift.

Momma's only words to Red and Rimjob before they piled into her car was, "Say nothing to 'em. Let it rest." She was wise beyond her years.

Rimjob wrapped up and took a good slug of his rye whiskey. "Where the fuck is Maximillian? If I remember the agenda notes as published, he was on the guest list, was he not? I have questions, goddammit." Rimjob was only asking what the others were thinking. "Something's not right with this picture."

Kramden was thinking aloud. "I know he's been away, but still it's not like him to miss a chance at a grand entrance when he knows we'll all be hanging on his every word."

"Relax, brothers, he's always marched to his own drummer. You know that. Maybe now, more than ever, since..." Johnson trailed off.

"Well, isn't that the whole point of tonight?" Rimjob was mystified.

"You know him, he was primping, planning on being fashionably late, but I'm guessing the Scotch took hold, or he met some gal in the bar. He'll get here." Johnson was making an excuse for his pal, and each of them sitting around that fire knew it.

Kramden pointed out to the boys, "I'm guessing Goldie's just on narco time. You know how irresponsible us narcs are. Fuck, just ask any of the bosses, yeah?"

It was probably the Scotch, but Quinn's mind had wandered into the past and for some perverse reason, his last Christmas with Suzy....He could picture it so clearly, the view through the frosted windowpanes revealed dim lighting and an immense, over-stuffed club chair nestled in front of a ripping fire. Inside, ancient oak crackled at the hearth, there was a comforting aroma of smoke and glove leather. Lying alongside him was Justice, his big, elderly golden retriever, his chin on Quinn's slippered foot, snoozing. Dean Martin was crooning "Baby It's Cold Outside" with Brenda Lee's "Blue Christmas" queued up next. Tiny colored lights bejeweled the handsome silver tip in the corner, presents tucked under the lower branches. A wooly afghan pulled up to his chin, and a copy of The Onion Field *opened and perched on his chest. In his battered hand, a hot buttered rum in a heavy mug, with just a hint of nutmeg. Suzy fixing something wonderful in the kitchen.*

Quinn swiped at his eyes and came back to the present when he registered Kramden's boss comment. The barb had been aimed at his time supervising the vice and narco boys. Christmas triggered another memory...

CHAPTER 12

The Best Blow Job You Ever Had

Christmas was a magical time of year. If you were a dope dealer, it could be iffy. It's true there's little that tickled a bunch of narcs more than a series of Christmas search warrants. Especially if the target of their warrant was some box of shit who had earned their scorn, disdain, and contempt.

Just seeing John Doe Douchebag, handcuffed on the couch next to his crying wife Jane, who'd also be in handcuffs, brought a smile to the faces of the previously offended lawmen. These same six or seven long-haired, well-armed narcs would be ready to join the Douchebag family in the Christmas tradition of unwrapping splendidly packaged treasures under the tree. They'd pillage, if not plunder the rest of the Douchebag domicile to locate the contraband that the court had deemed worthy of search. That would be fun. There was nothing like unwrapping that new vibrator or bong, just a few days before Christmas.

This day was one of those days. Three Christmas warrants in the bag and all by midnight. Two of the three warrants yielded big seizures, including a lot of firepower. Besides the usual shotguns and handguns, at one location the narcs seized a rocket launcher, some artillery simulators, and half a dozen hand grenades. One patrol type suffered a sprained knee, which was a splendid excuse for an attempted licking of a triage nurse at Big Mo. Four bad guys were off to the slammer and two to the local emergency room because of their flagrant lapses in judgment.

A good day, all things considered. Typically on a day wrapping up before the bars did, this group would journey to a local watering hole for libations. That is in fact what they did. Here, the target bar was Bini's Tavern in Tempelton, just over the Stock-town Borough border. Not ideal, being in a neighboring city, but it was only about 100 yards outside of Bristol City.

Bini's wasn't a cop bar, in the main. It was a narc bar. Narcs across the county ended up there routinely to share in good fellowship, a few games of pool, and large quantities of strong drink. One might encounter a patrol guy, maybe a smattering of detectives from time to time. Even a civilian mis-wandered in there occasionally. It was a bar, for sure, but mostly, Bini's Tavern belonged to a select crowd. There should be a mention that there were, more often than not, a few wenches of questionable character in attendance. The narcs liked that.

Most bars run dark, and Bini's was no different. Not that sprayed-on black cottage cheese ceiling, strip mall type of shit hole. More homespun and warm. Used brick, a stamped tin ceiling, and a gracelessly aging pool table dominated. The green felt was worn on the cushions, a minor tear often glued but never fixed. One of the inlaid sights placed along the rails, repaired with a smear of epoxy, was now yellowing and cracked.

Weathered and almost free of finish, the long wooden and zinc bar was showing its age too, but in an agreeable, ripened way. No armrest, but someone long ago installed a bronze foot rail that would be solid long after Bini's was a bar of the past. The back-bar was complemented with the usual mix of spirits, on and off brands, and the ubiquitous linear stretch of the mirror. The silvering had long ago started to erode, leaving long dull streaks of dark gray glass to break up the aesthetics.

On every shelf, taking up every exposed wall space were pictures, framed and not, new and old, depicting their reality. Dead cops, rookie cops, narco cops, cops currently in jail. Sometimes they were the same thing. Pictures of about three generations of police cruisers, some of them broken and splintered. A couple full of bullet holes. Police patches from a hundred different departments covered the walls as if applied by a shotgun blast. And for the holiday season, a couple of strings of red chili pepper lights provided the neural pathway for Bini's Tavern.

On this occasion, five veteran narcs propped themselves on the shabby bar stools, long necks and vodka predominating. Liar's dice was in progress, at a couple of bucks a game. Anecdotes and testimonials, fabricated and some not, were featured in exuberant proliferation.

Emory Melmon was at the far right of the group of seats, closest to the shitter. That was good and bad. Melmon was downing vodka grapes at an impressive rate, although it didn't seem to alarm anyone in the least. They just heard about it later.

As a younger Patrick Quinn waited for Perry, the barman, to haul the next one over to him, he felt a guy slide onto the stool to his right. Not paying attention, he glanced in his direction. Short, doughy, and possibly pigment-free, the guy was damn near translucent. Quinn ignored him. He appeared to be a civilian. Easily ignored.

They were rounding out a game of dice, when Quinn felt the elbow of translucent-man nudge him, at least that's what he thought. He looked at him, but he seemed disengaged. Back to escaping his atypical substandard gambling strategy, until he got the nudge, again. When Quinn turned, clear-boy was looking at him and nodding towards the bar. When he followed the gaze, there was a bindle, a coke bindle on the bar at Quinn's elbow. He slid it across in front of him. The idiot didn't understand he was in a cop bar. Perhaps besides being translucent, he was blind. A lamentable combination. Pat slid the dope back in front of him. "Not interested, man."

How annoying. He was in his favorite public house, trying to relax from a hard day at work, just like Ward fucking Cleaver, and some asshole was trying to sell him a controlled substance. What the fuck!

A couple of drinks later, Quinn had forgotten that translucent-man existed. His luck had turned, and he trounced a couple of his brothers in a game of ship, captain, crew.

Did the idiot just nudge him again? He turned and sure as shit, the guy slid that bindle down the bar in front of him again. He picked it up and stuffed it in clear-man's shirt pocket. "Look, pal, I'm trying to enjoy myself here. I'm not interested in your fucking dope," Quinn shot back. Shaking his head, it was becoming harder to ignore the idiot.

As hard as it is to believe, it wasn't five minutes later when once again, Quinn gets the nudge. Now he's technically and formally pissed the fuck off. He turned to translucent-man, but before he could say a word, the guy put his hand on Quinn's knee, giving him a conciliatory squeeze. Now Quinn didn't have some metaphysical clairvoyance, but he was sure he understood the meaning of the grope. The guy leaned in and murmured, "If you don't want my coke, I'll give you the best blow job you ever had."

To be honest, if Quinn were to accept a blow job in his bar, it would not be on the opposite end of translucent-boy. It offended his sensibilities and sense of manful decorum. The guy had challenged his masculine propriety. And…not to forget, he was already deep into the greyhounds.

Quinn yielded and leaned into the guy, saying, "I gotta hit the head. Meet me out in the lot in a few, and we'll talk about it."

Now, as professional narcotics agents, they had a few tricks up their sleeves. One of them was the high sign they'd share if they needed backup or some kind of support. Quinn gave that nod to Gene "The Head" Beckman, his task force partner and office mate, and walked into the can. Within 60 seconds, The Head joined him. "What's up?"

Quinn told him, "Head, you're not gonna like this, but that asshole sitting next to me's going to jail. Nothing I can do about it." Quinn told him he wanted some cover out by his car. Pat added he looked harmless enough, but he knew the clear-one "was holding."

A couple of minutes later, Quinn strolled back into the bar and the guy was eyes on him. Quinn just nodded to him and headed out the door for his car. On his way out, he surveyed the parking lot and picked out a couple of his hammered colleagues engaged in trying to be invisible.

Quinn leaned back against the passenger door of his undercover car and within seconds the idiot showed up in his peripheral vision. Quinn's plan was to change up and tell him, "Let's try that blow." As in most dope deals, even undignified little ones like this would surely be, the situation was fluid and unpredictable. Translucent-man squared up in front of Quinn, and as he started to speak, he threw his arms around Pat's neck. He wasn't throttling Quinn, he was trying to mate! Quinn wasn't sure how it was done in the queer community, but this wasn't working for him. Quinn pushed clear-boy back to arm's length and gently popped him on the snoot, three or four times. Translucent-man declined to continue standing.

It should come as no surprise they couldn't come up with a pair of handcuffs. So, clear-man, aka Louie Patero, sous-chef by trade and a moron by habit, lay crumpled on the pavement. He whimpered and promised he wouldn't move, and they believed the poor guy. After spilling the contents of his pockets, four one-gram bindles of coke was the take.

A minor congregation from the bar and the street watched the show. Melmon asked Debbie of the famous aunt/niece tag team of Debbie and Jackie Wax, to call the PD and request an assist. They had "one in custody."

It wasn't long before a Tempelton PD cruiser pulled into the lot. It took them about 90 seconds to size up the situation, and in that annoying way cops can have, they re-fucking-fused to transport Louie to their city lock-up. They also suggested everyone in that parking lot, and that included Louie, were drunker than skunks. You couldn't deny the blue suits were right, yet the boys remained petulant, causing an outbreak of finger-pointing with a "fuck you" or two being slung at the Templeton coppers.

Again, in that annoying way cops could have, they just drove off. That left Quinn and his brothers with a pudgy, bloodied, drunk, gay chef whose poor judgment caused the shit show in the first place! For many reasons, they couldn't just cut him loose and they had the fucking dope they needed to get booked into evidence.

They snugged Louie into the passenger seat of Quinn's undercover car. Amidst a flurry of incessant apologies, Quinn took translucent-man to the booking trailers himself. Narcs don't like to appear at booking. They know too many people on the inside. After a fair bit of begging, a kindly county sheriff's sergeant took pity on Quinn and lightly incarcerated Louie himself.

Early that morning, in the parking lot of West Al's Marine, four of the fellas drank a red beer toast to clear-boy. "Here's to staying positive and testing negative. Merry fucking Christmas, Louie!"

Louie skipped bail and fled to, of all the ridiculous places, Alaska. There was a felony FTA warrant, should he slide back into the state, so maybe he was smarter than given credit.

Quinn knew the Louie news because about a year later he received, at the PD no less, a handwritten letter from translucent-man. A year later, he hadn't stopped apologizing. Quinn said he was just getting it off his chest. Louie even put his return address on the letter. Dumb fuck.

The boys had a good laugh at the assault on Quinn's manhood, and the "Christmas Crook" working so hard to get locked up. It was always a marvel to lawmen how certain folk could talk themselves into getting arrested.

RJ sipped his drink and recollected.

"My first and best CI came to me from a good old-school burglary dick. We called him ZZ because he was a dead ringer for Billy Gibbons of ZZ Top fame. ZZ was a longtime meth cook and had had a bad business experience with the local chapter of the Outlaws. They had let him take the beef for almost getting caught with 2 pounds of freshly manufactured meth. ZZ tossed the dope and a sawed-off shotgun during a pursuit with the State Patrol. With his record, the state cops could put him away for a year just on the parole violation. They didn't need the dope or the gun. ZZ held his mud, didn't squeal on his Outlaw buddies, and figured they owed him his share of the 10-pound cook that had spawned the whole affair. The Outlaws saw it different and said that ZZ owed them for the 2 pounds that he had tossed out the car window. They settled things amicably enough; they stomped the shit out of ZZ and took his Harley, but they agreed to keep him on as a cook. Just business, you understand…"

CHAPTER 13

Stairway to Heaven

It started out as a tip about a bunch of Outlaw motorcycle gang members hanging out in a bar in a little Ozark mountain town. They called the bar The Vault, and folks alleged the Outlaws were wearing an Arkansas rocker on their colors and were slinging crank like crazy in the little out of the way tavern. RJ didn't know what to make of Arkansas Outlaws operating in a different state, but he wanted to find out. Johnson saddled up the G-Harley and got ZZ the informant to be his road dog. ZZ was a good pick because he had no history with the Arkansas Outlaws, however he knew a lot of other Outlaws, and could drop some names. The bar turned out to be a former 1800s bank on Main Street in a burg that the interstate never came near.

RJ and ZZ backed their bikes up to the curb in front. Looking at the bikes outside was disappointing; dressers and sportsters, even one Jap bike masquerading as a big American 2 cylinder, nothing a self-respecting Outlaw would get caught dead on. Still, RJ and ZZ had ridden over 80 miles to get there, it was a fine early summer evening, and they were thirsty.

The inside of the place was a bit trendier than most of the biker bars RJ had frequented, but the interior of the old bank had a 40-foot antique mahogany bar and back-bar imported from some 1800s establishment. The motif included a handful of vintage pool tables. RJ had split a couple thousand bucks of undercover funds with ZZ when they started out. ZZ had a gift for gab, and he was great at buying dope, guns, or whatever.

RJs theory was always: put a federal case on a guy, see how much time he could do. A lot of guys, including hard-ass bikers, opted to get on the federal team rather than do the federal time. The goal was to find the source of the drug. With methamphetamine, that was the lab. There were many ways to work back to a lab. Sometimes it involved following the chemicals back to the cook site, other times the agents would stay on a known cook until he led them to a likely manufacturing place. More often than not it involved a series of hand-to-hand buys, the arrest of the seller, and the seller's decision to give up information in exchange for a lesser sentence. That was the plan for the evening; RJ and ZZ wanted to find an Outlaw and make a first buy. There was always the outside chance that ZZ could talk his way into a job if the Arkansas Outlaws were looking for a cook.

Unfortunately this particular night was "wannabe-biker night" at The Vault. Instead of Outlaws flying colors, all RJ saw was pudgy middle-aged guys in black leather. Some had big eagles emblazoned on the back of their jackets. Real tough guys. Maybe somebody would want to sell some diet pills. Fuck.

RJ was usually a pleasant drunk, but for a number of reasons this evening he was working on being a mean drunk. Ironically he and ZZ were the only "authentic bikers" in the bar, and as the evening wore on and the beers flowed, the wannabe-bikers wanted to talk biker talk with RJ. One particularly obnoxious pus-gutted specimen leaned into RJ and opined that most outlaw bikers looked scary, but didn't have a lot of riding skill.

ZZ, whose memory had some large meth-sized holes in it, remembered RJ telling him about taking motorcycle lessons at the State Patrol academy, and how the instructors there were so talented they could ride a big cop Harley up and down flights of stairs. Not that RJ had done it in his 2-day class, THE INSTRUCTORS HAD DONE IT!

Anyway, a tiny chemical flashbulb popped in ZZ's brain and he bounded to RJ's defense and challenged the entire bar: "I'll bet any one of you motherfuckers a hunnert dollars that Rick (RJs current UC name) can ride a bike right up the front stairs of this rudey-poop shithole, and another hunnert that none of you motherfuckers can!"

He then fanned out his newly acquired $1000 of G-money on the bar for emphasis. Easy come, easy go for ZZ. No one could fault ZZ for his zeal, or his authenticity. Common sense questionable? Maybe.

"Nobody got a hunnert?" ZZ was on it. "What's the matter? Nobody's old lady give 'em any walking around money? You motherfuckers need to get on home…probably past your fucking bedtime!"

Just when the challenge seemed unanswered, and things were calming down, the damn bartender chimed in and told ZZ to shut up or leave. ZZ informed the bartender that it was a private wager and to mind his own fucking business. The wild bunch were all busy studying the labels on their beer bottles.

A pair of beefy bouncers started moving in on ZZ. "Time to go, asshole!"

RJ, who still had some shred of sense, laid his arm on ZZ's shoulder and whispered, "We don't need this!"

ZZ was still thinking how much fun it would be to split some heads, but knew RJ's rules were to maintain a low profile. He scooped up his $1000, drank the rest of his beer, and slammed the bottle down on the bar before turning to leave.

All would have gone smooth if Pus Gut hadn't followed them outside. Just as RJ was throwing his leg over the Harley he heard Pus Gut snicker from the top of the stairs.

A slightly drunk RJ just snapped, and that pent-up-mean came pouring out. He fired up the Harley and spun a circle in the street before he lined up on the stairs and Pus Gut at the top. The seized Harley Springer had plenty of power owing to the previous crook owner's investment. RJ set his sights on Pus Gut and flew up the stairs chasing him all the way through the front door of the bar. Pus Gut running for his life, and bouncers trying to knock RJ off the bike.

ZZ could have, and should have, gotten away, but he was back in the bar trying to collect his bet. To his slightly fuckered-up way of thinking, the punks in the bar owed him several hundred dollars.

RJ had knocked one fat bouncer on his ass and was trying to maneuver the bike back out the front door. ZZ saw the dilemma of an inward opening door and the remaining bouncer intent on dragging RJ off the bike. ZZ's time in prison taught him a lot about ending fights quick and dirty; he clapped his hands off the bouncer's ears and brought him down with a howl of pain, a thumb in each eye bought the bouncer's cooperation. A quick kick to the other bouncer's nuts kept him on the floor. ZZ was having the time of his life as a quasi-agent of the law.

Somehow RJ and ZZ swung the big door inward enough to get the bike out.

As it turned out, riding a Harley down a flight of stairs took more skill than going up, and RJ dumped the bike when he grabbed too much front brake at the end of the run. Timing is everything. Two squad cars arrived, and a pair of deputies came out guns first.

RJ's Browning Hi-Power sent the deputies into a frenzy when they found it tucked into the small of his back. It made their whole evening, in fact.

The holding cell was blissfully empty when RJ and ZZ got thrown in there by the deputies. RJ was sobering up quick and running through his options. He never carried his Customs ID when working undercover. Working around bikers could always get you stomped, but cop ID in your pocket could get you killed.

His UC driver's license would hold up for a while, but the protocol with DMV involved them notifying his agency if there was a law enforcement inquiry. Not good. RJ needed to contact somebody before things got too far, as in getting charged for a whole bag full of crimes.

When the deputies pulled RJ out to fingerprint and photograph him, he played the only card he could think of. "I can tell you guys where a meth lab is up here. I'll talk to a detective."

The deputies didn't say much, but RJ could tell they were thinking about it. He certainly looked the part. They put him back in the holding cell. ZZ, who had spent a third of his life behind bars, was grinning. "This is so cool! We never been arrested together before."

RJ thought, *Yeah, this is so cool. Fuck.*

An hour or so later an older guy in civilian clothes came to fetch RJ. This guy was a detective. Once sequestered in an interview room, RJ asked if Deputy Walt Brewer was around. Brewer was the name of a narc on the local drug task force. RJ explained to the detective that Brewer knew him and could vouch for his identity as a cop, more precisely as an undercover Customs agent. The detective gathered up his paperwork and left RJ locked in the interview room to ponder his future.

A while later the door opened and Brewer stepped in. "What the fuck, dude? Sheriff will be here soon. Fuck, dude!"

Brewer the narc brokered as good a deal as possible with the Sheriff; RJ would be released with no reports filed on him. ZZ was in a different boat though. He had neglected a meet with his parole agent, something that happened frequently with ZZ, and therefore had a parole hold in the system. ZZ would remain in the county jail until the Department of

Corrections came and collected him. The Sheriff felt justice would be served with ZZ doing a minimum of a year back in the State Penitentiary. For now, it seemed, ZZ would pay the price for their night of drinking fun.

In a month RJ would go to ZZ's parole hearing; he'd make up a supporting story. Again. And get ZZ released. Again.

The Sheriff's parting shot to RJ was, "You call me and ask before you set foot in my county again. You hear me?"

"Yes, Sir."

The sun was just coming up in the east when an exhausted RJ mounted up for the ride back to Capital City.

RJ was all over the board now, telling stories about him and Golden. He felt that he had to carry Maxie's end of the conversation until he arrived. RJ still had faith Max would show. He laughed out loud when he recalled one of Golden's jokes.

One evening at the Customs field office, he asked RJ to hang around for a fun surveillance. Their office in those days was a commercial space in a downtown shopping center. The three-level parking garage served the commercial tenants and the shopping public. The reserved parking for Customs was on the second level.

Golden knew that their boss, RAC Burchfield, was meeting a female bank manager at their favorite watering hole across the street from the shopping center. He was married; she was married, but that added to the fun. Golden had gone to the office key locker and got the spare keys to Burchfield's G-ride and moved the car to the bottom level under its reserved spot on the second level. It was a 2-hour wait, but it rewarded them to see Burchfield and his squeeze walk into the garage hand-in-hand. Burchfield walked the bank manager to her car where they made out, passionately. Golden and RJ were giggling in delight. Finally, the trollop started her car and drove off.

The real show started when Burchfield, with a mild bourbon stagger, went to where his car should have been. Then he stood there for a bit kind of looking like an owl as he tried to blink the missing car back into its slot. He lit a smoke and began a search, though with a pronounced lean. A lip reader wasn't necessary to get the gist of Burchfield's monologue. Golden and Johnson were in spasms of laughter. A confused Burchfield went to the pay phone by the elevators and made a call. The boys mused over the irony of him calling his wife to come and get him. Maybe he had called for a cab to get him home. It was neither. When the two police cruisers showed up, Golden and Johnson decided to break off surveillance. Discretion being the better part of valor and all.

The next day Golden would appear wholesome and innocent when Burchfield queried him about the prank. Golden was that good.

Quinn commented, "I was surprised that no one ever stuffed Golden into a dumpster when he was a rookie. He was always spraying mace in the AC vents of cruisers, and crap like that."

Kramden recalled a suspicion that Golden was putting dead rats in Detective Teddy Rusing's A.K.A. Dickface's desk, and rather artfully in the jar of jelly beans on top of the desk.

Maxie loved the joke. And then there was Major Meth, a man who played jokes on drug manufacturers.

CHAPTER 14

Major Meth

Golden and Johnson started working clandestine methamphetamine labs at a time when meth was king in the Midwest. The manufacture of methamphetamine had evolved and shifted from the sole purview of outlaw motorcycle gangs. The old-style meth, phenyl-2 propanone, or Prope dope required a cook who had some knowledge of chemistry. It was an involved process that required a minimum of 72 hours and metal catalysts to get the reaction going. Then the "new ephedrine method" came along, and virtually anybody could make meth. As one state chemist testified, "You mix ephedrine in any way with the right ingredients and you will have meth." Mom and pop cookers could get 30 kg kegs of Chinese ephedrine and by using either the red phosphorus/iodine reduction, or the hydrogenation method, make meth. The hydrogenation method working with thionyl chloride was a bit dicey, but once you got past that, it was just a matter of hitting the mix with hydrogen gas until it wouldn't take anymore. Perfect meth! Could even be done in a bug sprayer with a pressure gauge. Spend a little time filtering and washing with acetone, and you had a cash crop.

Sometimes in the course of a law enforcement career you encountered a giant in the field. Such a man was Major Meth, the DEA boss who was in charge of the regional meth lab task force. The Major was iconic within his agency and was genius enough to run the entire outfit. Neither Johnson nor Golden could figure out why a man of his background and brain power was heading up an obscure Midwest task force. The Major had been a Marine Corps officer, and later a CIA operative. He knew Ollie North, for Christ's sake! Golden and Johnson had a lot to learn yet about internal agency politics.

Anyway, Major Meth was an interesting character in a well-cootered SF Giants ball cap and horn-rimmed glasses, tall and lanky, a Marlborough perpetually dangling from his lip. Gray wolf eyes always roving…not nervous…maybe a little wary. Books had been written about his exploits south of the US border.

During one of Golden's early meth lab search warrants, the Major and his meth team were in attendance per protocol. After kicking the door in, a quick assessment of the target house revealed that for sure a lab was present in the basement, but no finished methamphetamine was evident. The law enforcement boys rolled up their sleeves for a long day of searching every nook and cranny for enough crank-related evidence to make a decent federal case.

Meanwhile Major Meth went to the basement to "tidy up" for a state chemist who was en route to process the chemicals. Apparently tidying up meant figuring out where the meth cook had left off in his process and finishing up that process for him. The Major knew that for the purpose of charging a federal methamphetamine case, meth in a liquid form counted just like powdered meth. There was an actual conversion formula. If the Major could figure out the clandestine cook's last step, he could continue the process to its end point. The Major was so damned smart that he knew how to make meth using any process ever devised.

He used to meet with cranksters undercover and compare methods and recipes with them. He was a genius!

The Major recognized an ephedrine-red phosphorus-hydriodic acid setup when he saw one. The cook was complete, and the red phosphorus had been filtered off. The batch still needed to be hit with some lye to neutralize the acid, a little dash of something to make it into an oil, and have some hydrogen chloride gas bubbled through it. Had he enough time, he would have filtered it and powdered it out too. As it was, the state chemist got a nice liquid sample that contained D-methamphetamine.

Later, at the meth cook's first appearance before a U.S. Magistrate, he seemed confused when the charging documents stated that he had 7 pounds of methamphetamine in his possession at the time of the warrant. The cooker kept arguing with his attorney that there was no meth in his house when the cops hit his place, and the attorney kept trying to tell the cooker that 7 pounds of meth was going to send him to the federal pen for about 119 years. When the court security men led him away, the crook was still screaming.

Major Meth merely chalked the whole "tidying up" incident up to the dangers of working around volatile chemicals and addictive drugs. A fellow can simply lose track of what he's doing.

The Major had a trusted partner in the war on meth in the Midwest, and that was a female Assistant U.S. Attorney named Beth Winslow. Beth was a nice-looking lady and sharp as hell, a bit of a spinster, but then maybe all that brainpower protected her from the silly antics of men. She did, however, seem to have a soft spot for the Major, prosecuting every meth case his team brought her way, and cheerfully answering her phone at all hours of the night to assist with federal search warrants. The pair took note of Golden and Johnson and their penchant for coming up with biker meth labs. Major Meth suggested that AUSA Winslow make a formal request to Customs to get them assigned to Major's merry band.

"I think I would have liked your Major Meth," said Quinn. "Sounds like he had the right attitude for locking up crooks. Didn't let technicalities get in the way."

"Maxie and I knew that we were working with a legend, though in hind-sight maybe that wasn't the role model we needed. I mean, we were young and wanted to make our own legends." RJ *stared into his glass for a minute before continuing the thought. "It's hard to follow the rule book when you're trying to get your own chapter in 'Greatest Cops of All Time.'"*

Kramden returned from the bar with a couple of plates of sausage and mustard. "Dive in, boys. What'd I miss?"

"RJ was just telling us about a little rule bending to secure a place in the narco hall of fame. Now days you better have an attorney on retainer or just stay in your office." Quinn winced as he said that.

Rimjob reached back in his memory bank and dredged up a legendary Quinn story that would surely get your ass canned in the current environment.

CHAPTER 15

Tougher Than Jimmy's Neck

BCPD Recruit Academy 171-F had 61 freshly shorn and scrubbed pink recruits, all working hard to start a career that many targeted in their youth. There was plenty of time spent struggling through procedural classwork and intensive legal instruction. For these youngsters, there were beaucoup classes that were fun and engaging. All of it was a new and exciting challenge.

Part of the reason many remember it fondly was that more than a few instructors were world-class. Most were journeyman police officers and detectives, they had so much experience to share and their methods to deliver their messages were frequently hysterically funny. They all had a passion to teach the young pups, and often it boiled down to not getting themselves killed, indicted, or divorced. Most of the recruits listened to at least two of these three pieces of advice.

Bristol City domesticated a young, transplanted officer in the early 1960s. He was a hard-charging, ass-kicking street monster, the Night Police's own, Pat Quinn. One of this academy's instructors referenced

Quinn as "tougher than Jimmy's neck." There wasn't a single recruit who could decode that phrase, though many of them used it their entire career.

Quinn spent over 30 years in the service of Bristol City, and as one might expect, not all of it in the good graces of his department or the city administration. The city fathers were a frequent target whom he referred to as "nincompoop windbags." Most of the recruits thought that was hysterical. Who the fuck says "nincompoop"?

Quinn was the subject of more than one absolute monument to police work. One afternoon, during a break from back-to-back classes of "Organizational Matrix and Chain of Command" and the ever-popular "Introduction to Criminal Law," a small group of the recruits were shooting the shit in a nearly empty classroom. Joining them was another of their instructors, Tony Masero, 25 years on the job and a rapidly graying sergeant in the MPD, or Mounted Patrol Division (read cops on horses, typically referred to as the "Mounties"). He was sitting over the edge of the table drinking a Tab and regaling them with the cop stories they craved.

His Pat Quinn story went something like this:

After five years as a beat officer in San Diego, California, Quinn made the move east, purportedly to satisfy his young, first wife who was habitually out of sorts. She missed her Midwestern life, her family, and especially her mother who lived about twenty miles north of Bristol City.

BCPD scooped Quinn up, always on the lookout for bright young officers, especially from what they assumed to be the more progressive law enforcement of the left coast.

It cost him in salary and lifestyle to make the move, but Quinn worked to convince his brethren it was the right thing to do for his marriage. The little woman, Lorraine Quinn, bolted for Cincinnati, Ohio, about seven months after setting up their new homestead. It appeared she preferred the company of her new beau, a Roto-Grip Bowling ball salesman for fuck's sake.

Back in '62, the new year in San Diego rang in with a bang. Quinn was pushing a police cruiser through what is now the Southeastern Division, in the neighborhoods of Skyline and Lincoln Park. Gritty even then, this oldest section of Lincoln Park, between Imperial Avenue and Ocean View Boulevard, took up the bulk of Quinn's patrol time.

On a warm, late afternoon in January, Quinn was berthed at Las Cuatro Milpas, an old joint even in 1962, in the Barrio Logan area. He was off his beat, by a lot, but in those days, a cop could flat cover ground, with little traffic stopping his progress. The yearning for those pudgy tamales and steamy bowls of chorizo was more than a young swashbuckler could resist.

According to Masero, Quinn had quaffed one of his favorites from Cervecería Modelo and dug in his pockets for change to leave as a tip. Paying a lunch tab was frowned upon by most cops and often they'd stiff the owners, not just here but anywhere they got the free meal. Not Pat Quinn. He knew they wanted him and other troopers in the door, as a deterrent to crime if nothing else, but he felt their service deserved payment.

With his back to the door, Quinn talked with the very hard working owner of his favorite Mexican cookshop when he heard two pops. Before he could turn, a third. This one perforated the big front window of Las Cuatro Milpas and drilled Raphael Ochoa in the middle of the forehead, blowing the back of his skull off and marinating his sister María Isabel in his brains.

Quinn unholstered and threw his arm across the shoulders of the stunned María Isabel, crashing them both to the floor. Telling her not to move, he belly-crawled, pooling blood and brains into the front of his uniform shirt. He peered cautiously out the corner of the same front window only to see a single white male, with a handgun in his left hand. The suspect casually walked to a powder blue and white, Chevy Bel Air parked northbound, heading away from Quinn's position. The guy slid into the driver's seat and started the engine.

Quinn sprinted for his patrol car. The white guy was already moving and picking up speed by the time Quinn got underway.

What Quinn didn't know was that the white guy, Denton Hawley, was three for four. His first two shots killed DeMarco Santin and Hewitt Pierce, both San Diego County Sheriff's Deputies. Just minutes before, the deputies had attempted to serve an arrest warrant on Hawley at the front door of his mother's shop, "Angela's Sewing & Alterations." DeMarco took the first round in the mouth, Hewitt took the second in the chin. Neither of them heard the other hit the ground.

Quinn never made it back into the chase. Hawley had disappeared into the sinking, evening sun.

Disheartened and feeling for the victims, including his unmet but brother officers, Quinn sat with detectives from his own department and recounted the gruesome details. Events slammed on the brakes when radio traffic advised that Denton Hawley had been spotted and was under surveillance. Radio traffic indicated cops had seen him through the front windows of some Skyline bungalow, still carrying that mother-fucking pistol.

Masero, slugging back Tab and now chain-smoking cigarettes, was becoming more animated in his narrative. He said that Quinn just bolted from the squad room. The detectives tried to slow his departure, but he'd have nothing of it.

Inside of 10 minutes, Quinn arrived on scene, siren wailing. Oddly enough he found himself right back near his own Skyline neighborhood. On the same block as today's True Vine Missionary Baptist Church, there was a congregation of another sort. Sheriff's Office squad cars and San Diego PD cruisers blanketed the block in which Hawley was now captive. On sorry little lawns, in driveways, blocking streets in and out of the neighborhood, police vehicles were everywhere. In the dark blue of approaching night, the atmosphere was electric.

Over the course of the next 30-45 minutes according to Masero, they made many attempts to get Hawley to give himself up. They didn't know if he had hostages, but it didn't seem that was the case.

The press had gotten wind of the situation, and they too were trying to squeeze into the scene. As usual, they weaseled in exactly where they weren't wanted, weren't needed, and where you could count on them to be in the way. The *San Diego Union* had a reporter and photographer burrowed in behind the on-scene lieutenant's car. Jesus, what assholes.

On a diagonal, several patrol cars away and hunkered down behind a 1957 Ford Customline police cruiser, Quinn awaited some resolution that would make him feel better.

In today's world, these situations would include SWAT teams, command posts, and hostage negotiators. There would be hours of trying to talk the suspect down, placating and providing milk and cookies until they could hopefully bring it to a successful conclusion. That depends on your perspective, of course. They did things differently in '62.

"Who the fuck knows why…the guy just gave up." Masero added, "Frustrating as it was, he'd had enough, I guess."

Denton Hawley yelled out the front door of the modest Spanish style stucco bungalow, "I'm giving up. Giving up. Don't shoot." Every cop on scene trained their service revolvers at the front of the house, anticipation spiking. A sergeant out front yelled back for Hawley to throw his gun out the door. In what seemed like a very long moment, the arched wooden front door cracked open…a hesitation…then Hawley chucked a .357 Smith and Wesson Model 19 out the door towards the lawn.

It was good it wasn't the Sunday edition of the *San Diego Union* that hit the streets the next morning. The Tuesday edition had less readership and fewer consequences, even if the photo was above the fold and on page one. Masero explained that the picture of Quinn, though grainy and in black and white, was still clear enough to understand the situation. The caption below the picture told the nut of the story in less than fifteen words. "SDPD Officer Patrick Quinn, throwing a surrendered pistol back to the suspect."

Yup, Quinn being the consummate young lawman of the early '60s had had enough of coddling the douchebag. When Hawley's handgun took a bad bounce on the turf, it landed practically at Quinn's feet. Doing what any right-minded police professional would've done, especially under the cover of darkness, he dumped the remaining rounds and tossed the gun back to Hawley. One might make a supposition why he chose that course of action. Then again, one might not.

The press roasted Quinn. Not like today's idiot, agenda-driven press might, but there were questions. And answers, but mostly non-answers. The nincompoop windbags did exactly what you'd expect. They covered their asses and lied to beat the band.

Remember this was 1962. Police brass had a different mind-set. Hawley was taken alive. No more innocents were hurt or killed. And, Quinn was well thought of for the most part, even if a bit unorthodox. Ten days on the beach was his sentence.

Quinn became a star on the choir practice circuit, toasted and re-toasted, and for about six months he couldn't buy a drink.

During multiple rounds of interrogations, it turns out Denton Hawley saw the uniformed Pat Quinn through that big glass window at Las Cuatro Milpas and determined he was a threat to his escape. Quinn was lucky. Ochoa was not.

Deputies DeMarco Santin and Hewitt Pierce remained dead. María Isabel was just starting her dark journey into alcoholism. In 1979, just prior to her death, she was still fighting the demons.

Kramden had another legendary Quinn story to tell, but Rimjob was oh so pleased with the sound of his own voice that he bulldozed over Kramden and leaned into one of his latest sexual exploits…

Quinn drops the ash from his cigar in Winny's mouth. "Damn it, Rimjob, your dick? Really? After that story, you launch about your dick?" He just shook his head.

Rimjob grinned. "So we're laying there, in throws of post-coital delight. And in my usual endearing way, I'm stroking her hair, kissing her. Soft, butterfly, sugary-dripping, motherfucking kisses on her shoulders and neckial region. I'm pretty sure I detected a stirring, so I ratchet up my moves. I'm pegging in the red."

Johnson can't bear it. "Post-coital delight. Where the fuck did you come up with that?"

Quinn offers, "He's still reading *Cosmo*."

Rimjob knocks back the last of his drink, easily ignoring his former partners. "I whisper some kind of really neat bullshit, guaran-fucking-teed to moisten." Animated now, the warmth of the rye starting to take effect, Rimjob continues, "Understand now, I'm being really fucking romantic. Actually not so romantic as to require a second date, but romantic enough to qualify for a continuing roll in the hay."

Johnson's eyes rolling, he just slides the bottle Rimjob's way.

"So with her face just inches from mine, in that hot, gravelly, sexy voice, she leans in… 'your face smells like my ass'!"

Kramden spewed his drink. Quinn just smiled.

CHAPTER 16

Heckle and Jeckle

Mike Cutler was living proof of the old cop adage, "We don't catch the smart ones." Officer Ron Johnson was only in his third week of the field training program, assigned to day shift under the careful tutelage of Field Training Officer Chris Mercer. It was a quiet Sunday morning with little traffic out. The radio call was simple enough; respond to the Lakeville Shopping Center to a reported man down. The reporting party would meet the cruiser in front of the Kut-n-Kurl beauty salon.

The reporting party turned out to be the newspaper deliveryman, not a paperboy, but a guy that goes around filling the newspaper vending machines, in this case with the big *Sunday Times*. As Johnson and Mercer approached, the man pointed at the door of the beauty shop. As the cops got closer, they could see a guy lying on the floor. "He's been like that since I called 911," the newspaperman offered. Mercer peered inside the shop, cupping his hands around his eyes. Johnson was watching Mercer for some clue as to what he should be doing. It was worrisome that Mercer did not seem overly concerned about the body on the floor.

"What do you think we should do here, Officer Johnson?"

"Uh, we should find out if he's injured or dead....Uh, call an ambulance, and ah...maybe a fire truck to break the door open?"

"You're right, Officer Johnson. We could do all of those things, but why don't you get on the radio to dispatch and have them call the owner of the beauty shop? Tell 'em that we need them to open up so's we can look around."

"Yes, Sir."

The lady that owned the business showed up about 20 minutes later with a large ring of keys and opened the heavy metal-framed glass door. As Mercer crossed the threshold, he told Johnson to put handcuffs on the body. A confused Johnson complied. As soon as he started manipulating the crumpled man by looking for wrists to handcuff, he could tell that the person was alive. How had Mercer known that?

The interior of the shop appeared to have been ransacked, drawers opened, stuff strewn all over the floors. Even the beauty chairs were lying on their sides.

Mercer asked the owner if she kept any serious cash in the shop, and she said no, just a tin box for petty cash. Mercer grunted to himself and told Johnson to search the suspect. Things were coming together for Johnson. The man's pockets were stuffed with costume jewelry, really cheap stuff, and a fold of cash that had about $60 in it.

Mercer walked back to the crumpled and now handcuffed man. He looked down at the figure for a moment before nudging him in the ribs with his boot. "Wake up, shit bag! Time to rise and shine! Officer Johnson, meet Mike Cutler, doper, burglar, and all-around waste product."

Mercer explained what had happened to Officer Johnson. Cutler had pried a roof hatch open over the beauty shop and used a short rope to lower himself to the floor, whereupon he stuffed his pockets with whatever looked valuable. Then came the problem of getting out. The doors were all dead-bolted and his rope was too short to get him out the way he came in. So the intrepid burglar tried to stack beauty shop chairs to make a ladder. It had all tumbled to the ground, knocking Cutler's dumb ass out. The odor coming off of Cutler hinted at the copious amounts of alcohol involved.

"Congratulations, Officer Johnson, on your first felony arrest!" Mercer was smiling.

Three years had passed, and Ron Johnson was a seasoned patrolman. He happened to be working the same beat as he had as a brand-new rookie with Officer Mercer, though he was now working graveyard shift.

Officer Ron Johnson was in a serious discussion with his graveyard shift beat partner, Officer Max Golden. Because of their similar time on the department and their propensity to get into shit, or otherwise stir things up, they had been tagged Heckle and Jeckle. The senior of the two, Heckle (Officer Ron Johnson) was explaining why they urgently needed a confidential informant. Jeckle (Officer Max Golden) was nodding in agreement.

"Jeckle, we will always be small time if we don't start developing snitches. We'll never be street monsters, let alone detectives. Shit, they could transfer us to day shift!" Jeckle bristled at the threat of day shift. "Let's watch Brett Bollinger's house tonight…shake down anybody we see leaving. If we catch somebody holding, we tell 'em they gotta snitch or else."

The plan was beautiful in its simplicity. Everyone in the free world knew that Brett was a coke dealer. The narcs knew it well, but were trying to work that into something bigger. They had shut Heckle and Jeckle down when they went to the narcs with what they thought was probable cause for a search warrant of the Bollinger home. The dynamic duo were disappointed when they were told to leave Brett Bollinger alone. However, the narcs didn't say anything about shaking down his visitors.

A couple of cars had come and gone from Bollinger's place, but calls for service kept them from making the car stops. At 1:30 in the morning, Jeckle came on the radio. "Northern, B11."

"Go B11."

"I'll be out of the vehicle with a suspicious person, 2300 block of Lakeville."

"Roger B11. Unit to fill with 11?"

"Northern, B12, I'm a block away. I'll handle."

"Roger B12."

Jeckle could hear Heckle's squad car coming the entire time, assuredly more than "a block away." The big 440 Dodge sounded like it could suck pigeons off the telephone wires when Heckle put his foot into it. Moments later the darkened cruiser slid up to Jeckle and his suspicious person. Heckle jumped out. "Hello, Mike Cutler. Long time, no see."

Cutler did not seem at all happy to see Officer Johnson.

"Hey, shit bag. Where you coming from?"

"No place."

"Must be coming from somewhere…everybody does. I just came from Lakeville Park, so where you coming from?"

Jeckle chimed in, "I'm pretty sure I saw him leave Brett Bollinger's place."

Cutler visibly squirming now.

Heckle, "Well up jumped the devil! Brett Bollinger is a drug dealer! Mikey, you weren't at a drug dealer's house, were you?"

Cutler wanted to rabbit, but his drug-addled brain telegraphed his move about 4 minutes before his feet could get going. Jeckle wrapped a large gloved hand around Mike Cutler's skinny neck and marched him over to the front of the cruiser. With his other hand he started turning out the contents of the hype burglar's clothing. On pocket number two Jeckle came up with two decent-sized glassine bags with white powder in them. It was enough to charge anyone with possession for sale.

"Uh-oh. Mikey, I'm so disappointed in you. I think this means you have to go to prison." Jeckle snapped his handcuffs on Cutler's skinny wrists.

Cutler now blubbering and blowing snot bubbles. "I can't go to prison, man," he wailed.

"Should have thought before you scored from Bollinger. I agree with you though, a little skinny shit like you will not last a week in prison. Some big Aryan Brother is going to punk you out. What do you think, Heckle?"

"I think you're right, Jeckle. About a week after he lands in Big Muddy, you'll be able to turn a moped around inside his skinny asshole!"

"Big Muddy?" Cutler sobbed.

"Yeah, sure. Big Muddy, Mid-Central, Ozark, it's all the same. Your skinny ass. Big Nazi boyfriend with a dick like an anaconda."

"Puhleeeeeze, you guys, I can give you something. I can give you Bollinger. You just saw me go there, I can buy from him!"

"Mikey, Mikey, Bollinger is so yesterday. He's small-time. We could have Bollinger right now if we wanted him. Nope, gotta be something bigger and better than that."

Cutler, still snuffling, screwed his face up in concentration trying to think of who wouldn't kill him right away.

If he got his dope from Brett Bollinger, that limited the dealers he could give up. Heckle had an inspiration because Cutler needed anywhere from $200 to $400 a day to support his coke habit. He had to get that money from someone. "Let's think, Mikey! When you break into those nice peoples' homes and steal the shit that they worked so hard for, who do you sell it to?"

Cutler was nodding his head as he followed Heckle's logic, not even realizing that he was tacitly admitting that he stole people's stuff and fenced it off. Then the idea of snitching on Fat Patrick and the consequences that would follow scared him more than Heckle and Jeckle. They might arrest him, but they wouldn't kill him. In true crook fashion, Cutler sensed some daylight and started lying. "Um, you know, I just sell stuff to people who want stuff."

"That's bullshit and you know it, Mikey!"

Heckle and Jeckle had Cutler by the balls. However, not being detectives or narcotics officers, they didn't handle Cutler with the immediacy the situation called for. Seasoned investigators would have not let Cutler out of their sight until he was signed up and producing. Or maybe it was the incessant radio calls that forced them into giving Cutler the bullshit High Noon ultimatum they did.

"You have exactly one week to come up with your fences. All of 'em! Meet us at Lakeville Park next Wednesday night at midnight. By the swing sets. Don't be late, Mikey." Jeckle's powerful gloved right hand gave Mikey's neck another squeeze to underscore the penalty for tardiness, then he removed the cuffs.

Cutler realized that he was free, at least for the moment, and shuffled off into the night. He wiped his snotty nose on a shirtsleeve without breaking stride.

"Think he'll come through for us?" Jeckle asked.

"No tellin', but we own his ass with that eight ball of coke."

On Wednesday night Cutler didn't show at the appointed time and place. Between Heckle and Jeckle they managed to keep Lakeville Park covered for an hour. Not an easy task with calls for service coming at a brisker than usual pace for a Wednesday night. When the duo could get face-to-face, they discussed what to do with their new unreliable informant. Heckle spoke first. "We gotta find him, plain and simple. The little douchebag is not taking us seriously. Now we gotta put the fear of God into him."

Jeckle nodded in assent. "For what it's worth, I'll check his mom's place on Sandalwood."

"Is he drivin' anything, or is he getting around on LPCs?" Jeckle knew from experience that LPC was some of Heckle's Marine-speak for shoes, or Leather Personnel Carriers.

"I don't think he's had a car in at least a year."

"All right, we need to do bar checks at the Lakeville Lounge starting now!"

Jeckle nodded in agreement. "I don't think he is stupid enough to go there tonight, but he'll show up there eventually, sure as God made little green apples."

It took until the following Monday night to corral Cutler. Heckle parked in the alley behind the Lakeville Lounge and eased in the back door. Out front Jeckle made a slow pass with his marked cruiser. It was a time-tested system the duo had used before. Lounge-goers who wished to avoid the law would make for the back door to avoid the cop out front and walk into the waiting arms of Heckle or Jeckle. Mike Cutler wasn't that smart. He was still peering out the front window when Heckle walked up and stood beside him. Cutler about jumped out of his skin when Heckle cleared his throat.

"Hiya, Mikey. Missed you the other night!"

Out in the alley Heckle and Jeckle launched into a heart-felt description of Cutler's future and the dangers of not meeting with his handlers at the appointed time and place. Cutler whined and cried and swore that he was trying to line something up for the cops.

He was given until Wednesday night again. Heckle and Jeckle were new to the informant game and thought they needed to establish a routine. They foolishly named the same time and place. And again Cutler did not show.

"This guy is pissing me off!"

"I know, Jeckle. I'm thinking he is not taking us seriously. In fact, I think he's clowning us."

"I think we will have to talk with him privately. Out past the landfill."

"Yeah. One of us has to scoop him up, the other needs to check that it's clear. Make sure no one's dumping a car, or a body. This has to be a private talk."

It took two weeks of searching before a simple radio call signaled Heckle. "Meet me at the dumpster." Heckle recognized the code and responded, "Give me 10."

An already anxious Cutler ratcheted up about 12 notches more on the terror scale. At first he thought Jeckle was taking him to jail, though it was odd he wasn't handcuffed. Then he realized they weren't headed for the station, but toward the outskirts of the city. He was begging Jeckle for answers, but Jeckle just kept herding the black and white into the darkness.

When Jeckle turned down the darkened road to the landfill, Heckle was in position. When he saw Jeckle's headlights approaching, he flashed the headlights of his own cruiser twice. Slowly.

Finally the cruiser rolled to a stop, and before Jeckle doused the headlights Cutler could see the other police cruiser just sitting there dark and ominous. When Jeckle opened the rear door, Cutler wedged his skinny doper ass down between the seat and the floorboard doing his best human ostrich imitation. Jeckle grabbed an ankle and neatly plucked the little hype out of the car.

"Outta the car, shitbag!"

Cutler flopped around in the dirt. "No, no, no, noooooo!"

Heckle switched on his flashlight. "Get up, Mikey. Quit acting like a cunt!"

Jeckle pulled Cutler to his feet in the flashlight beam.

Heckle, very business-like, "Mikey, I need the names of all of your fences now. No bullshit."

Cutler started naming names, but they were little pooh-butt names. Nothing was making Heckle and Jeckle's socks go up and down. Mikey clung to Fat Patrick's name like it was the Holy Grail. Finally Heckle took Mikey by the elbow. "Come over here, Mikey, I want to show you something."

At the edge of the dirt and gravel road was a deep ditch. Mikey struggled to stay away from the precipice. Maybe he should give up the Holy

Grail, and then he was tumbling into the darkness. Two ear-shattering booms, each with its own ball of flame. Mikey screaming and holding onto himself in the bottom of the muddy ditch.

"Shut up, Mikey. You're not hurt...yet! You can see how easy your life can end out here. Nobody's around, and nobody will ever look for you! We need a name, Mikey...your last chance." Then the single sharp beam of a flashlight illuminated Cutler in the bottom of the ditch.

"Okay, okay! Goddam! It's Patrick!"

"Patrick who, Mikey?"

"I dunno his last name, he's just Fat Patrick."

"Where do we find Fat Patrick?"

"He's a bartender at the Eight Ball. You can't tell him I told! Pleeeeease, he'll kill me!"

"Shut up, Mikey. He probably won't kill you, but I'm still thinking about killing you right now!"

"Ohhhhhhhh, gawd! Pleeeeeassssse!"

"For fuck sake, just shut up, Mikey. We ever have to come looking for you again, you're coming back out here. And it'll be with a shovel."

Heckle and Jeckle climbed into their cruisers and left. They left Mikey to his own devices to get out of the ditch and walk his narrow ass back to town.

Two nights later on a Sunday night, Officer Sean Benelli, neighborhood resource officer for the Lakeville neighborhood, asked for a meet with Heckle and Jeckle. They liked Benelli because he wasn't your typical day shift, schoolyard, friendly neighborhood resource officer. Benelli was more of a street monster and had taken the resource officer gig because it allowed him the time to investigate things in his area to his heart's content without having to run calls and have all the dispatchers and half of the cops mad at him for not pulling his weight on the ever present backlog of calls. It was Benelli's stepping stone to becoming a detective. Something that Heckle and Jeckle also desperately wanted.

They met up at their favorite McDonald's just as it was closing up. It was their favorite because at closing time they would give all the food under the warming lights to the cops for free. The manager liked having cops around when he was closing up and preparing the bank bag for deposit.

Benelli was leaning against the fender of his cruiser and biting into an hour-old Big Mac. He pushed his wire-framed spectacles up the bridge of his nose and looked at Heckle and Jeckle when they pulled in. The studious-looking glasses didn't go with his hulking weight lifter's physique. After each had grabbed a burger and fries from the pile on the hood of Benelli's cruiser, he opened the conversation. "You guys will not believe the crazy ass story Mike Cutler told me tonight."

Heckle and Jeckle munched without comment.

"He said you guys kidnapped him and took him out to the dump and used him for target practice. I told him he was nuts and not to smoke anymore of that rocked-up coke. It's frying his brain. I shut him down. Don't think he'll tell anybody else that story."

Heckle and Jeckle could only nod.

Heckle and Jeckle were unable to use the information about a fence, so they passed the information on to the property crimes detectives. The detectives were able to locate Cutler and bring him down to the precinct, and soon detectives were debriefing a surprisingly cooperative Cutler about Fat Patrick's fencing operation. Cutler's only request was that the detectives never leave him alone with Heckle or Jeckle. Ever.

Weeks later the detectives, using Mikey Cutler to do introductions, were well into a successful undercover sting operation on Fat Patrick and a host of other fences in the Northern District.

One evening as Heckle and Jeckle were clearing briefing and heading for their patrol cars, they were met in the hallway by Captain Bob Sellers, Chief of Detectives, and also head of internal affairs.

"Good evening, boys. A word?"

The two cops followed Sellers back to his office. Sellers took a seat in his high-backed desk chair. The boys remained standing.

"Relax, boys. I wanted to thank you for turning Mike Cutler for us. It turned out far better than expected."

Heckle and Jeckle smiled and looked at each other. "Thank you, sir," they said together.

"You know we have some openings coming up in the Bureau. I'd like to see you both apply. I like your initiative and gung ho attitude!"

Heckle and Jeckle beaming. "Yes, Sir!"

"Have a good shift tonight and be safe out there."

"Yes, Sir!"

As they turned to leave Sellers' office, he spoke one last time. "Oh, and boys, no more recruiting trips at the landfill."

Out in the parking lot the pair wondered aloud how Sellers knew, but then Bob Sellers knew everything.

"Sellers and I, we're only a couple of academies apart. He was so quick." Quinn recalled of his old friend Bob Sellers. "The administration didn't hate him, and he was smart enough not to bad-mouth them, even when they had it coming. Kept his mouth shut unless he had something positive to say."

Johnson followed. "Almost exactly like Kramden. No, wait! It was nothing like Kramden," he said, grinning.

"It is possible that a time or two, I may have shit in my mouth with the administration, but they were such a fucking group of needle-dick idiots. They needed my advice and counsel." Kramden was most unconvincing.

Johnson poured Quinn a Scotch, but continued needling Kramden. "And look what a career you carved for yourself, Officer Gleason. Another 10 years or so on the job and you might've been promoted to senior parking attendant!"

Kramden responded, "I could've crushed that job, my friend. Working day shift with weekends off. What's not to like?"

Quinn, still reminiscing about his old friend, "You know Bob was adept at side-stepping disaster, keeping his dick out of the dirt, but let me tell you fellas, he was one ass-kicking street monster in his day. He was the first one into the battle, and he could hold his own like nobody I ever met. Nobody I would've wanted more in my corner."

Considering that Pat Quinn had been a Golden Gloves boxer, that was quite a recommendation.

"And he was so old school," Kramden added. "He kicked ass and took names, just the way it was supposed to be. The first team I was assigned to out of the academy was Sellers' squad. He was a God to me."

"To lots of you boys," Quinn added.

"If you needed advice, hell, if you needed probable cause, by God he knew just how to make that happen. He may have been old school, but he knew how to play the game." Kramden beamed thinking about his old boss.

Like all of them, RJ had a soft spot for Bob Sellers. "Yeah, he made a huge impression on me and Maxie when he didn't fry us over that stupid Mike Cutler deal. I remember being a junior detective and having the on call duty on a Friday night. It was early October cause the World Series was on. Patrol guys found a body in one of those fleabag hotels over on SE 23rd. Dude was an addict and had OD'ed. I'm hating my life cause I had to dump my beer and quit watching a clutch game. I get there and determine no investigation needed. The burned spoon and the spike on the nightstand tell me what I need to know. I still have to wait for the ME's people though, and being the start of a weekend the body snatchers were backed up. And then out of nowhere Captain Bob Sellers, Chief of Detectives appears. Mind you, it's a Friday night, and the Series is on! At first I thought he was just checking up on one of his rookie detectives, making sure I hadn't screwed up The Black Dahlia murders or something. That wasn't the case. He's carrying a sack of White Castle burgers, two big cokes, and a transistor radio. We spent the next two hours listening to the game, munching burgers, and just shooting the shit about when he was a junior dick. A small thing, but I would have followed him into hell after that night. I was sorry as hell when he passed."

"Everyone was sorry, RJ. Fucking cancer. One day he was on the job, and it seemed like it was just a couple of weeks later we buried him. I ended up with his job and the promotion, but what a shitty way to get it. I would have stayed his lieutenant until we both retired. Goddammit!" Quinn was getting emotional by the time he got the words out.

Kramden needed to steer the group away from Bob Sellers' tragic, untimely departure, so he rolled into his own coroner story. "Can somebody tell me why you always get these calls during a fucking heat wave?"

CHAPTER 17

The Spoiling at The Hollywood Cashmere

"The body may not be moved without permission of the medical examiner, district attorney, or county attorney having criminal jurisdiction except in cases of an affront to public decency or circumstances where it is not practical to leave the body where found, or in such cases where the cause of death is clearly due to natural causes."

That's what it says in the paperwork from the Office of the Medical Examiner.

"Following notification of the OME of a death and the subsequent investigation, the OME will make arrangements for the transport of the body from the death scene or medical facility. Transport from the place of death to the OME will be by means of a contracted body transport service or designated funeral home."

Summer in Bristol City was blistering hot. Temperatures in the 90's and 100's were the norm. The third week in August that year was humid as fuck. Kramden's uniform had bonded to his flesh, and he was more than sure that one of his balls had glued itself to his thigh. He could feel beads of sweat trickling down his chest, under his Kevlar vest. The 20 pounds of armament and protective gear he was wearing (duty belt, loaded .357 Smith, two speed loaders, mace, handcuffs, baton, bulletproof vest, flash-light, radio, and mic, knife, tape recorder and in Jack's case, an extra mace pouch with two Romeo y Julieta cigars) felt heavier on days like that.

It had also been one of those days that was frustrating to a beat cop. The afternoon began with two burglary reports, back to back. Time-consuming and uninteresting. A cursory canvas of the neighborhood looking for someone who saw something or was at least willing to admit it, followed. It wasn't in depth. It was just collecting contact info for the detectives. A boring, blister of a day.

Kramden didn't have time to write either of them up when he caught a crash. It was out on the freeway and in Highway Patrol's jurisdiction so no paper to write, but until they showed, it was Kramden's gruesome. A middle-aged, management type working for a local pipefitting company somehow lost control of his 280ZX, spun it out, and launched himself up a concrete bridge support. If Kramden hadn't noticed the crumpled license plate frame sporting the words "280ZX Fury," he wasn't sure he could have identified it, such was the damage. The little red sports car had wedged between the underside of the overpass and the 45-degree concrete support. About 20 feet off the roadway surface, it was just a scrap metal carcass, purging itself of fluids.

Kramden and the arriving paramedics labored to find purchase, making their way up the bridge support. They knew that Fire was on its way, so Kramden advised dispatch to let them know of the tenuous grip the car had gained under the overpass. The concern was obvious; that it would let loose and slide down the support to the highway below, wiping out any of them who were trying to effect the rescue.

Daniel Evens DeClark, a white male, 49 years of age, was in the middle of that devastation. It was difficult to even identify his body parts, as the energy from the crash had contorted his physical structure.

His torso was face up, the lower half of his body folded over on top of him. His femur had shorn loose of the hip and had exited out his rectum. Daniel was alive at that point, blood spilling from him in rivers. It was heartbreaking to hear him struggle to say, "I don't want to die."

Daniel lost his life under that overpass anyway. The paramedics couldn't even get IV lines into him. He said no more. God was merciful to him.

Fire stabilized and secured the car in place. Displaying audacious bravery and insane talent, they pulled it off. Sometime later, under Fire's strict supervision, Midnight Towing fashioned a way to lower the car down to the freeway pavement. The highway cops and Fire, with their extrication tools at the ready, awaited the coroner.

Jack heard later that evening, after the coroner had done his thing, it took over two hours to extract what was left of Clark from his car. Even for guys that have seen it all, they said it was a ghastly affair. For the family, there was a modicum of, Kramden guessed, good news as Clark was at least intact. An open casket was still a possibility if it was important to them.

As Kramden was clearing the crash, dispatch cheerfully advised him he was "clear for J4," meaning he could grab a bite to eat. To be honest, he wasn't thinking food, but cops compartmentalize. He'd put what he'd just experienced away and would deal with it sometime later. Maybe that night at choir practice. Or six months down the road, having coffee with his partner. Or…he'd just avoid it all together.

Kramden ended up at Beto's, one of Bristol City's few decent Mexican joints, with his best buddy who shared the adjoining beat, Ron Johnson. They both had an early dinner of steak picado, refried beans, rice, and a stack of steaming tortillas. Two iced teas revived them from the day's activities on their beat. With two hours left on their shift, they were planning on knocking back a few G&T's when they went off duty. That was not to be the case.

The call "10-105 possible dead body" could not have been more disappointing. Kramden was engaged in pre-choir practice mental calisthenics and this was going to likely fuck that way up. It didn't help that the radio dispatcher who Kramden fondly referred to as Lucretia Shitmouth, assigned him the detail. He knew she did it on purpose; she had a hard-on for him. It may have had something to do with the fact that a few months back and about five hours into a virulent choir practice, Kramden had gotten into a beef with her. It appeared he called her Lucretia Shitmouth. And a cunt. Not good form when the target of your dissatisfaction can send you on any shit call their heart desires. And Shitmouth's heart was malicious and spiteful.

Thanks to his social blunder, Kramden was aimed at the Hollywood Cashmere Mobile Home Estates. It was on the I-270, a six-lane rip through the heart of the city, squeezed in between Dollar Dave's Used Cars and a pawn shop.

The Cashmere's name was a misnomer as it was, in fact, a waste yard of dilapidated, 50s and 60s era, piece of shit mobile homes. Some sitting on bare tire rims, the rubber having dissolved long ago. A few were more permanent structures but were actively falling down in slow motion. There was an American flag out front, and Jack appreciated that, but it was the two-foot size you'd hang at the stern of your 21 foot Chris Craft.

On arrival at the Hollywood Cashmere, Fire and paramedics were already there, standing out front. Kramden pulled into the driveway, parking on pavement that had eroded into nothing more than a gravel easement. Maybe this would be "unfounded," one of his favorite dispositions. He was still hoping to meet the boys for cocktails.

When he stepped out of his cruiser, Kramden realized it was the stench of putrefaction that kept the others from the ramshackle mobile home. Fuck! He grabbed his Streamlight and stuck it in his sap pocket. You never knew what you'd be digging into.

Kramden met the teams assembled outside of Unit 8. There were knowing looks, and perhaps even a hint of a grin. Fire advised him this was an attended death, and that he'd been dead for a while. That was pretty fucking obvious.

As it says in the policy of the Office of the Medical Examiner, in an attended death, "The physician in attendance at the last illness of a deceased person who, in the judgment of the physician, appears to have died of natural causes while in the care of the physician, shall certify the cause of death to his best knowledge and belief."

Here, Mr. Erling Andreasen had died of complications of hepatocellular cancer. When writing his report, Kramden had to look that up to understand it was essentially liver cancer. According to Andreasen's doc, he'd been battling it over two years, was in treatment, and his death was not unexpected. The medic had seen him just five days prior in his office.

Because of Erling's attended death, the Medical Examiner would not be coming; the body transport people would. That was way quicker. In fact, the J. Wincel Company, Mortuary Transport Service had just pulled up in what looked like a plumber's hearse.

Fire and the paramedics were more than happy to leave, and Kramden envied them. Since he'd have to take the report on this, he grabbed a jar of Vicks, jamming about half up his nose and headed for the front door.

The aluminum siding was uncommonly warm even on this scorcher of a day. Kramden pulled the screeching front door open, and two things happened. First, the hot, almost liquid stench washed over him like a putrid wave. In a blink, he also understood the broiling effect. In the squalid little living room was a space heater, on full blast and pumping out enough British Thermal Units to melt the wax candle next to it into a pool.

Dead bodies, in that heat, started smelling, sometimes within hours. Most loosened their sphincters, so the body would smell of feces and the spreading bacteria would wreak havoc on the body. Here Mr. Andreasen, a morbidly obese Danish fellow, was laying nude on his side on a tattered couch, in front of the melted candle and the blasting space heater. Just the heat, was almost untenable.

Besides his obesity, the combo of time and the added thermals from the space heater had bloated Andreasen's body even further. Filled with all kinds of gases and liquids, the body is only so large and the excess needs somewhere to go. The secretions formed from putrefaction oozed out of his mouth, eyes, and other orifices, his body's tissues were breaking down and peeling back to release all that built-up gas. The obnoxious fluids puddled on the couch next to his body and pooled on the carpet.

Kramden unplugged the space heater, pulled open a sliding window, and stepped outside, gulping fresh air. Since fire and paramedics had already noted his death and had spoken with his physician, at least he didn't have to confirm the death. He could have, from the Circle K down the street.

Kramden joined a stout, tattooed Boz Scaggs look-alike, Jacoby, and his partner Charlene. She was a dikey blonde with big tits and a single gold tooth featured between her pillowy jowls. Kramden laid out what he knew to Wincel's body baggers. Neither of them seemed concerned. It was what they did for a living. Every day.

The Office of the Medical Examiner makes a special point to outline in its policy pertaining to contracted body transport services: "Please bring with you any personal biohazard protective gear (gloves, aprons) that you may need to make the removal. Be mindful that you are responsible for the removal of the body and that the assistance of our staff with lifting or transport is not a part of their job. This is done as a courtesy. We will make an effort to notify you if the habitus of the deceased may necessitate you bringing additional staff."

Back in those days, biohazard was a word that, as far as Kramden was concerned, only scientist types might use. Lifting or transport isn't part of the OME's job, nor his, but in those days you did what you could to help.

Kramden could see the heat waves coming off the top of the trailers across the park. "Fuck me," he muttered to himself, it was hot. After a slug of iced coffee from his thermos, the three of them trudged up the rickety single step and re-entered Unit 8. This time Kramden took more time to observe the surroundings and the conditions as he'd be writing a report, albeit a short one.

Andreasen's place was a fucking train wreck. Today, we'd call him a hoarder. Books, magazines, clothes, tools, dishes, most of them dirty, were piled high in the tiny mobile home sink. Assorted sports memorabilia covered almost every flat surface in the place. There were narrow trails cut through the debris from the back to the front of Andreasen's tin box home. Greenish gray carpet leaked out from under the remnants of his life.

The tiny kitchen spoke to his disease. Prescription bottles (Sorafenib, Regorafenib, and several other 'nibs'), funnels, box after box filled with medical supplies including sterile gauze, ointments, OTC anti-nausea medicine, syringes, and other detritus from his treatment. There were reams of medical marketing materials and research papers spread throughout the place. Most of it seemed about neoplastic processes, whatever that was, giving rise to targeted therapies. It was all above Kramden's pay grade.

Andreasen had hollowed out a grotto amidst his gallery of despair and misery. On his couch in his hovel, he had taken his final breaths. It was more than depressing.

The heat from the space heater had not only sped up the decomposition of Mr. Andreasen, but it had also aided in creating massive blisters on his chest and his stretch-marked belly. Blisters that would contain a quart of bodily fluid each. And there were several of them. In his nude repose, this dead guy was literally dissolving in front of them.

Jacoby and Charlene made a quick survey and decided they needed a "scoop," sort of a cross between a stretcher and a dustpan. They'd literally shovel Andreasen's remains into a "Bio-vue," extra heavy-duty, body bag. They positioned the scoop alongside the corpse, with the body bag close at hand. With the baggers at his head and mid legs, they rolled him into the scoop. Unfortunately for them, two or three of the horrendous blisters on his chest and stomach ruptured, douching them in fetid body secretions. Kramden leaped backward even though he was out of range. The closer two sputtered and swore and attempted to wipe the shit off. Kramden had seen enough and left Charlene and Jacoby to their business.

They took some time to wheel Mr. Andreasen into the J. Wincel Company, Mortuary Transport Service hearse. Not only did they struggle to get the fat him out the skinny trailer door, but it turns out he was "more liquid" than they thought.

"The notification of the next of kin is the responsibility of the law enforcement agency," according to the OME and BCPD policy. Kramden doubted it would surprise the family, but he wanted to get it out of the way. It was a task he loathed.

This wasn't a typical day on patrol in Bristol City, but it wasn't uncommon either. Death can be ugly. The boys in blue see it all. That's why they compartmentalize.

You know, live, don't die, repeat.

Quinn rattled the cubes in his glass as he tried to verbalize what effect that had on a young cop. "We did things somebody has to for the citizenry. Just like those poor body baggers. I think you get used to it, at least to a point."

Kramden thought about that. "I don't know, boss. I mean, I agree, some of them, the natural causes deaths, you could accept, even the ripe ones. But there were so many others…"

That made RJ think about Maxie. Some dead bodies were a hell of a lot harder to get past than others…especially the ones you had a hand in. He glanced at his watch. What the fuck was Maxie doing anyway?

CHAPTER 18

You Don't Forget These Things

Grief is a hard thing to quantify. Even when you're grieving, you don't really understand the depth of your own pain. You don't understand how to swim to the surface of grief and catch a gulp of fresh air. You only know you're sinking and that the horizon is slate gray...you can't see it ever becoming a sunrise again, pink with optimism. Grief may be needed, all the stages, but when you're in the middle of it, there's routinely no moment that lifts you, that makes you feel better about where you are. It's a personal thing. You sometimes shed it over time or you can carry it with you. It's possible to carry it with you. Many do.

Cops are asked to treat third-party grief as if it were the Grand Slam Breakfast at Denny's. They are asked to attend the most gruesome of moments in the lives of everyday people. They must share in the darkest moments a mother, father, or family can have. Then the expectation is that they'll just call it another assignment handled and get back on the beat. This is what they do. They do it every day. It's expected.

If they're involved in a shooting, even a clean one, they'll put them on paid leave, take their firearm, and force them to see a shrink. If they go to a fatal accident, an unspeakably grisly knifing, or any of the more routine but ghastly tragedies that cops are commissioned to attend every day, well, that's just business as usual. No one sends them to the company shrink. No one comforts them. All their partners are going through the same shit. There is a reason cops self-medicate. It's a tough gig. Some get through it relatively unscathed, some don't.

Max Golden partnered with a guy, a great cop. T. Steven Knorden was one of those guys that had "it." His gregarious personality and brilliant smile drew you in. Charismatic. Whip fucking smart. There wasn't a Night Policeman on his shift that didn't enjoy working with the guy. And Max was at the top of that list.

T leaned a bit quirky. He worked harder than most, but wasn't hesitant to say, "Never put off till tomorrow what can be done the day after tomorrow just as well." He was type-A, for sure, but self-deprecating and full of good humor.

Golden once chided him for missing a court date. "Life's tough, my brother, but it's tougher when you're stupid." That made T howl with laughter; he knew Max never meant a syllable. T was tough as nails, but with a soft side that many never saw. Max was one of the lucky few.

The Kansas City Southern Railway Company hauled freight through Bristol City; agriculture and minerals, some chemicals and petroleum too. On January 23rd, 1981, at 4:04 a.m., a brand-new SD40-2s, KC Southern's 3,000-horsepower road switcher diesel-electric locomotive was traveling south through the city at 41 miles per hour. As it crossed the Lyman Street grade crossing, the "active" automatic warning devices, in this case, flashing lights and barrier arms activated.

Maximum Golden got the call, "Vehicle versus Train." That was a call that had ominous written all over it. He poured the coal to his cruiser, emergency lights flashing in the darkness. He didn't bother with the siren, there was little traffic.

Dispatch continued, "Fire engine company 12 and ambulance on the way." The city equipped each engine company with basic life support equipment, and in a "Vehicle versus Train," there was a high probability that it would get used.

Max was first on the scene. The force of the crash had pushed the wreckage down the tracks at least a hundred yards. It was obscured by a mangled chain-link fence, heavy underbrush, and an entanglement of roadside debris.

Max grabbed his flashlight, pushed through the thicket of shrubbery, and scrambled over the tangle of limbs and chain link. Dust still hung in the air, and Max could hear the respirations of the massive locomotive in the dark. As he dropped to his feet on the track-side of the fence, he swung his Streamlight across the second car of the hulking train. It was on the tracks and appeared intact. Pushing down the tracks, he made his way past the railway engine.

Max paused, trying to make sense of what he was seeing. Stunned, shocked. Overcome with suffocating emotion, Max found it hard to push himself forward.

Responding to a silent burglary alarm, T drove around the descending barrier arms at the Lyman Street grade crossing. The oncoming Kansas City Southern crushed T and his squad car.

He was only 26 years old with a young wife he adored. Why he slipped those barrier arms is still a mystery, over 20 years later.

T's passing tore the fabric of Max Golden's heart.

Six weeks later, Max and Steve Rimfro had worked as beat partners for 12 shifts. It wasn't reasonable to believe that what happened next could occur over the course of just 41 days, but it did. Most cops wouldn't have a run like this over the course of a career. But then again, many would see much worse.

March 16th. The day before St. Patrick's Day and the first of three days off. A dangerous combination for a bunch of young cops looking to get their party on. Most of Max and Rimmer's team planned on St. Paddy's together. It would be epic. Max wouldn't show, he wasn't ready.

Max was on his J4, meal break, having the basic burger at Gil's Great Big Burgers. Skimming the *Post-Dispatch* sports pages, his mind wasn't on it, but it was a habit. Typical radio chatter churned in the background. After you've been doing the job for a while, it's easy to go on autopilot and isolate the radio traffic that's important, to differentiate it from the more routine communications. Just as he was about to hit the street, he heard Rimmer, 4S43 requesting a fill-unit. Rimjob immediately appended his request, "10-18 urgent and send a bus."

Max didn't understand what Rimjob had going, but Rimmer was just 500 yards from his last cheeseburger. He jumped in his car and bolted across the intersection, red lights up and siren wailing. Once across the eight lanes of traffic, he spotted Rimjob's cruiser, in front of Millbrook Pharmacy. Rimmer was struggling with a bloodied female, obviously drunk or stoned off her ass. In her arms was an infant, couldn't have been over six months old. On the ground at her feet was a six-inch blade.

As Max leaped from his car, Rimjob shouted: "Take the baby." The female, later identified as Tina Coffee, was punching and slapping Rimmer with one hand and clutching a very tiny Sabrina Coffee with the other. It took some effort to pry Sabrina away; Rimjob more than had his hands full.

As Rimmer was cuffing Mrs. Coffee, Max noted that Sabrina was not looking at all right. She grew limp in his arms, and her deep brown eyes fluttered up under the lids. Rimjob guided the stoned bitch to his patrol car, and Max pulled Sabrina up close listening and feeling for respirations. It was obvious she wasn't breathing. His hand on her chest, Max could feel a heartbeat, but she needed help. He could hear the ambulance en route.

Max started mouth to mouth on Sabrina, standing there, in front of the pharmacy. People paused on their way to get their medications or cosmetics or whatever, some with their mouths wide open. Sabrina's little arms hung limply, her legs dangling. She wore a tiny little two-piece outfit that twisted around her from her mother's struggles with Rimjob. It exposed her belly. More store patrons were gathering, and Max wanted to cover her stomach but he didn't have enough hands. It seemed wrong not to cover her little tummy.

Max kept up the artificial respirations, in his mind encouraging her, begging her to breathe. It didn't feel to him like she was getting the air exchange she should have. It seemed like their mouths and cheeks would balloon with air but he couldn't feel her chest rising as it should in rescue-breathing. He checked again for a pulse, and this time there was none. A MedStar Ambulance guy slipped up beside Max. He took Sabrina from him.

"Tell me" is all he said.

"I don't think she's getting air at all and no pulse now." Max cringed, noting that blue pallor starting to show on Sabrina's lips.

By that time Rimjob had rejoined Max who was wondering what the hell had happened while he was dealing with the drugged-out and violent, so-called guardian. Max filled him in. They turned and walked towards the ambulance to looked in on Sabrina but there was no time. The rear doors slammed, and the bus tore out of the parking lot, code three.

At the end of shift, Rimjob and Max were at South Patrol Station, both of them wrapping up reports. Rimmer explained that Tina Coffee got into a beef with the hired help inside of the pharmacy. When Coffee became abusive, they asked her to leave, which she refused to do. They called the cops and Rimjob showed up. With some difficulty, Rimmer talked her outside. Before he had the chance to call for back-up, Coffee, still holding Sabrina in her arms, labored to pull a six-inch kitchen knife from under her blouse, gashing her ribs. Luckily, for all three of them, it just clanked to the pavement.

Rimjob slipped over to a bank of phones making that tough call to the medics at Big Mo. He wasn't on the phone long when he hung up. He didn't say a word, just sat down. Max knew.

Sabrina Marie Coffee, five months and four days old, died that afternoon. Max never had a clear airway, she wasn't getting air from his repeated attempts to inflate her little lungs. All Max was sure of, was that he had failed her.

Hours later one of the MedStar Ambulance guys joined Max and Rimmer at Brick's. He was a young kid, younger than Max even, and you could tell it shook him. It turned out that Sabrina, during her mother's drunken rampage, had swallowed the blue crayon she had in her mouth. It lodged in her airway and prevented any lifesaving exchange of air. She had died of complications after they'd removed the crayon. Turns out she had an underlying medical condition.

At three in the morning, a hammered Max leaned against his personal car just outside his apartment. He was uncommonly pained. He didn't understand why Sabrina's passing hit him with such force. For him to get misty was just not something he was used to. *Well, fuck me,* Max thought. He'd just have to get over it. He had to testify in court in five hours.

About three weeks later, on the first warm night of the new spring, Max was on patrol in his brand-ass new, Ford Crown Vic. His police cruiser was smugly the top shelf of police machines. It was to this point a great shift. Little paper, but the calls had been interesting as hell.

Max responded to an armed robbery they squelched within moments of its report. It just so happened that Officer Tony Sei was in the parking lot of Tanto's Auto Parts when the idiot that just robbed the place fled on a Kawasaki KZ750 LTD motorcycle. He made a turn around the side of the building, and Tony, he swore unintentionally, using his patrol car, bulldozed the dirtbag and his stolen bike into the flank of the brick building. A pursuit of 7 seconds. A record!

They also had a shooting and a minor foot pursuit in the first couple hours into the shift. This is why the boys in blue went to work every day. They'd just cleared Tanto's when Max received a radio call to assist Fire on an unknown medical call just a few blocks away.

Max landed at an apartment on Queen Anne Court, a three-story, 24-unit, lower-income housing block. Rimjob pulled in right behind Max. He knew they'd beaten Fire to the call, as they had about a three-mile run. Rimmer and Max oriented themselves in the complex, then headed for a set of concrete and wrought iron stairs on the far side of the small property. As they approached, they could hear a bawling. Not screaming, but a dreadful, aching wail. It was painful to the ears.

Max took off running and hit the ground level landing, then the stairs, two or three at a time, with Rimjob on his heels. At the first switchback in the stairs, Max glanced up to see a young female, 23 or 24 years old, crying and holding an infant in her arms. He hadn't gone one or two more giant leaps up the stairway and she launched the toddler into the air, directly at Max. She traveled at least 12 feet, maybe 15 in the air, downstairs.

Thirteen months old, Brinique White landed in Max's outstretched arms, knocking him down a step and back into Rimjob. As he tried to tuck her in close, protecting her, afraid she'd hit the stairs, she let loose a dreadful howl. It took a split second to finish the flight of stairs and to recognize that he had a very burned infant in his arms.

At the top of the stairs was the apartment Lakedra Thompson-White shared with her daughter Brinique. Max yelled at the sobbing Lakedra to get him a clean sheet or a towel. Door wide open, Max looked for a soft spot to lay Brinique, the carpet would do. Rimjob threw a cleanish sheet on the carpet, and Max laid Brinique atop it.

The beautiful toddler was burned, everywhere. Max's brain couldn't manipulate the data to understand how this could happen but amidst Lakedra's bawling, they came to understand the horror.

Brinique, a recently walking toddler, had been in the kitchen with her mom. An electric frypan, filled with boiling oil for supper's french fries was on the counter. Brinique, pulling herself along the cabinets, reached up and pulled on the cord draped over the counter. The fryer upended and dumped the searing oil directly over the top of her. If that wasn't bad enough, she stood in the spilled oil which fried her tiny feet.

No sooner had Rimjob and Max heard the details than the Fire Department poured in the door. Archer Ambulance was 30 seconds behind. Fire had the sterile burn sheets they always carry, and they laid those out and put Brinique on top. Then they poured over her a version of distilled or sterile water they carry just for those purposes. Brinique's gasping sobs broke every heart in that room. They bundled her in the sheets, but not before Max noticed that the bottoms of her feet were cooked away by the scalding oil. He could see bones.

When the paramedics transport gravely injured persons to the hospital, a fireman will often accompany the attending ambulance guys, supporting any lifesaving processes in play. In Brinique's case, the firemen had a second urgent call come in, in their district, and Max volunteered to go to Big Mo. Rimjob said he'd go, but Max pushed forward. Rimmer took stock of the fact that Max was trying to suppress the tears in his eyes.

As the ambulance burrowed into the night, red lights and sirens blazing, Max watched the paramedics frantically attending to Brinique. They had Max holding a monitor attached to the toddler while they intubated the child. He could hear the ambulance driver on the radio, advising the hospital of Brinique's vitals.

As they swung on to the emergency room apron, Brinique was failing. The rear doors of the ambulance swung open, and there was already a crew of about four or five standing with a gurney. The toddler was in the ER in 30 seconds. Doctors, nurses, and others swarmed. It was a frenzy of activity, orders being barked, everyone committed to saving her. The

ER doc in charge asked Max what he knew and he spit it out. Max couldn't imagine he'd been very helpful.

In what was probably a couple of minutes, but seemed like hours, Max heard the same medic say, "We're going to have to cut down." Max had seen this procedure once before and had at least an inkling of what was to happen. A venous cut down is an emergency procedure in which a vein is exposed surgically, when the docs need to get a needle into it and it's difficult or impossible to find. Brinique needed fluids in a bad way and this was the only way. At least that's how Max remembered it.

Brinique's wailing never subsided. It didn't change in its magnitude even as the doctors started to cut into her arm.

Being of no use to the ER heroes, Max left the little draped cubicle and went to the nurse's station. Often you'd know people there. The Night Police were in the ER often. Tonight was not one of those nights where he'd find a familiar face. He wished there was someone there to shoot the shit with. Just some idle chatter would have been a diversion. He could have, but didn't want to go back to his beat. He needed to know how things were going with Brinique.

Max didn't have long to wait. The ER doc came out and found him, maybe 40 minutes later. He told Max that Brinique's burns covered 80% of her body, second- and third-degree burns. He said, she never had a chance. Her little heart had just stopped.

A couple of hours after shift's end, Max finished his reports. He knew where he'd find Rimjob, and there he was at the bar at Brick's. He was sloshed, on the edge of melancholy. They had a few drinks, and Max told him, "She didn't make it, Rimmer." Somehow Rimjob knew. They didn't discuss Brinique or the call any further.

On the first Saturday in April, Rimjob and Max had just cleared their swing shift briefing and were walking to their cruisers. Rimjob was pissed. Their swing Captain had reamed him over his observations submitted in a written report. As is normally the case with the brass, the Captain wasn't there, was misinformed, and was way the fuck out of line asking Rimjob to change his report. Rimmer refused. Rimjob would pay the price before they would eventually find a witness who corroborated his statement. The Captain never apologized. It was beneath him. Prick.

Interrupted mid-bitch, dispatch advised Fire was responding to 10-52, an "Ambulance Needed" call. The Night Police didn't normally respond to these, but this time Fire, though responding, had a very long run to get there. Rimjob and Max both answered up, responding. Sometimes a couple of minutes could make a difference. As they boiled out of the parking lot, dispatch alerted them, "Additional. Reporting party advises an infant not breathing."

Max wasn't sure what Rimjob was thinking, but he knew the words "please don't let this be a bad one" were going through his mind. Though he tried to shake it off, a dark unease settled over Max.

Rimjob and Max arrived one after the other at 303 Randyjean Court, just across the street from the Union Pacific tracks. At the curb, hysterical and sobbing was a young woman, red hair, in a robe and slippers. As they poured out of their cruisers, she was hyperventilating, pointing to the house. "Tell us what's happening! Where's the baby?" Rimjob implored. She simply could not speak, she was so overcome with emotion. Rimjob tried to push her towards the house, and she just folded, collapsing in a heap. He tended to her, and Max ran to the house and banged through the screen door.

Where the fuck is this kid? He scanned the living room, the kitchen. Nothing. He ran down the hall. There was no baby in the bathroom. He threw the shower curtain aside and nothing. A bedroom just outside the bath was likewise empty. Nothing in the closet but clutter. He ran to the last bedroom. At the threshold of the door, he looked and nothing. "C'mon, kid, where are you?" The closet was open, and he looked inside. It was empty. The bed was a mess of bedding and pillows, he yanked that off, and the bed was…empty.

As Max turned back towards the door, he noticed behind it, a pile of the light plastic that's used at the dry cleaners to protect your clothes. It hit Max, and in the same moment he thought, *Oh, no.*

Max yanked the door open and amidst what must have been a dozen of those discarded bags was the baby. An eight- or 10-month-old, David Allen Southland was on his belly, the bags wrapped around his lower body. He was wearing a light blue, feet at the bottom pajamas with tiny squirrels on them. Max didn't know why he remembered that fact, he just did. He pulled David from the bags, rolled him over, and kneeled next to him in one quick move. He checked for a pulse and breathing. Nothing. Max started CPR on young David.

Rimjob burst into the room just as dispatch advised that the responding fire unit had been involved in an accident. Another engine was being dispatched. The paramedics were on their way, but they were coming from Mercy Hospital and that was a long run.

Rimmer kneeled next to David and Max and relayed that Dianne Southland, 23 years old and first-time mother, was being tended to by neighbors. She was a wreck. Rimjob pulled from her that her husband Philip was away on business. Preparing for his trip, he'd hung his dry cleaning on the back of the bedroom door. He shed the bags as he put his clothes in his suitcase. Later, he wouldn't remember he hadn't thrown them away.

Max kept up with the CPR until Rimjob put his hand on his shoulder. He said, "Let's switch." As they'd been trained to do, they did just that, a coordinated hand-over. Rimjob started the chest compressions and rescue breathing. David was so small that two adult men couldn't share the duties like you would on an adult. It was exhausting work and made sense to trade off.

Max didn't know how long it was, but it seemed forever when two paramedics came charging through the door. A fireman right behind, loaded with lifesaving gear and more medical electronics. In another synchronized move, Rimjob and one of the paramedics switched spots and CPR continued.

As Rimjob and Max backed out of what was now a very cramped bedroom, it was such a pitiful sight. David looked so small surrounded by all the professional lifesavers and a mountain of gear. They listened as one of the paramedics appraised the emergency room at Big Mo of the situation. It was matter-of-fact and professional. They couldn't decide if it sounded good or bad, but they were still doing CPR and that wasn't good.

Little David didn't make it. He passed away at the hospital an hour after he arrived. Knowing the ER docs, Max and Rimmer were sure they made a heroic effort to save him.

It turns out that Dianne Southland was home, ill with the Hong Kong flu. She'd fallen asleep in bed after a dose of antihistamines. She hadn't intended to fall asleep. She expected her husband home from his trip to Cleveland at any moment, and she and the baby were waiting up for him.

Somehow David had made it off the bed and crawled behind the door. He burrowed into the plastic bags where he asphyxiated. When Dianne found him, she didn't understand what to do, didn't know CPR, didn't know how to help. Scared and disoriented, Mrs. Southland was unprepared to assist her son in any meaningful way.

The coroner found there were no indications of SIDS or foul play. The baby died of asphyxiation. Simple. An accident.

It was not simple for Philip or Dianne Southland.

Surprising to both Rimjob and Max, it wasn't simple for them either. They met after shift for a couple of beers, but neither wanted to do it in town. They didn't feel like a choir practice or hanging out with the other Night Policemen.

As they sat at the bar at Mumford's on St. Charles, they each nursed a Jack Daniels, neat. Neither of them liked the shit, but it seemed like it might be quick medication. They both wanted to be with each other, but neither of them wanted to discuss it.

Three times in six weeks was a lot to hold so close. A lot to keep inside. It was also a lot to expose even to the partner they'd shared it with.

They didn't fix a thing at Mumford's. They clung together needing comfort and having nowhere else to go to get it. No one "on the outside" got it, and mostly, they probably didn't care. They didn't shed tears, but both agreed "enough was enough." They wanted no more dead baby calls. After more than a couple Jacks, they were both a bit in the bag. They resolved they weren't taking those calls anymore. "Fuck 'em, we just aren't gonna go."

But of course, they did. That's what they paid them to do. There was no paid leave. There was no psychiatric support. For most, there was no chaplain. Most of the Night Police just didn't want to share the real stuff, you know feelings and emotions and shit. It was too warm and fuzzy for them. No one suggested it was smart, that's just how they rolled.

There's nothing surprising about why many cops can't stay married or why they drink like fish or why some eat their guns. It's a hard act.

"No wonder we fucking drink! Shit just gets too real sometimes." And with that Rimjob knocked back the rest of the whiskey in his glass. "You know I think it was within a week of that homicide, the one with 4 little kids, that Dave Joseph ate his fucking gun. Poor fucker."

Dave Joseph had been a Night Policeman, and then fellow detective with the group. It was a painful memory for Kramden and the others. "I thought he had it made. He was so on his game, all the time."

Johnson added, "I knew he had some problems. Fuck, we all did. He'd moved in with his folks, for crying out loud. Didn't know he was a big gambler, or at least was into some Shylock for money. Maybe that was a factor. Maybe it was just about those dead kids. Maybe it was everything. I don't think anyone saw that coming."

Rimjob just nodded in agreement. "Not me, for sure."

"That bitch of an ex-wife was in his shit every chance she got, but I never thought it even ruffled his feathers." Quinn sipped his Scotch. His cigar was now one long ash teetering over his lap.

"You know, he didn't talk much about anyone he was close to, did he? I never thought about it, but I guess he just kept the personal shit bottled up, more than most. Guess I remember he talked about his folks now and again, more than others on the job. He was close with his old man."

Johnson interjected, "Yeah, and I think that's why he lined the tub and the bathroom with plastic before he blew his brains out. He didn't want it to be too gruesome if his folks got home before the body baggers got there. I'm sure that's why he called radio and told them to send a wagon...before...well, I guess he had no more to say."

"Remember that tall goofy-looking ambulance jockey, the one who crashed the wagon into Captain D'Antino's cruiser?" Before anyone could answer, Rimjob

continued, "He told me they only had like a three-minute response time and Dave still had some twitch in him when they arrived. Poor fucker."

At the Seneca's concierge desk, Max asked the always unflappable Mort if the Caddy was available for a trip over to Solly's. It was on another run. Mort suggested to Max that he have a drink in the lobby pub and Mort would come get him when the Caddy arrived.

The bar at the Seneca was an understated space, all dark paneling and greens. Just what you would expect of a grand old dame.

Golden handed his cashmere topcoat to a hat-check girl. It was that kind of place, the kind that Maximum Golden could get used to again.

At the bar itself, a very attractive redhead sat next to a guy with salt and pepper hair. He obviously had some years on him, but handsome none-the-less. They were having a serious conversation. Too bad, *thought Maxie. Could be fun to see if he still had what it took.*

He took a seat at the bar close enough to watch her, but not so close as to be ungentlemanly. Long time since Max had taken a woman to bed in a fancy hotel room. His couplings the last five years had been no more than rutting sessions. A sexual release in a third-world environment.

He ordered a Scotch and allowed himself a little fantasy about taking the redhead upstairs.

Too soon she stood and took her purse from the bar. She gave her companion a peck on the cheek. "That was one of your best lectures tonight, Jimmy. I was fascinated." A squeeze of the older man's shoulder, and she headed for the coatroom and the door. Max couldn't help but follow her with his gaze. When she left, he turned back to the remainder of his drink.

Jimmy had watched Max Golden when he had entered the bar. He had taken in the big shoulders and narrow waist, and the moment of hesitation as Max had surveyed the whole bar before entering. Hard to explain, but normal folk just walked into a bar. The gentleman struck up a conversation to confirm his suspicions.

"If she had stayed on a bit, you might have had a chance with the lady. I was hopeful myself 'til just a minute ago when I got the older brother treatment. Crash and burn." The accent was Irish.

Golden hoisted his whiskey glass to the gentleman and replied, "Story of my life with the ladies."

They drank in silence for a while, each man wondering what might have been. The older man eyed Golden before he spoke again. "Ah, we may be better off without them. They'll shorten your life, you know." Jimmy had resigned himself to the fact that he would return to his hotel room solo on this night, but he wasn't done drinking and he hated drinking alone. "Slide down this way and I'll buy you a conciliatory drink. Maybe we'll swap a lie or two."

Golden was still thinking about the redhead when he climbed the barstool next to the man offering wisdom about women. Max offered his hand. "Max Golden."

"Jimmy O'Reilly." The man had a warm, friendly grasp.

"So you're Irish," Max observed.

"As Irish as Paddy's pig. No, there I go again, can't seem to help myself. That's a lie... ethnically Irish I am, but it's Chicago born and bred. Truth to tell, the accent is affected, but helpful in my current situation."

Golden lifted his fresh Scotch to his host. "Thanks. So what is your current situation?"

"Former priest, religious expert, famous author, and lecturer of note!"

Golden raised an eyebrow, but it fit, he could see the guy as Father O'Reilly.

"I know what you're thinking, lad. How'd I lose the collar and cassock? Again, in the spirit of honesty, I'm a fallen angel. The church threw me out on my bum years ago."

Golden nodded in understanding. Jimmy had been at the drink for a while before he got there.

"But enough about me. I saw how you checked the place out before you came in. I'll bet you wanted to take the corner booth over there with your back to the wall, facing the door. But you wanted to sniff on that redhead, so you took a seat at the bar. You're a

cop or a soldier. I can tell by the way you carry yourself. So which is it? Just tell the good padre all." Jimmy rubbed his hands together in anticipation. He savored the prospect of someone to drink with and swap stories.

Max Golden chuckled at Jimmy's powers of observation. However, there was a third category of wary human besides cop or soldier. He pondered Jimmy's offer for a moment. Would it feel good to tell someone the truth? Talk to some perfect stranger and tell him every fucking bit of it?

"Tell you what, Jimmy. You're right on several counts, but how about you tell me your story first? Getting kicked out of the Catholic Church sounds a lot more interesting to me."

"Max, mine is the same sad story warned of in Galatians 5:21–'Envy, drunkenness, orgies, and so forth…that those who do such things will not inherit the kingdom of God'… Nor is it tolerated by the Church here on earth."

"Well, that sounds intriguing. At least it wasn't little boys." Sometimes Maxie couldn't help being a smartass. He regretted the comment and offered his apology. "Sorry, Jimmy, that was uncalled for. Let me buy you one."

Jimmy asked the bartender for another Kilbeggan on the rocks and toasted Golden when it arrived. "Here's to a quick death, and an easy one."

Golden could drink to that.

"It was the damn war that started me on the path of the fallen. To doubt my vows. To lose my way. Crawled deep into the bottle for a while. Right out of divinity school and getting ordained I volunteered to be a Navy Chaplain. Wham-bam and there I was in a war in a jungle. A frightened young man trying like hell to help even younger, more frightened men. I was a Sky Pilot. You know what that is, Max?"

Max didn't and shook his head. "No."

"A Sky Pilot helps those fallen boys on their last journey. It's different for all of them. Some want their mamma, some wanted to get a message to their wife or a girlfriend back home. Most wanted me to introduce them to God. It was the young black men I remember most, they would clutch my arm fiercely, the death grip I suppose, and implore me to get them right with God. More precisely, 'Get me right with the Man,

padre, get me right with the Man.' Then they would jerk, or rattle, and they were gone. I wasn't worthy of that job, Max!"

Golden looked at his watch. He should be going. The boys were waiting, but there was something he craved in the brutal honesty of this conversation that he was having with Jimmy.

When Mort appeared to tell him the Caddy was ready to take him to Solly's, Max declined. "Sorry, Mort, I'm going to stay awhile."

Maxie ordered another drink, and he turned to face Jimmy straight on. "Jimmy, does the pain ever get so great, so heavy, that…you know…?"

CHAPTER 19

Face Down

There's a concussive dissonance a blink prior to the splintering of a wooden door frame that often indicates that narcotics detectives are requesting admittance. If on the inside some douchebag's engaged in cooking methamphetamine, it can be a teensy worrisome. On the noble side of the door, they're ready to earn their pay.

Crank was some popular shit back in the day. It'd produce a buzz that was superior and lasted way longer than the cocaine high. Irresistible to the frugal offender. It reeked, many said, like freakishly bad feet, and it had long-term effects that were scary if you thought about them. Most cranksters never thought about them.

Manufacturing meth was mostly in the domain of criminal motorcycle gangs. The Outlaws, Bandidos, Hell's Angels, Pagans, and other groups of like-minded and dysfunctional lunatics owned the meth biz.

Manufacturing the dope was the key to their supply chain. To do that, they'd have to recruit some defrocked chemist or another reprobate with a year of chemistry and a GED to manage the process. Sometimes they'd use some poor half-wit who could get through a recipe but was too fucking feebleminded to know jail or the morgue was in his immediate future. These ass clowns would occasionally detonate themselves and, if lucky, a couple of their dirtbag buddies. Sometimes their Christmas chemistry kit didn't quite behave as expected.

Serving a search warrant on a clandestine lab was a dangerous business for just that reason. Toxic and often very flammable chemicals such as Ether, Phenyl-2-Propanone, Acetone, Benzene, Methylamine, Formaldehyde, and many others were often present. Bunsen burners and other sources of ignition were always in the mix. In short supply were safeguards, either out of sheer ignorance or profound carelessness.

Taking down a clan lab was also risky because cranksters had a fascination with guns and they were almost always present. Most of them were paranoid from the crank they used and whatever other mental defects they had. Most had criminal records, and most had done time. Staying stoned was a lifestyle choice that carried over into the lab as well.

Not having an affinity for the constabulary presented its own problems for the narcotics agents.

One early morning or late night, depending on your perspective, 15 seasoned narcotics agents assembled in the corner of a field of strawberries. If it had been light, they'd have seen the carpet of green stretching for miles. Steaming coffees, kicking cold feet in the dirt, their silhouettes were outlined by headlights. They were a loose gaggle awaiting an operational briefing to begin. As the last narc came barreling in, Sergeant JT Mavis gathered them together to go over the game plan.

A search warrant had been granted hours before, for this clandestine meth lab. In a ranch style home, on three white oak covered acres, it was on the only foothill in the county. Ian Clark, a legendary crank snitch, worked for Agent Don Pennerton and he'd been inside, within hours of their assembly in the strawberries. As reflected in the search warrant affidavit, Clark had seen an active, working lab, three suspects, two males (one previously identified who had records for dope and weapons) and some unidentified skanky biker broad. Clark told the narcs he'd seen at least six or eight weapons inside. Typical.

Three of the task force troops surveilled the place prior to gaining the warrant, and there'd been no activity for the last 10 hours. No reason to believe there were others inside, but then again, you never knew.

The entry team's glide path would be down an unimproved dirt road, across the face of the hill, and down into a small clearing. Their approach into the clearing was wide open, so they'd have to take advantage of the darkness and their stealth package. They didn't actually have a stealth package, but they were sneaky. Being less than two miles away meant they'd be knocking at the door in short order. After bailing out of the vans, the entry team would politely knock and request admittance.

In those days there was no such thing as hazardous materials teams. The task force was on its own handling the explosive and toxic potentialities. The fire department was their go-to, to assist with the chemicals. Compared to what's known today, they weren't lax about safety but they were ignorant as to the real risks and mitigations. If they considered a clandestine lab major (often they wouldn't know until the door crashed down), they would team with DEA or state DOJ, bringing more resources to bear.

The entry team for this operation comprised nine very experienced narcotics agents, including five that all worked out of the same office. Don Pennerton, Rich Mercado, Jack Gleason, Tommy Lincoln, and Steve Rimfro were a tight team, and the bosses routinely assigned them to "do the door." Kicking a door off its hinges upon entry was considered a sexy job amongst the narcs. Because of the danger involved, it was often the catalyst that created a very strong camaraderie amongst entry team agents. And, the five of them had a lot of experience together.

Their operational plan had Kramden giving the "one-o-five" or the "knock and notice" for the search. Tommy would be on the battering ram with Rimfro. Don and Rich would follow with the rest of the entry team. The balance of the team would spread out on the exterior.

They wrapped up the briefing, Sergeant Mavis advising, "Be safe, boys. We know they've got a lot of firepower in there." With that, the crew split into three groups, in the three vans idling amongst the strawberries.

As they climbed aboard, Mercado in his typical, slow Mexican drawl, stressed to the team, "Juboys, get jurmotherfuckers out."

There is anecdotal evidence that upon entry in high-risk situations, there is a propensity for lawmen to deploy expletives with an overabundance of enthusiasm. Motherfucker is the favorite. They can use it as many as seven times in a single phrase to show emphasis. In this ritual, they all spit a few outbursts of staccato "motherfucker-motherfucker-motherfucker-motherfucker-motherfucker!" It always caused a smile or two and had a relaxing effect for upwards of three seconds.

Once the narcs boarded whatever conveyance would transport them to their objective, a sobering seriousness would settle in. In the rocking tight squeeze of the van, the entry team, would gear up. They checked weapons and ammo, vests and tactical gear. There'd be the sound of shells being racked into shotguns. Radio checks and last-minute, silent moments.

Mercado always kissed his St. Christopher and crossed himself, although by design he wouldn't step foot in a church. As an altar boy, Father Justino Oronas Madrigal made him kneel on pebbles when he got caught reading the Sunday comics. That was enough organized religion for the young Mercado.

All geared up and focusing on their own personal thoughts, they careened towards Clark's clan lab. They couldn't see shit out of the covert vans. They knew it was time to do their business when their van skidded to a stop and the driver announced, "Go, go, go!" or something equally creative.

Kramden's team slammed to a stop in the front of a dumpy, derelict, single-story ranch house. Exactly as described in the affidavit for the warrant. The usual selection of rusting and rusted out abandoned cars was in place, just as they somehow knew they would be.

The van door slid back along its squeaky track, and they boiled out into the darkness. They could hear the bodies and gear from the other vans hitting the ground, hard. Grunting and suppressed, softened sounds of running feet were barely audible. The teams were taking their places around the house.

Kramden's team, slipped to the front of the residence. Pressed against the walls on either side of the front door, they paused for the count of five, letting the others get in place. It bunched Tommy and Rimjob in a tight space on one side of the door with a 30-pound, "forward-weighted, close-quarter" entry-ram in hand. Kramden was opposite them, with the rest of the entry team lined up like arranged dominos behind. A window in the front door was boarded over. It didn't offer a view inside, but it did provide cover.

In the penal code of this state, it's recorded: "To make an arrest, a peace officer may break open the door or window of the house in which the person to be arrested is, or in which they have reasonable grounds for believing the person to be, after having demanded admittance and explained the purpose for which admittance is desired."

The prescribed scenario is supposed to be something like, "Police! We have a search warrant! Open the door!" This is the part where you wait for them to answer and open the door. Or…you hear furtive movements, potentially destruction of evidence or escape. That's when the door comes down.

Reality is different. "Police! We have a search warrant!" Immediately and in unison, the door's blown off the hinges. "Open the door" follows. Usually. Narcs know the douchebags on the other side are often prepared to dump product and to kill them "completely to death," given the opportunity. They like to narrow that window of opportunity. The latter version of "knock and notice" would be deployed that morning.

A simple hand signal, one, two, three. Kramden growled, "Police, we have a search warrant!" Tommy and Rimjob swung the ram at the knob and caved the door, sucking the frame in behind. Somewhere in the mix, "Open the door!" could have been said. Kramden jumped the splintered door, hanging from a single hinge with the rest of the entry team right on his ass. He and two others went left, heading for the hallway. Others headed right and plowed under a white male trying to right himself on the couch. They could hear Mercado, "On the ground, motherfucker! Don't chu move, cabron!" They were sure he'd called him a cocksucker, though they didn't know how he knew.

They quickly cleared the dump of a kitchen and made the hallway. Hustling down the narrow, dark corridor, cover was nonexistent, and they'd already given up stealth. They cleared a bedroom and approached the second when the door burst open.

One David "The Packer" Odom lunged through the door with a .308 rifle in his hands. They were so close to him, both Don and Kramden had the same instinct; they smacked The Packer upside the head with their pistols at the same moment. He dropped like a bag of rocks, unconscious long before he hit the deck.

Rimjob cuffed Odom. Don and Kramden moved to the last door on the left. More narcs poured down the hall past them, towards the very back of the house.

The bedroom door was locked, but just for a blink. One big old 12D boot mowed it down, and the two of them burst into the tiny, grimy chamber. That made four people in a cramped shit hole of a bedroom. In the bed was a white male, tattooed, long hair, naked, and later identified as Landess Otis Taylor. One of his threesome was a loaded, Ithaca Featherlight 20-gauge shotgun tucked in alongside of him. On her belly on the other side of Landess was the skanky biker bitch described by the CI, Clark. Both of them must've been partying hard the night before because even with two doors down and the awesome rumble that's more than a dozen narcs flooding the joint, these two were still groggily trying to rouse.

You could flick the rouse switch to "right the fuck now" by screwing a 9mm into the forehead. It seemed to have just that effect on Mr. Taylor. The blonde, hands stretched to the headboard, face buried in the pillow, was already weeping. "This can't be." But alas…it could.

With the Ithaca secured, they pulled the sheets off of both of them, it appeared they were otherwise unarmed. Kramden told blondie to roll over, keeping her hands above her head. She was wearing a "Spank Me" t-shirt and baggy granny panties. Ugh.

Kramden did a double-take. *What the fuck!* He yelled, "Boss, in here, right now!" Don was also immediately in on the non-joke. When Mavis joined them, his eyes popped out of his head. "Boss, you got to keep Rich out of here." Sergeant Mavis did an about-face and vanished from the room, heading straight for Detective Mercado.

It was one thing to find a skanky biker bitch in granny panties in bed with some tattooed ass clown, but it was altogether different when that woman was the wife of one of their partners. Especially when that police detective was in the living room, pumped full of adrenaline and armed to the teeth.

While they secured the two losers, the boss man had to secure Mercado. He was a stereotypically hot-headed Mexican. And he'd have been the first to admit it. However, since he'd torn his thigh open on the trashed door hardware on entry, his mood could have been better as well.

Rich and his wife Gail had a history of separations and general dysfunction. That wasn't noteworthy amongst the narco clan, but Rich leaned jealous, to be sure. Coming across this disgrace, in front of all of his brothers, would not go down easy for Detective Mercado.

As a matter of course, back in the day, they'd "bag" the suspects they took into custody. Meaning they'd cover their heads, usually with a pillowcase, so they couldn't ID any of the narcs. Once they handed them off to the uniformed guys, and they were on their way to the hoosegow, they'd pull the pillowcases. It was noninvasive. Hell, it improved the looks of a lot of suspects.

Kramden was standing in the doorway when they loaded up the sobbing and pillow-cased Gail Mercado into the back of a squad car. Rich stood between Mavis and Don in the open front door watching, in silence, blood leaking out the gash on his thigh. He'd gotten over his initial "I'm gonna fuckin' kill this bitch" moment and had morphed to something closer to pensive. Kramden noticed Rich's Smith and Wesson wasn't in his holster. He assumed the sergeant was hanging on to it. Safe keeping.

The balance of the entry team had in fact located the lab, in the back bathroom, modified for the purpose. It wasn't in operation, and the narcs didn't think it had been, but they found some finished product and a lot of chemical precursors. It wasn't a complete bust, but it wasn't what they'd hoped for. Next time.

Beyond Taylor's Ithaca, stolen of course, and the .308 rifle, they also collected six handguns. Every weapon was loaded. Again, typical.

Tommy Lincoln interviewed the guy who'd been plowed under trying to get off the couch. He was still face down, handcuffed, the ubiquitous pillow slip over his head. He'd been more than cooperative and hadn't moved an inch since they'd cuffed him. It tickled the boys when they heard his name, Gonzo Alphonse. A 24-year-old bartender.

Tommy was taking some last evidence photos as Kramden tilted Gonzo into a more upright position. It wasn't ideal to interview someone with a 200-count linen bag over their head, but they didn't need much from him. He was adamant that he had no connection to Odom or Landess. He told the narcs he was just crashing there with "a Lynette." Turns out she was some other skanky biker bitch and was out selling Avon or stuffing her snoot full of some fine peanut butter crank. Gonzo had no record, and they couldn't find any intel that connected him to the other nitwits. He was a reasonable sort and convinced them he wasn't part of the lab operation; he wasn't a certified, accredited biker or even an associate. Gonzo was the definitive example of "wrong place, wrong time."

They decided they'd 544 Gonzo, cut him loose without charging him. Taylor, Odom, and Rich's wife were all going to be charged with 579 violations. Statute 579, in all of its many variations, covered most of the drug-related offenses in the state, including possession of methamphetamine for sale, manufacturing drugs, narcotics or controlled substances, possession of certain chemicals intending to use them to make crank. Oh, and there were gun charges including felons possessing, blah, blah, blah. It was serious stuff.

Tommy and Kramden were the last to leave the ranch house. They'd already told Sergeant Mavis they'd do the paperwork and cut Gonzo loose. They had to pack up the last of the gear spread around the site, check to make sure they had everything that belonged to the city, county, or state, and grab any incidentals. They needed to make sure there wasn't any identifying information left at the scene either.

So Kramden sat next to Gonzo on the couch, which reeked of dog piss. He explained they wouldn't charge him; they'd cut him loose. The narcs couldn't leave him in the house since he didn't live there. They'd take him down the road, off-load him, and let him figure out how to get home. He was seriously grateful.

They secured the place, and Kramden guided Gonzo out the door to his undercover ride. Fortunately, one of the team had driven it up from the strawberry fields after the raid. Kramden was driving a Z28, not ideal prisoner transport, but they tucked him in the passenger seat and Tommy took the back. They drove about a mile away and made a left onto another agricultural-type, dirt road. They only went a few hundred yards and pulled over. Kramden got Gonzo out and led him to the edge of the road. He told him they'd cut him loose, but there were two rules they expected him to follow.

Oh shit, oh dear, was Gonzo ready to go along with the program. "Gonzo, listen to me," Tommy said. "We're gonna point you out into this field. I want you to walk straight ahead. Just walk. And…I want you to count. I want to hear you count to a thousand before you take the fucking pillowcase off. Don't turn around, don't look back. I'm fucking telling you, Gonzo, just keep walking and counting. When you get to a thousand, you're on your own. Got it?"

Gonzo was so happy, he damn near snapped his head off the stalk nodding in affirmative understanding. They watched for a bit, just to see what he did.

The poor mope, the bag on his head, was blindly staggering into the field. "One hundred and twenty-seven, one hundred and twenty-eight, one hundred and twenty-nine…" They drove off.

About 20 miles down the road, on their way back to the office, Tommy said, "Fuck me. I left the fucking camera back at the house."

"You have fucking got to be kidding," Kramden said with all the sensitivity he could muster. Which was none. As they say in the narc business, they "flipped a bitch" and headed back.

This time they bypassed the front door, having secured it with two by fours and nails just 45 minutes prior. Around back, they slid open a window and slipped back in through the kitchen. Guns drawn, they made their way to the front of the house. Startling them both, standing in the living room was Gonzo. "Oh, noooooo!" he wailed.

Kramden barked, "Gonzo, on the couch, turn the fuck over. Face down, right now!" And you know he did. It was actually pretty fucking funny. Tommy, Gonzo, and Kramden all laughed, out loud.

They didn't ask the poor fucking mutt to walk and count again. They felt for the guy. They left him on the couch, face down, no cuffs. Tommy yanked a beer from the fridge and stuffed it in Gonzo's palm before they left.

"Poor fucking Gonzo, couldn't find his ass with both hands and a flashlight!" Rimjob *wasn't one to mince words. "One advantage we had over the bad guys is there were some stupid motherfuckers out there."*

Quinn added, "Not to mention some very unlucky SOBs."

"And a few naïve slobs who just couldn't help but stand on their own dicks." Another Rimjob *classic.*

RJ *took a moment to relight his cigar that had gone out during his visit to Solly's aged water closet. After bringing the stogie back to life, he offered, "I always liked the cranksters, at least as a general class of crook. Liked 'em better than gang bangers, ghetto rats, or some of the other flavors. Plus Maxie and I had so damn much fun working them!"*

CHAPTER 20

Methamphibians

Later that year Resident Agent in Charge Burchfield selected Golden to be the agency representative to Major Meth's DEA regional methamphetamine task force, but he couldn't assign one-fifth of his staff to a task force. By then Golden and Johnson were almost inseparable as partners, and they agreed privately between them that if Golden was going to the task force, so was Johnson. They knew they had a new boss coming, and it was unknown how he would feel about that. Better to ask forgiveness than to ask permission, and *the manual is for sheep*.

Their respected boss, RAC "Tex" Burchfield, had accepted an upward transfer to headquarters in DC. His replacement, Wally Hubble, was a balding, nicotine-stained little monument to nepotism from Wood Hook, Oklahoma. It took the boys about four minutes to figure out their new boss. The scuttlebutt on Hubble involved a massive fuckup of omission on his part when he was a street agent. Seemed his lazy ass did not tell the Secret Service about a righteous assassin with plans to kill the president. The fallout went all the way to DC, and yet miraculously a buddy from Oklahoma could still get him the RAC job in Capital City.

The manual called for RACs to be present on all high-risk operations conducted by the office. Hubble quickly established that he could relegate this responsibility to a senior agent so he could remain back in the office with his cowboy boots up on his desk, smoking a Kent, and yammering with some good old boy halfway across the country about the sorry status of the agency, what with hiring women and blacks and all that shit. Hubble termed it the "Cunts-an-Runts" program, though by either definition he could qualify.

Through subterfuge, namely the threat of the Special Agent in Charge showing up, Johnson and Golden got Hubble out on a crank search warrant. Prior to the door kick, Hubble positioned himself well back behind a car. Sweat streaming down his pasty face, looking ridiculous in a wrinkled raid jacket and ball cap. Nothing like leading from the rear. Besides being lazy and useless, the man was a physical coward. It disgusted Johnson and Golden. They were used to bosses like Pat Quinn and Bob Sellers, or their latest hero, Major Meth. Guys who had been there and done that. Guys that you could go to for answers, and guys who always had your back.

Hubble didn't have the balls to tell RJ that he couldn't go to the task force. So on a bright sunny June day Golden and Johnson reported in to the DEA task force to begin a two-year reign of terror on meth-makers that would take down over 250 clandestine labs.

The boys knew several of the task force crew from the meth cases they had initiated, but now formal introductions were in order. There was a new task force boss now, DC having sucked the Major into its orbit to write legislation for controlling precursor chemicals. A burley Scots-Irishman name Mike McGee was the new guy. His pedigree went from D1 college fullback, to Marine Officer, to LA County Sheriff's Office, to Bureau of Narcotics and Dangerous Drugs, or BNDD, which later became DEA. It disappointed Johnson and Golden that they would not be working for the Major, but McGee with his hearty laugh, bone-crushing handshake, and porn-star mustache, seemed a fair replacement.

There were other new faces too. Two first-posting DEA agents had just reported in, a pair of bookends named Randolf and Roberts. Much like Johnson and Golden, the DEA boys had been local cops before and they were ready to rock. Some veteran members included two local officers. There was Dusty Rhodes, a Capital City Police Detective on his fourth or fifth divorce, too broke to even pay attention. Dusty lived in his G-car, or in the task force office. A master of long-term solo surveillance because he had nowhere else to go or be.

And then there was Bobby Meyer, a Sheriff's Deputy with perpetual drama going on with his fiancée. Normally Bobby was a manic riot of comedy around the office. Whenever things went south with the fiancée though, it was depressive Bobby, and he would turn into a suicide-bent alter-ego named Buddy.

Bobby/Buddy would prowl the DEA office looking for interesting places to commit suicide. His running monologue described poses and places to shoot himself. It was not unusual to find Bobby/Buddy with his head in a file drawer and his duty gun at his temple. "Look! If I shoot myself like this, my brains will stay in the drawer! Smart, huh?" No one in the office found this strange or alarming. It was just Bobby.

Later on Golden would engage in gun games with Bobby.

Bobby never drove the big cases, but he was a great worker bee, surveillance partner, and when needed for undercover action, Bobby played the perfect ex-con parolee. He had huge shoulders and chest stacked on a narrow waist that only comes from years of prison length workouts. Dress Bobby in an untucked flannel shirt, old blue jeans, and a pair of prison boondocker shoes, and he could buy crank or chemicals all day long, if you could keep the street monster cops from rousting him on a parole search.

The office space that housed the task force was in an older two-story professional office complex occupied by dentists, doctors, and CPA firms. Inside the task force, the walls were adorned like a Smithsonian tribute to the American culture of methamphetamine. The seized denim vests of outlaw motorcycle gangs were nailed up on the wall. The task force had its own patches and denim 'cuts' depicting Laboratory Retrievers, and Ghostbusters style "Lab Buster" patches. A cop-made meth lab detector consisting of a road flare with stabilizing fins fitted into a crossbow was nailed to a support beam. In one corner a huge 72-liter triple neck flask, complete with the tall glass condensing columns, cheerfully bubbled air bubbles to a bunch of goldfish. A corkboard displayed a kaleidoscope of methamphibian life. The photos, art, and poetry of the culture. Three-legged pit bulls, six-toed cats, and stanzas proclaiming, "I love you motherfucker even though I know you're fucking my sister too." It was damned near Japanese haiku shit in its symmetry.

The parking lot behind the building was reserved for the tenants of the complex. Before the task force, it had been the domain of doctors', dentists', and accountants' Mercedes, BMWs, and Cadillacs. The task force brought a collection of seized vehicles pressed into government service. IROC Camaros, an old El Camino SS, and lowered blacked-out pickups, now nestled among the professional luxury cars. The chopped Harley motorcycles set off car alarms. Task force members favored Wayfarer sunglasses, boots (cowboy or biker), and leather jackets. Male agents sported more facial hair than a Civil War reenactment. The female agents went for hair piled high and gobs of mascara. They fit in with the professionals and clientele of the Town & Country Professional Building like a dick on Santa Claus. The tenants were mortified, if not terrified, by their federal neighbors.

Members of the task force worked night and day. Worked hard. Partied hard. Most days you couldn't find the line between the two. Golden and Johnson found themselves among a group of guys and gals who were crazier than they were, at least in the beginning. When the locals anywhere in the Eastern District stumbled onto a meth lab, the task force got the call to come and dismantle it. Depending on the stage and type of cook, meth labs could be flammable, or explosive, and were always toxic, if not deadly. Airtight suits, boots, gloves, and breathing gear were the order of the day. Who ya gonna call? LAB BUSTERS!!

Ripping up and down the state, 24 and even 36 hour days were not uncommon, a long surveillance rolling into a search warrant and hours of dismantling a lab and categorizing the evidence. Driving back to the office in the middle of the night and stopping at McDonald's reeking of a meth lab; high as a kite from just handling the shit. Back in the car eating Big Macs renamed McCrank burgers.

The big cases might have over a dozen locations to search simultaneously, calling for multiple raid teams from multiple agencies. The briefings were a law enforcement cast of thousands, kicking off at 0400 in the morning to have all the teams in place for a 0600 showtime. Meth crooks all favored guns, thrived on paranoia, and were fascinated with explosives. Lab team boss McGee liked to have Golden or Johnson spend a few moments during the briefings reminding the search teams of the protocols for dealing with explosives, or suspected booby traps. Golden loved to yuk it up by fumbling up to the podium wearing a pair of myopic coke-bottle glasses, putting his wristwatch right up to his glasses to check the time, and then addressing the assembled cops about the need to call him for any booby trap or explosive. It was a crowd pleaser every single time.

Kramden, more than a little tipsy now, was conducting a symphony of opinions on one of his favorite subjects, the oft-maligned confidential informant. He was the product of a classic Jesuit education and had brain power that he seldom advertised. It didn't hurt that every Night Policeman, ever, had plenty of opinions about CIs and for a host of excellent reasons.

Often the CI was some tatted-up wastrel, doing his best to manipulate the cops just enough to miss being a practice wife for a homeboy in the slammer upstate. Sometimes it was your basic businessman who got his dick in a ringer and would do almost anything to keep his wife and work from knowing he got caught diddling little Joey. Frequently, the snitch was a target of law enforcement who knew what the miscreant was up to and planned to use that against him. It wasn't personal. They merely wanted to move up the chain, to the malefactor running whatever criminal enterprise they coveted.

There was, however, one constant. One perpetual, unremitting truth. One unvarying universal fact that all undercovers knew: snitches are deceitful, cunning reprobates who need constant care and feeding to keep them from fucking everything up.

Kramden threw out a question for the students. "You ever have a snitch rat you out? On the street?"

Rimjob pondered the question, while Quinn poked at the business end of his cigar, a run in it annoying him, then he spoke, "Not me, but I remember that narc from Cambridge getting outed and it fuckin' near cost him, damn near bought the farm."

Rimjob asked, "The guy that got knifed in the back in some bowling alley?"

"Mermaid Lanes or something like that, yeah. Yeah, that was the guy." Quinn groused. "Think they had to take out a kidney. Poor fuck got retired over it."

Kramden slipped back into the lecture. "When Abraham and I shared that office, I guess I'd just made the bureau. I had, shit, one of my very first narco snitches, and I had him in one of those interview rooms across from the Robbery dicks. I'm in there listening to some load of crap from this guy when who come's sauntering in, a Polaroid in his hand, but that big walleyed SOB."

Kramden took a sip of his Wood Hat and continued. "Abraham was scary looking just standing there, right? Filling up the doorway, neither eye looking right at you. Anyway, he held the door open with his foot, and grabbed some rookie trooper just walking down the hall and drug him into the room. I don't remember who it was. No matter. So now, the rook, the snitch, and I were all confused.

"Walleye unpinned the badge from blue suit's uniform and told the snitch to take it. I'm thinking, what the fuck? The snitch ain't grabbing for the badge, so Abraham took the guy's hand and shoved the shield in it. Then he tells him, 'Hold it right here,' up about shoulder level. He told the blue suit to stand in next to the snitch. Then, Abraham whipped out his trusty Polaroid and snapped, I don't know, probably a dozen pictures of the two.

"That, my friends, is when Abraham got all magical and shit. He told my snitch that if he made the extremely poor decision to rat me out on the street, that he'd personally distribute those Polaroids around town, to all of my CI's dirt ball buddies. That poor fucking snitch was a dim bulb, for sure, but he got it...trust me."

There was an art to maintaining the confidential informant. That was chapter one in the Book of Abraham.

CHAPTER 21

Junkie Blues

Rosie Alba was a "crook-snitch." A crook-snitch being one who unwittingly introduces an undercover detective to their associates, friends, and relatives for the purposes of procuring drugs.

Rosie's life was complicated. Nothing complicated it more than the fact she was a PCP freak. She was a dumpy Mexican chick in her early 30s. Great big tits, riding way low. On most days you'd find her in an unwashed sundress and flip-flops. The flips always sideways on her feet, her heels hitting the pavement. She could have used a hair wash too, as she kept it rather swine-like. One of Bristol City's narcs described her as "A no *Fast Times at Ridgemont High* jezebel. Just low rent, bottom of the jizz sump, junkie-assed goods." She needed work.

Unfortunately for everybody involved, she had twin girls, 18 months old. It was tragic. And there was never a moment Rosie wasn't stoned. Ever. She couldn't keep three sentences in line with a protractor and a compass. Because of her drug abuse, she couldn't understand even basic mothering skills. And, she didn't care.

Kramden had tapes of her on the "hello phone," the one used in BCPD's undercover offices to talk to and record their crooks. She could go on for 20 minutes without a single coherent thought. Those poor fucking kids were always crying in the background.

Kramden met Rosie at the Lakeside Lounge while working Artemis Wicks. Artemis was snitching for Kramden…who the fuck wasn't he snitching for? He was working off beefs with departments across the state. Maybe the Stateys and the Feds too? Just to put it in perspective, Artemis was a guy who'd snitch on his own kin if they were dope dealers. They were, and he did.

Wicks was sipping an Old Style at the Lounge and was in an expansive mood. Stoned too, as usual. He told Kramden, "Rosie's a freebie. She can do PCP and tar," a very low grade and cheap form of heroin. Kramden liked freebies, so Artemis duked him, introducing him to Rosie. Within two drinks, Kramden noted that Rosie was flirtatious and distasteful, yet she was trying. It wasn't working for the young detective.

Two weeks into the investigation, Kramden had made four KJ buys with Rosie in Bristol City and neighboring Menhome. Small shit, but still a PCP case was good business. For whatever the reason, Rosie confirmed that she was warm for Kramden's form. For him, a chilling thought.

Next, she started calling him on the hello phone and in her very special, fuckered-up way, she called him "boyfriend." Kramden knew to get this stink off him, he'd need the healing ablutions that would be her incarceration.

A few days later, Kramden was sitting at The Ravenite slugging back greyhounds and shooting the shit with the barman. Rosie walked into the gloomy, foul-smelling tavern, blotto. A blooming romance, her man at the bar, briefly flashed across her temporal lobe. Briefly. During the jukebox record change, which it appeared Rosie thought of as an intimate moment, she leaned into Kramden. Not wanting to go down that road, he switched gears. "Rosie, I always wanted to try heroin. Can you make that happen? And trust me, I ain't gonna use no needle." Of course, she could. Oh and "maybe we could do it together?" she said.

Wouldn't that be fucking peachy? Fuck me, Kramden thought.

Ten days later, Kramden gathered stinky up in his official undercover vehicle, and they were heading south to Blairsden, to meet two "dudes who could take care of business." Kramden had his doubts.

Back in those days, narcotics agents seldom wore wires for a simple hand-to-hand narcotics buy. It was a painless procedure if all went as planned.

As the two of them got into the neighborhood, Rosie said, "It's right near the high school." For what it was worth, Blairsden had a population of about 300,000 fucking people and she thought it was by the high school.

"Okay, which high school, Rosie?" Kramden asked patiently.

"High school? You know, the one on that street right here. You know."

"No, Rosie, I don't know. You've gotta help me out here, Darlin." Kramden figured sweet-talking her might help.

Narco partners, TJ Mavis and Tiny Dave Whitling had planned to pick up the surveillance of Kramden and Rosie as they turned off I-65 onto Gilbert Joseph Avenue. Their blueprint was to set up on the suspect house once the two arrived. Kramden let Rosie work out the "get there" details. Mistake.

The Villa East barrio may have been an urban dumpster, but it wasn't without its charm. During their expedition in the hood, they saw a handful of ancient Chevys and Fords, most of them nicely tricked out low-riders. Surprisingly, not one of them was currently being stolen.

Try as they might, the narcs couldn't turn up any intel on the crooks to help pinpoint the place that Kramden and his snitch were headed to. Rosie insisted her connect was "Disiderio and his brother." That was all the details she had. Amazing she remembered that much.

It took several trips through the shit hole neighborhood, "driving right by the fucking place each and every mother-fucking time," according to Kramden. Then voila...she spied the brothers in a driveway. The house, a trash heap flat top, plunked down on a weed-filled lot, a lawnmower almost dead center in the front, which hadn't moved for a decade, weeds towering around it.

The Ybarra brothers, it turns out, were well-known, low-level dealers in heroin and PCP. They had about 15 arrests between them, and both had weapons histories. Kramden and his surveillance team did not know that.

Rosie and Kramden parked and headed for the driveway. He just glimpsed Whitling setting up two streets to the north, which felt a bit better. The brothers Jessie and Heriberto (as opposed to the aforementioned, Disiderio) both sported sagging jeans and boxers, sans shirts.

With just a moment to take it in, their bare body canvases spoke volumes. Amongst many others, Heriberto was sporting a cobweb tattoo on his left elbow. Kramden was no body art historian, but he knew that reflected a long stretch in prison. Jessie, it seemed, enjoyed the pleasures of neck and face art. The three dots tattoo at the corner of his eye... his "mi vida loca," showed his association with the gang lifestyle. At that point, it was all Kramden needed to know. He hoped Sergeant Mavis had kept up and there were two guys backing him up.

Crunching gravel in the driveway, Rosie started jabbering in Mexican. Both brothers ignored her and stepped towards Kramden. Heriberto pulled out an eight-inch kitchen knife. Now to be honest, Kramden didn't really feel threatened. Heriberto had the shiv at his side, and Kramden assumed he wanted him to know he had it. He didn't like it, however, when Ybarra pointed the blade at his chest, and grunted to Rosie, "Who the fuck's the güero?" Kramden, doing the math in his head, hoped that White and Mavis wouldn't jump the gun and could make out that his situation was a hair less than menacing.

In one of Kramden's recountings of this tale, he noted, "Back in those days, I could deploy a hair-trigger course reversal like a big dog and Rosie would bring up the rear, I can tell you."

This may have been the first and only time Kramden appreciated Rosie slurring out, "S'cool, he's mi amante." Ok, now he was her lover… fucking-A, but now he was on board! She carried on, and Kramden could see the brothers Y relax.

Jessie asked Kramden, "What 'chu want?" and he responded, "I'm looking for smack," a decidedly white guy term. Jessie got a quizzical look on his face and smiled. "Look at'chu, you don't do dope."

Kramden could feel the decompression. It amused Jessie at this point. "You're right, but I want to try it. Rosie says I can snort it." Naiveté was fairly dripping off Kramden.

Rosie, God bless the girl, was enthusiastically rubbing her mama-rosa pendulata on Kramden's arm and confirming his play. In fact, Rosie was really looking for a taste or a sample of the heroin she thought she'd get when Kramden copped. In her world, it'd be better yet if she could make that happen while still loaded on KJ. Somehow they seemed to buy Kramden's bullshit, or maybe they just trusted Rosie. Perhaps they wanted to rip Kramden off and dump his body in the garden? Kramden's preference was the former.

Heriberto gestured with his head, suggesting, *Follow us, clueless and unsuspecting white fellow.* Down the side of the hot guava-colored stucco garage, Kramden could see they were going into the backyard or thereabouts. He glanced around. Whitling was still there, but no sight of Mavis.

Thinking to himself, *This may be really fucking stupid,* Kramden was scenario planning. *Think! Do I really need to make this case? Of course not, but, I'm young, I'm a narc, I am invincible according to me, and at this precise moment I have about 10,000 milizots of pure fucking adrenaline coursing through my veins. Oh yeah, I'm making this case.*

Midsummer and it was white hot. The sweat was just pouring off. As they made it to the back of the garage, the door was standing open, and inside was as black as Coley's ass. Heriberto and Jessie slipped in, followed by Rosie and Kramden. The "Reverse Parisian Advance" came to Kramden's mind.

One of the Ybarras whipped aside the shitty old drapes and lit the dump up. There were two iron and spring bed frames, each with a bare, skinny-ass mattress on them. *They must've gotten really used to the beds in county jail*, Kramden thought.

Heriberto sat on one, and said, "I got two bags for you, but we wanna taste." Not unreasonable in the dope game. Kramden would be more than happy to let them have that sample. His dope case would still count. But, before he had time to agree, Heriberto had already taken it for granted. Remember the refrain, *Follow us, clueless and unsuspecting white fellow?*

He said, "Eighty dollars, cabron." Kramden thought he should beat him down on the price, at least 10 or 20 bucks, but he wanted to get the deal done. As a novice doper, he wouldn't know the difference, anyway. Kramden pulled 80 bucks from a wad in his pocket and handed it to Rosie, then she handed it to Kramden's new pal.

Rosie and Heriberto tittered like schoolgirls. Kramden was clueless, and they didn't have the courtesy to speak English. Rosie reached between her gigantic knockers, Kramden swore her arm disappeared up to the elbow, and she pulled out a sock. It was her kit or intravenous narcotic accessories carryall. It was obscene; foul with body odor and appearing moist to the touch. Kramden did not touch. He wasn't sickened, but he didn't have an erection either!

He noticed Heriberto had two balloons of heroin in his hand. Where he'd secreted them, Kramden didn't see. He was currently pinching one of them to get their "taste," hovering over it like some scientist at a lab bench. Upon completion of his lab work, he flipped the two balloons with the balance of the dope to Kramden.

Okay, this case is complete, thank you very much.

When the three of them got ready to torch off the dope, they discovered they had nothing to filter the load. Jessie dropped to his knees on the side of the other bed.

Kramden was paying attention. That bed looked like an ideal hide for a shotgun, and he was bracing for undesirable festivities. Again, wrong. Jessie pulled out yet another sock. There was a pair!

The three amigos then cooked up a nice little batch of heroin. They use a red Bic lighter wrapped in black tape, the traditional and customary bent-back spoon, and the filthy sock number two, to filter the drugs they were about to inject into their veins.

Rosie went first (chivalry was not dead amongst junkies), then Heriberto, with Jessie getting the stank-end of the deal. Of course, they all shared the same needle. What could be the problem with that? And yes, engrossed in stabbing each other, it was easy to ignore Kramden. He was busy anyway, working out a graceful exit from this den of morons.

Kramden watched as Heriberto, a ludicrous grin on his kisser, advised: "Rosie, your arm." Rosie, who was in an almost Olympic class nod, slowly, very slowly, looked down at her left arm. There was a trail of blood from the injection site down to her wrist. She smiled. Paused. There may have been thinking? Probably not. Then, using her other hand, and again, very slowly, she wiped the blood trail aside. Her body was so soiled, that it left a clean patch under the blood smear, where she'd washed her arm with her own blood. While Kramden processed that, she licked the blood from her fingers. One must maintain sanitary procedures. Again, no erection!

This is the point where Rosie and Kramden made their dignified exit. They were in a good place. Rosie, Heriberto, and Jessie were all mid-stupor, sated, and willing to disregard Kramden. They had the money they wanted, the three of them got a free buzz, and Kramden hadn't been killed. Even a bit. And by the time Kramden got to his UC car, he'd have three new cases.

The Ybarras made it back home to state prison for some hard time.

Kramden ended up doing about 19 cases with Rosie and rolled up most of her pitiful group of confederates. She was disappointed when it became clear she wouldn't be marrying Kramden that spring.

Rosie, as expected, got jailed. Because of her twins, she just did token time. And the court, in its infinite wisdom, returned the kids to her. That turned out to be a mistake.

By now the Night Police were sharing a collective glow. The Scotch, cigars, and camaraderie having the effect they all were looking for. The laughter came quicker, the companionship felt deeper. It was the perfect escape from the real world.

Something about Rosie's story rang a bell with RJ. *"Hey, Kramden, didn't that snitch* Rosie *live right around the corner from Gene's Liquors?"*

CHAPTER 22

All Units, a Robbery in Progress

Section 570.023(1) of this state's Penal Code states that "A person commits the offense of robbery in the first degree if he or she forcibly steals property and in the course thereof he or she causes serious physical injury to any person." If you're convicted of robbery, it carries a two- to five-year sentence in state prison. If during the commission of a robbery, you discharge a firearm resulting in great bodily injury or death, they can sentence you to an additional and consecutive term of 25 years to life. For young lawmen, this is a seriously sexy crime.

Camille Ocampo was a 61-year-old Filipina from Cagayan de Oro, the capital of the Province of Misamis Oriental in Northern Mindanao. In the 1960s, nurses from the Philippines became the largest group of nurses immigrating to the United States, and Camille was part of that demographic.

Upon relocation to Joliet, Illinois, she met and married Byani Ocampo, one of the so-called "1946 boys," or Sakadas, the last large group of agricultural laborers brought to Hawaii by the sugar planters. The two met at the Rizal Social Club in Joliet and soon wed.

Friction was almost immediate between Camille and Byani. It came down to Camille being the primary breadwinner; Byani had a hard time with that. Social status was important to him, and cutting broom corn in the flats of Savoy was nowhere near as sexy as Camille's well-paying nursing salary. Byani's heavy drinking added to their troubles.

Fast-forward 21 years. Byani has been dead six years, he died three months before Camille accepted a plea deal for diverting the morphine and other opiates aiding Byani in the last stages of his battle with pancreatic cancer. Camille felt lucky to have her job cashiering at Gene's Wine and Spirits, a dumpster of a liquor store in Bristol City's South-end Borough.

On a quiet, warm summer evening, Camille's cassette deck played one of her favorites, Kapantay Ay Langit sung by a beloved Pilita Corrales. Her day off was just hours away.

G. Regis Temonti changed Camille's plans. Out of Anamosa State Penitentiary in Cedar Rapids just six weeks, he was still under control of the Iowa Department of Corrections, Division of Adult Parole Operations (DAPO).

Parking around the corner from Gene's, he nestled his dark blue 79 Ford Fairlane tight against the Goodwill Store. He pointed his ride towards the quickest route to southbound I-64. It wasn't by chance

Temonti took an Army surplus duffle bag from the backseat and headed around the corner. As he made the front of Gene's, he discarded the bag, the contents secured in his hands.

Camille first felt the interrupted breeze from the box fan on the floor. She looked up from the ancient NCR cash register, but her normal genial expression slammed head-on into a rictus of fear. It rocked her, looking down the twin barrels of that sawed-off, Remington Spartan 310 shotgun.

Camille's hands shoved skyward as she stumbled backward. Temonti, "Keep 'em up. I want the cash." She gestured with her head toward the cash register, and Temonti tried opening it. Crashing the buttons on the register and still unsuccessful, he hissed, "Open it!"

Trembling, Camille's hands were almost unworkable, but she got the till drawer open. She couldn't take her eyes off the shotgun. She didn't know a damn thing about shotguns, but she knew enough to be terrified.

Temonti rummaged the till and stuffed his pockets. "Don't move an inch." He tucked a bottle of Popov vodka, the cheap fuck, under his arm and started for the front door. He paused and turned back to Camille. Without a word, he raised the Remington towards her and fired one 12-gauge round of number eight shot from about seven feet away. The 410 lead pellets, traveling at 1,100 feet per second carved out a baseball-sized chunk of Camille's inner thigh. With it was the effective removal of her external genitalia.

The inertia from the blow threw Camille's feet into the air, and she crashed on her shoulders and back at the base of the rear counter. The injury to her inner thigh severed the femoral artery, and she was already on her way to hypovolemic shock. That occurs when you lose in the neighborhood of 20% of your overall blood supply. As a result, your blood pressure drops and your heart can't pump enough blood to the rest of your body. As she lay crumpled beneath the grimy counter of Gene's Wine and Spirits, her life ebbing away, Temonti bolted.

Two young patrolmen, beat partners and best friends, were at the home of a young, smokin' hot bartendress from one of their local hangs. Actually, they were visiting with the parents, drinking ice tea, just shooting the shit hoping Della would show up. Doris and Reese got a kick out of the interest the boys in blue showed in their daughter.

Two tones on their radio indicated a serious call was following. Both patrolmen paused and listened up. Dispatch advised, "All units, a robbery in progress."

Adrenaline dump was the nonclinical term cops used to describe the body's sudden release of adrenaline. Initiated when the brain perceives a high-stress event, it prepares them for "fight or flight." In law enforcement, the threat of imminent physical danger is a common contributing factor. With a big hit of adrenaline, tunnel vision, sometimes called target fixation, would set in. Fine and complex motor skills diminished and short-term memory could shut down, leaving the responding officers with little more than primal, emotional instincts to operate with. Street cops learned to cope with it.

Absurdly to many, young officers often found the adrenaline dump a draw to the business. It was for these two troopers. Leaving the hospitality of Doris and Reese behind, they ran for their cruisers.

Detective Curtis Threading, a robbery-homicide investigator, was just finishing up his solo, cheap, and altogether lousy dinner at Wyndyms. Cardboard Salisbury steak, peas, and possibly carrots, with a smear of pureed potatoes, the exemplar for TV dinners. He was getting used to cheap and lousy. Jennine Threading had filed for divorce just weeks prior, and she'd already drained their bank accounts. A temporary restraining order was already in place. Fucking lawyers. Curtis picked up the two tones on his handy-talkie radio. He dropped five rumpled singles and what change he had on the table and headed for his car.

As Detective Threading slipped behind the wheel of his black Chevy Monte Carlo, his handset barked, "A robbery in progress, Gene's Wine and Spirits, 1653 Sundale Ave., cross of Taylor. RP advises one down, shooter fled on foot. NFD." No further description was what he expected seconds into a fresh call like this. Interrupting his train of thought, "Fire and paramedics en route."

Threading was only three blocks away. A red light flipped down from the visor, siren blasting, he was at Gene's within 90 seconds. Good thing, too, as Camille didn't have much time.

As Threading slid his G-ride to the curb, he surveyed the scene. He saw no one fleeing on foot, no cars leaving the area. An elderly man, wearing of all things a bowler hat, was just entering Gene's. He barked at him, "Police! Outta there! Outta there, man. Get the fuck outta there!"

Startled and confused, the dapper senior took a few clumsy, backward steps, moving away from the door.

Threading entered the liquor store, his Colt Detective Special drawn with a purpose. He studied the interior, looking for the shooter and the "one down." At first blush, the suspect wasn't in sight. The gravely wounded Camille lay right at his feet. She was already shocky, profusely sweating, and gushing blood from between her legs.

You didn't have to be an emergency room medic to recognize an arterial bleed, or that she was on her way out. Threading pulled her sodden sundress aside and could see the gaping crater inside her thigh. The blood pumped out in a deep red, viscous flood, so-iron-rich-it-can-only-be-blood smell.

On his knees, he slipped his hand into the dreadful wound. He knew enough to try to clamp the artery to stem the flow of blood. Rhythmical sprays of crimson soaked him. It ran down his face, soaking through his JC Penney's "Best Bet" white cotton shirt. It was like unscrewing the nozzle from a garden hose with the water running, the spray everywhere. In what seemed like forever, but was just seconds, he slowed the blood flow. He could just reach a box of towels under the counter. He wadded a couple up and added it to the dam he was creating. Camille was still alive.

As Threading tried to retrieve his handset from the pooling blood, a civilian slid into the tight space next to him behind the counter. Out of breath, he described to Threading seeing a tall white guy in a black T-shirt run for his car, parked behind the Goodwill. Unable to release the pressure holding inside Camille's thigh, Threading nodded towards his handset. "Can you help?"

"Yeah, I think so, what do I do?" was his response.

"Push the big button on the side, say the detective's okay, not injured, but you're assisting him. Describe the shooter and his car. Do it now!"

Officers Ron Johnson and Jack Kramden Gleason rocketed their cruisers towards the scene. They could hear the civilian giving the descriptions of the car and the shooter. Dispatch asked in which direction the shooter fled, and the civilian responded, "Shit, I don't know directions." Stammering, he added, "I know he went towards the railroad tracks." Both officers knew what that meant, and they headed in a direction to intersect it if they were lucky enough to spot the car. Johnson took a more northern route than Kramden, as additional units flooded the crime scene.

Both fire and the paramedics arrived at Gene's, assisting Threading in saving Camille's life. More details were coming from the scene, including the vague description of a sawed-off shotgun. A second witness added to the vehicle description, including a Bondo'd quarter panel and at least two bumper stickers on the trunk lid.

As Kramden hit a wide boulevard, in the distance he saw a blue Ford and sure as shit, it looked like a Fairlane. If he could have, he'd of put his foot through the firewall. "4S51, southbound Daly Boulevard, suspect in view, southbound." Dispatch repeated the transmission as Johnson moved to parallel, two streets north. "4S51, suspect northbound onto Timmons." That Bondo quarter panel was sticking out like a sore thumb. Kramden made a turn behind Temonti, and he saw the Fairlane, up over the curb, the driver's door open. "S51, he's bailed! Northbound towards the tracks, on foot."

Johnson roared down Villa Avenue, on his right the railroad tracks, north to south. As if looking down the barrel of a cannon, Johnson was hyper-focused on the ribbon of roadway in front of him. The velocity of his cruiser set at max, he was seeing it all in slow motion. He heard Kramden on the radio, in foot-pursuit, his radio breaking up. He made out "...tossed the gun."

To Johnson's left was a chain-linked enclosure topped with concertina wire, the home of Denex Steel Fabricators. As he thundered down the street, Temonti burst across the tracks, Kramden just steps behind. By the time he adjusted his brain to the changing situation and could bring his hurtling cruiser to a screeching, smoking halt, both Temonti and his partner had passed behind his patrol car. They bolted through an open gate and into the DSF compound. "Dispatch, I've got them both heading into DSF, northbound." He added, "Right behind you, Kramden."

As Johnson exited his patrol car, he unholstered and rushed toward the compound. A cloned pair of welders, leather aprons, shields up, each swinging the ubiquitous lunchbox were pointing behind a fenced enclosure at a water tower. "Over there!" they shouted in unison. Johnson running, saw only one path forward, and he vaulted onto the chain-link fence. His adrenaline push got him up and over the concertina with minimal injury.

Hitting the ground running, he heard Kramden, "Freeze, motherfucker! On the ground! On the God-damned ground!" When Johnson turned the corner, he saw Temonti, just starting to buckle at the knees. Kramden was pointing his Smith and Wesson at center mass.

Later, out front of DSF, they both leaned against Johnson's patrol car. Kramden confessed, "Never fucking saw you, dude. Never heard you." Those were the effects of adrenaline dump and target fixation. In this line of work, they had to battle it.

Camille Ocampo lived through her ordeal but battled her injuries until she passed, four years later. Grateful her rescuers had given her additional days, she listened to Pilita Corrales to the end.

They awarded Curtis Threading the department's highest honor for saving Camille's life. A waterskiing accident, the morning after he received the award, took his life. Ain't that a bitch.

Convicted of armed robbery and enhancements, G. Regis Temonti was sentenced to 30 to life in the Eastern Reception, Diagnostic and Correctional Center. The charges of attempted murder and assault with a deadly weapon had long ago been dealt away for the guilty plea. Unfortunately, this was prior to "three strikes," so his four previous convictions for firearms-related felonies didn't affect his sentencing.

On the morning of his intake at the E Reception Center, an inmate stabbed him seven times, including a coup de grâce to the right temple. His killer's still on death row. Karma's a bitch.

Quinn leaned in, more serious. "Can't remember how many 'suicides by shotgun' I went to, always gruesome. Hell, I've been to more shootings with you boys than I care to remember, but I don't often forget the shotgun calls."

Kramden stepped in. "Boss, remember that north-side shooting, Russel and Recil Tyver, those two douchebag brother-burglars—"

Quinn interrupted, "Oh, yeah, on Queensland Court. I remember those two."

"Yeah, Recil took both barrels in the belly and was on his way out. You put me in the bus to the hospital to get a dying declaration." Quinn, fingers to his lips, nodded, remembering the moment.

"I was so new," Kramden mused, "I'd never seen a guy fucking near cut in half with a shotgun. It definitely spooked me. Stuck with me too."

"Sort of put a damper on Recil's fun," Rimjob added. "Did you get the declaration? Did he give it up that his puss-bucket brother torched him?"

"As you might guess, that's what the report said, brother."

When a sub is put in at third base during a baseball game, you can count on the fact that the next ball leaving his opponent's bat will be blasted right at him. It's like that in law enforcement too.

CHAPTER 23

A .20 Gauge Headache

The Woodlands, Bristol City, was a wasteland. You seldom ventured there if you happened to be affluent or educated. There was one possible exception. If you wanted drugs, almost any drug of choice and you had just a little courage, the Woodlands was an express pharmacy for the non-prescribed.

The houses were clapboard, disheveled, often with cardboard in the random missing window. Broken bottles and the common debris of broken lives littered the potholed streets. Fire hydrants buried in weed-choked patches and hidden behind abandoned cars. It was not at all uncommon to have to step over hypodermic needles or used condoms if those things caused concern.

Jack Gleason loved working the Woodlands. A recent government census had found a population comprised of 97% addicts and assorted douchebags and 3% parole agents. It was a carnival for cops. Kramden couldn't have been happier when one of his cases landed him in the Woodlands.

This evening Kramden was working a snitch the narcs affectionately called several variations of Scrotum. And they considered that a huge upgrade for the burglar nitwit. He was about nine years shy of a college education, had a mouthful of corn nuts for teeth. He'd gladly give up his firstborn spawn for an eight-ball of crank. Just shy of 25 years old, he'd just finished up a two-year vacation at the Northern Territories State Prison. Ballsack was less than successful at everything he did, including burglary. He'd been out about 4 months and already he was working as a confidential informant for at least two police agencies.

Working with the Scrote was an adventure. You never knew when he'd show up stoned off his ass, but you could safely assume it was any time you had him out on a narcotics enforcement playdate.

Tonight was no different. With the setting sun reflecting a pale purple off the keloid scar tissue of his boney forearms, Testes showed up in his formal wear. A pair of jeans last washed during the first Reagan administration. A pair of flip-flops, and an ancient Cardinals sweatshirt. One arm of it was only elbow length. Dressed for success.

He was also Kramden's date for a party that was being assembled in the Woodlands. The narcotics enforcement officers knew of the likely group of miscreants that would attend. As a narcotics agent, Kramden was happy to buy dope from anyone willing to sell. Tonight, he'd targeted two female dealers, both of whom had extensive records for coke and meth sales. What made them interesting targets, other than they'd likely go back to the joint, was that one of them was Scrotum's sister. The other, his mother. There is no honor among thieves. Apparently, there is none amongst dope fiends either.

Back in the day, you had to qualify your informants before they were worthy in court. You needed to complete at least two undercover narcotics transactions showing your informant as credible, a stretch for sure, before the narco DAs would rack up cases with your CI in the middle. The repeat or professional rats knew the system, and they'd hook up two easy marks just to make the cases, so they could work off their beef. That was Nutsack's motivation for dumping on Donna and 'Lisbeth—sister and mother.

Elizabeth Hastings had a long criminal history, incarcerated in state prison twice. Once in Indiana, once in Florida. One of her convictions was for dope sales, and one was for pouring boiling water over her sleeping ex-husband, Wade. Wade survived, though she cooked one of his eyes to that fried trout-eye look. She had a sheet of many misdemeanor arrests, all of it having to do with booze, dope, and hooking.

Donna Hastings was just coming into her own as a meth dealer. She was just 25 but had priors that included an arrest for possession of crank that was hardly her fault. They had stopped her for drunk driving two years prior. When she stepped out of her rattletrap Ford Fiesta, she fell flat on her toothless face. The impact knocked the dentures from her mouth. Unfortunately for her, she was holding two bindles of crank under the hard palate portion of her prostheses. The patrol trooper was dialed in enough to note them in the pool of blood and broken denture material; he fished them out with his pen before Donna even came to.

This brain surgeon had two other arrests for possession of methamphetamine. They dismissed both of them so she could concentrate on her recovery and rehab. Not surprising to anyone in the business, it was an abject failure. Scrotum's sibling had no interest in recovery or rehab, she only had an interest in shoveling crank up her nose or pouring it into any of the very few veins she still had left to abuse.

The brood's father, Arthur Hastings Sr., hung himself on a loop he created with an extension cord. About six years after Ballsack was born he'd had enough and simply decided he'd be better off dead than lead his band of perpetually stoned, prison-bound nitwits. Kramden thought it might have been one of the best decisions of his short, fucked-up life.

Scrote, Kramden, and Detective Dave Joseph planned to meet at about 9 p.m., headed for the Woodlands to join the party. Joseph was Kramden's backup for the evening. He was handsome, well-liked, and was a terrific detective. He had a trajectory to make Chief in a few years. Unfortunately, Dave killed himself about three years later. Ate his Detective Special at 34 years of age. They heard he'd been battling depression and a bit of a gambling problem, though not a single soul they knew, knew of his issues.

At about 9:30 p.m., the three of them met at the Woodlands Sunoco for a quick get-your-shit-together briefing. They agreed, Ballbag and Kramden would drive over in his car. Dave would park nearby where he'd have eyes on the front window of 2241 Lakefire. If things went to shit for any reason, he'd look for random furniture ejected through the front living room window. That would bring the cavalry charging in to save Kramden's ass. It was a typical plan for the times.

This party would not be a catered affair. The chances of poached shrimp and an oaky Chardonnay were non-existent. It was more a shared-needle occasion. Perhaps there'd be Cheetohs and for sure there'd be Schlitz Malt Liquor, but beyond that, it would be weed, coke, and crank on the menu.

Tonight, Kramden would be Scrotum's pal, from rehab, the assignment he was currently ignoring. Even for him, this was a modest, uncomplicated scam he should be able to pull off, no problem. This was simple dope-dealing 101, lab, and lecture.

The front door was wide open, and clouds of weed poured out under the bare bulb on the front porch. They packed the house, mostly with local hoods and degenerates. It was a gathering of the waste product of the Woodlands. Kramden recognized two mopes from his days back on patrol, but he wasn't in the least worried they might recognize him. A beard, shoulder-length hair, and a bit of a different attitude was a fair transformation from the young street monster who used to pound this beat.

Ballsack and Kramden did what you do at a party. They drank beer, Scrote smoked weed, drank a little wine, and they mingled. An old Marantz receiver was pushing tunes out to some quality speakers. Kramden knew they were booty from some burglary.

It was early, and the party was lively. Nothing like it would be in three or four hours. Although Kramden looked everywhere, he couldn't find one stinking Cheetoh.

Early on, the Scrote introduced Kramden to his sister. More interested in snorting a line of crank off the back of her hand, she was less than convivial. It may have been early evening, but she was 3 a.m. fucked up already. Kramden told his CI to get it set up, they wouldn't be there all night.

If you could've dropped a net over this party, you'd have spent all night booking and processing warrant arrests, possession arrests, and transporting assholes to jail. Or giving them a lift to the emergency room. At one point, some douche fell over a backpack on the living room floor and clacked his jaw off the coffee table. He bit the last 3/4 of an inch off the end of his tongue. Good thing he was highly medicated. That could've hurt.

An hour later, Scrote and Kramden were making small talk with two skanky chicks in the crowded kitchen. Who came waddling in but 'Lisbeth, and she was mid-deal with a crank-head who was begging for just the tiniest bit of credit. They slithered out the back of the kitchen, credit appearing to be a long shot.

Nutsack pointed out a K-Mart male fashionista, trying too hard to look bad. "Kinda of off, you know, mentally. Crankster. King, deals in quantity, though."

Kramden asked him, "Quantities of what?" and Ballbag suggested it was meth.

Kramden kept an eye on him and overheard him whining, "They're all over me…fucking always on me." It sounded like it could be some typical crankster paranoia, but Kramden wasn't really in a position to hear much. He kept it in mind though.

Kramden stepped out and took a piss in the front yard. Okay, he wouldn't do that if you'd invited him to a party at your house, but he was way more than sure that in this crowd it was socially acceptable. He also intended to signal Joseph that all was well, and they were on track.

Kramden's stood there, dick in his hand, when Scrote and the sibling showed up alongside. You'd have thought he was waiting for a bus, they could've cared less. Donna said, "My brother says you want some blow? Says you got money?"

Kramden was laughing and trying not to piss on himself. "Just give me a minute. Let me zip up, for fuck's sake."

Once fully reassembled, the young narcotics agent turned, and she was standing there. In her open palm, two bindles of coke. "How much?" he asked.

"$110 apiece," she slurred. They completed the deal for a single bindle in about 30 seconds. Kramden was relatively sure that Joseph had probably seen the deal go down, it was that out in the open. Kramden pulled his ball cap off and turned it around bassackward. That's all it took to signal Joseph that all was not only fine, but also dandy.

Back inside Kramden suggested Scrotum find out if 'Lisbeth was still holding. He wanted to get the other one under his belt.

As Ballbag disappeared into the crowd, the aforementioned King sidled up behind him. Kramden didn't hear him coming. "Who the fuck are you?" The detective turned and sized him up. King wanted to know who he was with. Who invited him.

"Who the fuck wants to know, asshole," Kramden hospitably responded. They shared a stank-eye moment, but King had already moved on into the crowd. Perhaps Kramden took it too cavalierly. He thought, perhaps it wasn't the best judgment he'd ever displayed.

Maybe 15 minutes later, 'Lisbeth approached and Kramden gave her the ubiquitous party greeting, "Hey."

In a bit more circumspect manner than her daughter, she leaned in. "I got maybe an eighth left, that's it."

Kramden asked her, "Coke or crank?" not knowing what the Scrote had set up. Not that it mattered.

"Blow," she answered. Kramden surmised she and Donna must have split up their stash since they were selling the same shit. He told her he'd take a gram, but that was all the cash he had left.

'Lisbeth and Kramden had just swapped money for dope when he heard the first chilling clack of a shotgun being racked, a round shoved in the chamber. Before the hair could stand up on the back of his neck, he saw stars. The steel barrel of a Marlin Model 44, 20 Ga. punched him in the back of the head, almost knocked him to his knees. Kramden knew immediately it was King, the discourteous douchebag.

"Motherfucker," he growled. "Narc! This fucking pig's a motherfucking narc!" King announced to the group of stoners trashing the living room. Immediately the party grew quiet, all eyes on them. Kramden's hands were up at shoulder level. King shoved him forward with the shotgun, banging his head again.

Kramden, of course, rejected his description. "Hey, fuck you, what're you talking about?" King shoved again. Kramden was getting pissed he kept banging him in the head but he also wasn't discounting he was doing it with a .20 gauge. King continued pushing him towards the front door. As Kramden would describe, it was "so quiet you could hear a pubic hair hit the floor."

"Lighten up, dude. I ain't no narc. You're outta your fucking mind," he suggested. Even 'Lisbeth was slack-jawed at the prospect of an exploding narc in her midst.

King kept his tirade up. "Motherfucking, motherfucking narc cocksucker."

Even weaselly Ballsack pleaded, "Hey, man, he's cool. He's with me. What're you doing, man?" King must've felt truly dissed.

By this point, King had maneuvered Kramden out the door onto the front porch, still whacking him on the head with that God-damned shotgun. Kramden knew by now his cover guy would have them in view and he'd be working the radio, calling in the cavalry.

Kramden stepped down to the grass, and King gave him one more long shove, pushing him out toward the sidewalk. "Get the fuck out of here, cocksucker! Get the fuck out!" It seemed logical to Kramden. When he got to the sidewalk, he moved toward Joseph's position. Kramden turned, the crowd at the door was yapping anti-cop horse shit. Scrotum stayed tucked into the group. Luckily he was apparently no worse for wear.

It dawned on Kramden to signal Joseph he was okay. He ran his fingers through his hair; he did it more than once, hoping Joseph would call off the troops. Frustration set in when he heard two sirens in the distance, but just as quickly, they faded. Joseph was a good man.

When Kramden made it to his undercover car, not five cars down the block, he opened the driver's door to get behind the relative safety of it. Reaching into his pocket, he pulled out a "flash roll" of cash. He held it over his head and yelled back at King, "You stupid motherfucker! You could've made some cash…fuck you. Fuck you!" Kramden knew the motivation behind the dealer scumbags he dealt with day-to-day.

They de-briefed at Brick's later that night. Over longneck Schaefers and a few shots of 151 rum and tabasco, they discussed the relative merits of the evening. They ended up with sales of cocaine cases against mother Ball Sack and the sibling. Scrotum made it out alive. Good outcome, all in all.

Kramden's theory was that if King had thought he really was a narc, he'd have done the evil deed, and Kramden would have been toast. King felt disrespected. Too bad. Fuck him.

It pleased Kramden to no end when three months and four days after the party in the Woodlands, he bought four ounces of meth from King in a buy-bust. If the legislation had been in place, it would've been King's third strike.

King spent 11 months in SP-C, affectionately known as Carthage State Prison right there in Allen County. It seems he stepped on his dick more than once and was transferred to Northern Territories State Prison. Apparently, he really didn't get along all that well with his playmates.

King found himself housed in Cellblock D, a longer-term Security Housing Unit, or SHU, designed to control the most intractably violent prisoners. He was only there 19 days when they pitched him down a set of stairs, fracturing his spine and putting him in a wheelchair for life.

Too bad.

Quinn was sitting up straight by the time Kramden finished. "Jack, if I had known that douchebag King had pulled that shit on you, he wouldn't have made it to the pen at Carthage."

The boys knew Quinn was serious. Somehow the perp would have had a bad accident at the hands of one Lieutenant Patrick Quinn. In a rare moment of candor, Kramden clarified, "Boss, that's why we never told you."

The boys loved having their narco assignments in common. Being a Night Policeman and a narc was something they all thought of as a badge of honor. The cops they worked with, by and large, would almost never say it out loud, but they knew that many of the others looked up to them. They knew they were recognized for their cop-life experiences and the balls it took to play on that stage. Being truthful, it was part of the gig that drew them together.

RJ paused for another sip of whiskey. "It was good times, boys. Me and Maxie had arrived! Customs valued undercover work, and we were cocked and locked to deliver. Maxie wore a leather jacket with an honest-to-god fringe on it, black cowboy boots with sterling silver tips. He had kind of a stubble beard and looked like a poor man's Robert Redford. We were driving badass seizure cars with ZZ Top and other Southern fried rock blaring from the dash. We had our own nearly personal souped-up Harleys. DEA or Customs aircraft at our fingertips.

"Maxie would fly into some little airstrip and convince some crankster gangster to trade him a couple of pounds of finished meth for a keg of ephedrine. Worked almost every time too. I swear, those toothless wood hooks called Maxie, 'Sir!'

"The kids back in the Customs office were green with envy. I had no idea how deep that shit ran until later. All the same, Maxie and I had more cases than we could

write, so we were kicking down the crumbs to them. Easy cases putting a federal charge on a mope with a huge bag of crank."

CHAPTER 24

The Untouchables

Only their DEA boss and the US Attorney's office had any idea what Johnson and Golden were doing. Their Customs boss did not, and on any day or evening he had no clue where they were or what they were doing. That was for the best, as he had blood pressure issues already.

The big boss, the Special Agent in Charge at the Field Division, knew that the two relatively new agents led the division in federal cases submitted, and further, that they had just put a 1,000 pound meth case on one of the most vicious and notorious Outlaws of all time. With the murderous Outlaw locked up for life, law enforcement agencies across the Midwest got witnesses to come forward and finger him on over a dozen homicides.

About every two months, the Special Agent in Charge routed a written commendation for one of their cases to their boss. So as much as their antics and bullshit made Wally Hubble curse and fume and smoke, Golden and Johnson were modern-day Eliot Nesses.

They were untouchable, all right, but they knew the assignment couldn't last forever. It was a hollow threat, but RAC Hubble often threatened to bring them back from the task force when his frustrations with the duo reached the boiling point.

Golden and Johnson tried to avoid Hubble at all costs. They made what trips to the office they had to, and always after hours. A few reports dumped in Hubble's in-box were the only sign they had been there. Well, almost the only sign.

A bonus of an after-hours visit was pissing in Wally Hubbard's office plants. This caught on with the younger agents; Wally's plants eventually turned a sickly yellow. The clerical girls suggested that he may be over-watering.

On late night surveillances, the two always discussed options.

Golden leading off with his latest scheme. "RJ, you ever miss the Marines?"

"Yeah, sure. Pay is better here though."

"I've been looking at going back. Special Forces this time."

"Maxie, that's for 19-year-olds. We're in our thirties. We'd die in the first week of training."

"No. Check it out, there's a Reserve Special Forces unit in Springfield. You can join the Reserves and over a two-year period get qualified. It's for older guys like us. Then after you get your beret, you could go active. Whaddaya think?"

"I don't know, Max. Doesn't sound very conducive to family life."

"Exactly!"

A couple of months later, in the wee hours of another surveillance…

"RJ, you ever hear of Snow Cap?"

"The DEA thing down in South America?"

"Yup. It's military operations against the cartels in Colombia, Bolivia, and Peru. They send you to Army Ranger School before you go down there."

"Maxie, Hubble doesn't even like us hanging out at the task force, and we're in the same city. He will never support that, even if DEA would entertain having Customs agents on board."

"That's the thing. We quit Customs and join DEA. I talked to McGee, and I called the Major back in DC. They'll both recommend us. Major Meth knows Frank White. White's the head honcho for Snow Cap. We could get on just as soon as we finished the DEA academy! Come on, RJ! It's shooting cartel dudes in the jungle!"

"Max, let me think about it. My kids barely know who I am now."

"Alls I'm saying RJ is I can't go back to the airport field office. Can you imagine writing pirated VCR tape cases on a poor old mutt who filled his suitcase up with knock-off tapes in Mexico while he was catching some sun? I can't, and I don't think you can either."

Maxie. Always one to have the last word.

The risky behavior of Golden and Johnson continued to intensify.

Unscripted undercover meetings and drug buys with outlaw bikers. Trying to keep the facts and evidence and buy money straight in their reports got harder and harder.

RJ looked up at the ceiling of Solly's and shook himself, not quite believing he had survived it all.

"After two years on the task force we were tired of the work, or just plain tired. You guys remember that was the end of my marriage. Maxie and his wife barely spoke."

Quinn interrupted to ask if Maxie divorced then too. Quinn was trying to figure out the missing parts of the story that had led them to all gather here tonight.

"Not then, Pat. Maxie was unhappy though. Max worried me when he would start acting like nutty Bobby Meyer doing the gun to the head thing.

"Bobby would go into one of his suicide pantomimes, talking about shooting himself and all, then Maxie'd yell at Bobby to stop threatening to kill himself. Maxie would pull his own gun and point it at himself. Channeling Blazing Saddles, *he would declare, 'One more move, Bobby, and the Jew kid gets it!' At least Bobby and Maxie had the sense not to do their act when McGee or any other bosses were around. Vintage Maxie. It was funny, but dammit it was disturbing.*

"In retrospect, it was the best two years of our careers. Maxie talked about quitting Customs altogether and going into business. He had that latitude. You know his old man was wealthy. Anyway, the old man had often made overtures to Golden to enter business with him. The two weren't close, but dad would kick down thousands a year to Maxie. Kept him living in Maximum Golden style. They could have done well together, the old man's money and brains, and Maxie's balls and charm.

"I knew I'd be with Customs until I retired or died. I applied for a commission in the Reserves though. Maybe it was in answer to all of Golden's military schemes, or maybe I realized that I had to keep myself straight. Maxie was no longer interested."

Patrick Quinn was ever curious about "his boys." He could never know too much about their pasts, their histories. He nodded. Another piece of the puzzle fit together for him.

RJ picked up the thread of the Max Golden years. "For our next act we got to be Death-From-Above SWAT guys! Customs wanted to be like the other big boys and have SWAT teams, so it was a no-brainer that Golden and I would do it. It was another venue for out-of-office adventure. It was perfect."

RJ looked at the burned-out cigar in his hand. It had burned badly while he had been delivering his story.

Kramden was right there with a freshly snipped Ashton. "Try this, buddy. They have a good draw…it's smooth. You know, I didn't understand you guys were into so much undercover stuff over at Customs. I worked with the feds a few times. It was always major shit. Impressive."

RJ accepted the cigar and a light from Kramden. "It was a blessing that we got away from the UC shit. The lines were getting blurry. We were believing our own headlines, and that was dangerous. The SWAT thing was an improvement for us; we cleaned up and got back into shape.

"Although getting into shape started Maxie on another wild idea. He started looking into the French Foreign Legion. I think he sometimes saw himself as this sophisticated European misplaced on the American continent. You know because of his old man, he had dual citizenship and a German passport. Anyway, it was another Maxie scheme to get out of Dodge and not have to deal with his marital situation."

Rimjob held up his drink here, interrupting RJ. "Wait a minute! Go back! I don't care about you idiots playing Rambo. You mean to tell me that Maxie had that pretty Asian wife, and he was trying to shitcan her? What an idiot! That's my fantasy wife...little geisha broad with a sideways breezer that does everything for me and doesn't speak a word of English."

RJ sighed. "Rimjob, you little pervert, you already have a wife."

"Not anymore. I fired her lazy ass! She was a lousy housekeeper. Every time I went to take a piss in the sink, it was full of dirty dishes!"

Kramden called bullshit. "I know he's lying, cause there's no way Rimjob *can reach the sink with his tiny legs and tiny wiener."*

"You know what, Kramden? Fuck you! I got one of them kitchen step-stool things so I can reach stuff. Fucking asshole!" Quinn just smiled and motioned for RJ *to continue.*

RJ *had been the first to see Max Golden in several years, and he wanted to prepare Quinn a bit before Golden arrived.* RJ *leaned in close to Quinn. "Maxie…he's pretty fucked up, boss. I would be for sure. I mean how could you not, but…since Maxie isn't here, I'm going to fill in some of the blanks for you boys."*

Quinn waved it off. "Life's hard, brother. Then you better get right. It ain't like you got a choice, but tell us what you know, RJ*."*

CHAPTER 25

Junior G-Man

Max and RJ had returned to the Customs field office after their two years on the meth lab task force. Now that they were more or less under the supervision of Wally Hubble again, Johnson and Golden were saddled with more and more of the administrative tar, the sticky crap of collateral jobs that makes any police bureaucracy go 'round. Evidence vault custodian, range master, duty agent, and since Golden had over five years on the job, and therefore was a journeyman agent, he became a training agent.

For 20 years Customs had hired only those persons who had prior law enforcement or military experience. Something had changed at the upper echelons, and now there were new Customs agents fresh out of college with no experience. What a dumb fucking idea.

Chip Connor had been a star collegiate athlete at Penn State and had taken part in their ROTC program for all four years. Upon graduation and while awaiting his slot at Army Officer Candidate School, Chip went through the basic paratrooper course at Ft. Benning, a necessary step on his path to becoming an officer in one of the Ranger Battalions. His father had been an Army Ranger. Unfortunately for Chip, an accident during a night jump shattered not only his femur, but his chance to become an Army Ranger. Four months and two surgeries in Army hospitals gave Chip plenty of time to think about a civilian career that would put him closer to home and his college girlfriend Cynthia. While Chip communicated a lot with Cynthia during his recuperation, his gut told him she was moving on and did not embrace being an Army officer's wife. He had to get back home to New Jersey.

After getting his discharge from the Army, Chip took and passed the Treasury Enforcement Agent written exam, qualifying him for special agent positions with the Secret Service, US Customs, ATF, and the IRS Criminal Investigations Division. The image of being a steely-eyed Secret Service agent trotting next to the presidential limousine appealed to Chip. He just knew it would impress Cynthia too. As luck would have it, the much lesser known US Customs called first and offered him a position in the Midwest. Chip went to see Jim Sparato, a Secret Service agent near his home in Trenton. Jim had been advising Chip about the Secret Service hiring process. They liked what they saw in Chip and wanted to hire him when something came open; that looked to be several months out, however.

Sparato gave Chip his best advice. "Take the job. Do three years and get past being a conditional employee. If you don't like it at Customs, you can apply with us or any other federal agency and get accepted. Whatever you do, stay away from ATF, those guys are cowboys and don't have the best reputation."

"But the position is in the middle of nowhere," Chip whined. Sparato, already assigned to his third field office, was not sympathetic. He knew of Chip's desire to stay local and therefore close to his girlfriend, and being older and wiser knew that girlfriends, even wives, come and go, especially in the life of a special agent.

So needing a job of some sort, Chip accepted the offer from U.S. Customs in faraway Missouri.

Resident Agent in Charge Wally Hubble took a perverse pleasure in assigning a complete rookie to Max Golden. The office was expanding, and there were several new hires. However, most had come from other federal agencies, the military, or municipal police departments. All of those new hires had carried a gun before, and most of their training needs merely involved getting them familiar with the Customs laws and internal policies. A brand-new rookie was very time-intensive for the training agent and often strained one's patience. Max did not have a great deal of patience to begin with.

If there was a word to describe the 23-year-old Chip Connor, that word would be impetuous. Maybe 5 feet 8 inches and 150 pounds in a compact track star's body. Hair still in an Army buzzcut, though he had been out for over a year. His New Jersey accent grated against the Midwestern twang spoken in the office. He was whip smart and could only be expected to "go study the manuals" for so long before he was back at Golden's side wanting to do something "meaningful." Having been to neither the Basic Criminal Investigators school, nor the Customs academy, he could not carry a gun or perform any law enforcement duties on his own. He could accompany Max or other journeymen agents on routine field duties, witness interviews, meetings with informants, meetings with other cops or prosecutors. Nothing more.

On those occasions when there was no one to tag along with, Connor bounced around the office like a Super Ball in a tile shower stall, annoying everyone in the office. The other agents were trying to get the never-ending load of paperwork done and didn't have time for his nonsense.

Chip Connor realized that Golden and Johnson were the two high fliers in the office, and he considered himself lucky to have Max Golden as his training agent. Between the two of them, Max and RJ ran 90% of all the informants for the office and made 100% of the decent cases.

Even though their meth lab task force days were over, Max Golden and RJ were still narco cowboys at heart. That they were on the division Special Response Team just added to their aura. Connor wanted to be just like them.

Two months passed and soon enough Chip Connor was on his way to the Federal Law Enforcement Training Center (FLETC) in Glynn County (Glynco), Georgia, to begin his first 10 weeks of basic criminal investigator training. There would be another 10 weeks of Customs training down the road. The basic criminal investigator's course was much like a basic police academy; studying the laws of arrest, search, and seizure, physical training, shooting, and high-speed driving. At the end of these 10 weeks, Connor would at last be able to carry a gun when he accompanied other agents somewhere, or even by himself. He still could not participate in law enforcement activities without a journeyman agent present.

Progress reports back to the field office were a little less than stellar; academically the former Penn State Phi Beta Kappa grad was underwhelming, placing in the middle of the pack. He had been drinking way too much beer and doing the minimum amount of studying. Physical fitness was top notch as one would expect from a Division One track star. And then there was "the incident."

The security force at FLETC known as "Flet-See Five Oh" by the student body, was very exuberant in their enforcement of the law at FLETC, and they were not impressed with anybody's badge because every student there had one. Nor were the local law enforcement officers on the outside of the gate. Recreational drinking in and around FLETC required a lot of pre-planning and luck to stay out of trouble. After priming the pump at the FLETC Gay Bar, Connor and three other trainees headed out for the bars on St. Simon Island to see if they could improve on the male-to-female ratio that governed FLETC.

Chip Connor and friends failed on the planning aspect and the luck factor ran out at the foot of the St. Simon Island Bridge when a Brunswick

PD patrol officer saw them run the red light to enter the causeway. The Brunswick PD arrested Connor and three other agent trainees; one for drunk driving, and the other three for public drunkenness. Lucky for Connor he was not driving the car when they were pulled over, and as he sobered up, he remembered to provide the arresting officer with the name and telephone number of his Customs coordinator at FLETC.

Weeks prior when the eight Customs trainees that were part of CI Course 90-2 reported into FLETC, Special Agent Brian Ward welcomed them aboard and explained that he was their connect to Customs and their respective field divisions. He also laid down the law about screwing up in and around FLETC, promising termination if they broke the rules, but gave each of them his business card. "Call me if you get into trouble. Chances are that I can't do a damn thing, but call me."

When Special Agent Ward showed up at Brunswick PD at one o'clock on a Friday morning, he was none too happy. Two of the drunken delinquents were Customs trainees, and two were ATF trainees, including the driver of the car. The Brunswick officers were more than happy to turn the Customs kids over to Ward. It was a quiet ride back to the base. He told them to report to his office after the Friday training schedule was complete. Fortunately for Connor, Ward had been a classmate of Max Golden. No official report went to Connor's field division. Instead, Ward placed a call to Golden and gave him a heads up about his trainee. Ward and Golden had some laughs remembering their own exploits and close calls at FLETC. Max requested a phone call from Connor so he could deliver his own world-class ass-chewing to his trainee.

The always acerbic Rimjob had to insert himself. "Just shows how dumb the fucking feds are! Who could be dumb enough to let you two train anybody?"

Good question, RJ *thought. "Our shitbag boss, Hubble, thought it was funny to saddle Maxie with a complete rookie. Maxie didn't have the patience to mentor some Ivy League frat boy. Something was going to blow up, but Hubble was such a dick that he didn't care.*

"Man, oh man, how Maxie and Hubble would get into it after we got reassigned from the task force. Maxie's fuse was about an eighth of an inch long at that point, and his favorite blasphemy was god-fucking-dammit. Hubble had given him some stupid last-minute tasking, probably on a yellow sticky note because Hubble never liked the possibility of confrontation. Anyway, whatever it was, it was causing Maxie to launch into a triple burst of god-fucking-dammits. Hubble, terrified that the clerical staff would raise Hostile Workplace issues, told Maxie that that was enough god-fucking-dammits. To which Maxie just stared at Hubble. 'Wally, just how many god-fucking-dammits is too many god-fucking-dammits?' The office girls, as opposed to taking offense, were now laughing at Hubble and his beet-red face. Hubble stomped back to his office and slammed the door. Must've been a real strain on the little worm, afraid to confront a wayward employee and afraid of any complaints about his office to upper management."

RJ *was on a roll. It was obvious to the boys that* RJ *still harbored some real animosity toward his former boss. "I remember about that same time Hubble got a call from the US Attorney's Office bitching about something I had done. I was always stirring shit up there. I think they turned me down on a search warrant, and I went to a state judge to get what I needed. I didn't give a fuck who signed the paper, I just wanted to get the job done! Anyhow, Hubble, a tower of strength, hitched up his trousers and started bitching at me because some AUSA was giving him a little shit. So I said, 'Hey, Wally, how about just backing us up for a change?' This infuriated Hubble, and he was screaming at me 'to sit at my desk and not do another goddamned thing for the rest of the year!' To which I said, fine, put that in writing please, because when the Special Agent in Charge wants to know why I quit making cases I can show him your order. That sent him back to his office to slam the door and have an illegal indoor smoke."*

Seems somebody kept calling the Division Office and complaining that RAC Hubble was smoking in the office against federal workplace rules.

CHAPTER 26

The Lesson

Two weeks later Connor was a graduate of the Basic Criminal Investigators Course and was back in the field office complete with a badge, gun, and a sack full of desires to make cases and arrest bad guys. Golden squashed this notion with the admonition that Connor was to do no enforcement action on his own and must have a journeyman agent with him. Problem was Max found Connor to be a major annoyance and a hindrance to his own somewhat unorthodox methods of making cases and therefore did not include Connor in many of his endeavors. One of Max Golden's off-the-books endeavors was the courtship of a local businesswoman and former Miss Arkansas. It was not like he could have his trainee wait outside in the car.

Ron Johnson was more tolerant of the exuberant young agent and let him tag along on some of his cases. RJ was sympathetic to the kid's failed Army attempt and his desire to be a top-notch federal agent. The kid could only do that by getting his hands dirty out in the field.

RJ well knew of Maxie's preoccupations. He took on the job of setting Chip Connor up with his first informant, a good stepping stone to making a case. Informants, because they were all past, present, or future criminals, had the ability to get into places where criminal activities were going on, but one always had to keep in mind that today's confidential informant is likely tomorrow's defendant. The successful management of informants took a firm hand and a well-tuned bullshit meter. This was a good starting point for the fledgling agent.

RJ introduced Chip Connor to Luther, one of his older, not so wild informants. When he wasn't driving his big rig, Luther spent a lot of time in bars and was always at the fringe of something in the meth trade. After a "come-to-Jesus" talk with Luther the CI, RJ told Connor that he could run Luther and try to get enough info on some lightweight meth dealers to get search warrants. RJ admonished Connor about keeping him in the loop. Quite a sight; the diminutive Chip Connor in his nylon military fliers jacket, buzzcut, and aviator sunglasses meeting with the big old Okie truck driver in his cowboy boots and cowboy hat. RJ had to laugh.

Since Luther was not working off a beef, he was in the category of mercenary monster. He sold information for money. RJ showed Connor how to get undercover funds for paying confidential informants and purchasing evidence. He schooled Connor on the rather onerous process of keeping up with the government's $2,000 in case money. Luther, a documented confidential informant, had to sign a receipt for every dollar given to him by Connor, and Connor would have to write a report documenting the information obtained. Johnson monitored Connor and gave him sage advice about keeping the government funds separate from his personal funds. "Trust me, Chip. You put G-money in your wallet, and it will eat your money up!"

RJ and his fiancée Liz had met on the meth lab task force. Liz was a blue-eyed beauty from State Narcotics, and to the amazement of cops all over the state, the crazy Customs cowboy had won her heart. All true and then some, the pair had emerged from the pyre of two failed marriages to start a home out in the country together. They had set a wedding date for late that summer.

Connor was spending more and more of his off-duty time with RJ and Liz at their home. Connor's own living situation was frugal and bleak. As a federal employee, he could get a room in the Bachelor Officers Quarters (BOQ) at the nearby Air Force Base. It made sense; why spend the money leasing an apartment when one half of Connor's first year would be at the federal training facility in Georgia. In either location, Connor's domestic life had all the charm of a Motel 6 room with a writing desk and a wall locker. The warmth of Liz and RJ's hearth and Liz's great cooking were an obvious draw for a lonely kid 1,500 miles from home.

Besides the food and companionship, Chip Connor enjoyed using RJ and Liz's telephone. There was only a payphone in the common area of the BOQ, not a very intimate method for talking with his girlfriend back East. As it was, RJ and Liz overheard Connor talking to Cynthia and they knew that things were not going well. Cynthia had graduated from college and was now a department store management trainee back in New Jersey. She had a new career and a new circle of friends and coworkers, which included guys. This was disturbing to Connor.

On an early Friday evening in April, RJ and Liz were planning dinner and looking forward to doing some major landscape work in their backyard that weekend when Connor pulled up in front of their house in his red sports car. There was nothing unusual about having him drop in, though they would have preferred to be alone that night. For several weeks the three had been training for a marathon and Connor crashed on their couch or in the spare bedroom several nights each week to accommodate the long early morning workouts.

Liz was gracious about Connor's unscheduled appearance and set another place at the dinner table. It was obvious that Connor had had a few Friday afternoon beers at the Officer's Club before heading out to Liz and RJ's place. Liz figured a good solid meal would soak up some alcohol and the kid would crash on the couch. Dinner didn't have the desired effect on Connor. He was in a party mood.

After having two more beers from RJ and Liz's fridge, Connor began pestering them to go downtown for some drinks and dancing. This didn't fit RJ or Liz's plans, but they took pity on Connor and agreed to go on the conditions that they would only be there for a couple drinks, meaning two, and Connor would let them drive because he was already over the limit. The three loaded into their pickup truck for the 20-mile trip to Capital City.

Blackbeard's Bar was located in Old Town Capital City. It was a popular joint for the younger set. It had bars on the ground floor and the basement, and both were packed on a Friday night. They found a small table downstairs, and the first round went without a hitch. Johnson and Liz were enjoying the music, and Connor was checking out all the young ginch.

Then Connor's pager started buzzing. It was Luther the CI paging on a Friday night, wanting to trade some tidbit for some government cash. RJ advised Connor not to encourage Luther the Mercenary Monster by answering pages on a Friday night. Luther would never page RJ on a weekend. He knew better than that. He never gave information that needed immediate action. Connor was eager though, and headed out of the bar to find a payphone where he stood a chance of hearing what Luther had to give up.

Connor came back 15-20 minutes later, longer than a CI phone call should take. He likely had a drink or two upstairs. After another beer at the table with RJ and Liz, Connor wanted to dance. Alcohol slows some folks down. In Chip Connor's case, it often made him even more frenetic, like rocket fuel mixed with testosterone in the little PT stud's body. Soon he was up working the bar line asking women to dance. Most of them were with a date. RJ could see that Connor was making an ass out of himself, and some dudes, all bigger than Connor, were looking like they were about tired of his shit. RJ jumped to his feet and started talking fast to avert a bar fight. "Sorry, folks. My cousin here just got back from the Gulf War." RJ playing off of Chip's goofy buzzcut. "He's still trying to sort some stuff out." The big dudes told RJ to rein Connor in because somebody would punch his lights out if he kept it up.

Liz had fresh beers on the table and a plan. "Drink up, cause we are going home after this round." Connor's pager started buzzing again, and he was up and moving before RJ could stop him. He was gone longer this time, and Liz and RJ were concerned about him. They both looked at their watches. They were ready to go home. RJ stood up. "I'll go find him." Johnson suspected that Connor had detoured through the bar upstairs, but he was not there. A check of the payphones out on the street also came up empty. Back at the entrance to Blackbeard's, Johnson asked the bouncers if they had seen a little buzzcut dude in a nylon flight jacket.

"Yeah, you know him?"

RJ got a sinking feeling. "He came here with me and my girl. I'm looking for him so we can take him home."

"Good luck with that. Cops are looking for him too. We wouldn't let him back in because he's too drunk. Then he flashed some kinda badge at us and tried to push his way in. We threw his ass in the street. That's when he flashed the gun at us, and we called the cops. Hey, is he some kind of cop?"

"Not really," Johnson muttered. "I need to find my girl and get going."

By the time Johnson and Liz made it outside, there were three Cap City PD squad cars on the street in front of the bar. Shit! Two cops were talking to the bouncers, while a sergeant sat in his squad car. RJ thought he had seen the sergeant before, maybe at a search warrant. He wished he knew the guy better, but he didn't. RJ took a chance, and he walked up to the car and presented his credentials. "Hey, Sarge, I think one of our rookies is the guy you got called about. If you can cut some slack on this, I'd sure be grateful. Could you call me if you find him? I'm looking for him too."

The sergeant took Johnson's card with his pager number on it. "A lot depends on if Blackbeard's wants to press charges, you know. If they do and we find him, not a lot I can do."

"Thanks, Sarge. Any help is much appreciated."

Johnson and Liz went back to their truck and started their own search. Connor had to be on foot because he rode with them to the bar. He had left his car parked in front of their house over 20 miles away. The Customs office, however, was only a few blocks away.

No joy. The office alarm was on, and the lights were off. RJ unlocked the door, and he and Liz stepped inside. He turned off the alarm. No Connor, but the office was a good place to call Connor's training agent. RJ called Max at home. Max Golden had not heard from his trainee that evening. He filled the phone wires with god-fucking-dammits for several minutes before calming and trying to figure their next move. Because Johnson had identified himself to the sergeant, the PD knew that Connor was a Customs rookie if they wanted to come looking for him.

The bigger issue for Johnson and Golden was whether to tell RAC Wally Hubble. Not telling him could bite them on the ass later, but if they called him that evening, or even waited until Monday to tell him, Customs would fire Connor. Simple as that. Much as the two journeymen agents wanted to strangle young Chip Connor right that moment, neither wanted to be a rat, nor had they ever told Wally Hubble anything about anything they had ever done. Neither would piss up Wally Hubble's ass if his guts were on fire. Why throw him a bone now? The two agents agreed to call if either heard something about Connor.

Johnson and Liz drove around downtown for a while longer, including Old Town, though they stayed away from the street that Blackbeard's was on. After 45 minutes of searching they got on the freeway and headed south for their home in the country. After exiting the freeway RJ and Liz were on the dark two-lane road that headed south to their country home. A taxi cab passed them heading northbound. Taxis at one o'clock in the morning were rare out in the country. A mile down the road, there was an all-night Shell station. Sort of an outpost at the edge of rural nothingness. Lo-and-behold…who was at the gas pumps putting fuel into his little red sports car? Apparently Connor had taken a cab from downtown all the way to RJ and Liz's place to retrieve his car. RJ and Liz were incredulous as RJ idled up to the pumps on the other side of one Chip Connor. Connor in a drunken haze was oblivious to 6,000 pounds of Ford diesel idling next to him. RJ got out and went over to Connor who displayed a slight sway as he filled his car.

"What the fuck do you think you're doing?"

Johnson got Liz to drive Connor's car back to their house, and he loaded Connor into the pickup truck. "Do you have any idea how much fucking trouble you are in?" This seemed an appropriate conversation opener.

Connor had his head resting against the passenger window with his eyes closed. "Ron, I'm really drunk right now and I don't feel so good."

"No shit. Just wait."

When the trio got home, Liz guided Connor to the spare bedroom while RJ called Max to let him know they had found Connor.

Saturday morning dawned bright and clear, a beautiful spring morning. RJ and Liz rousted Chip for a hearty breakfast of sausage, eggs, pancakes, and fruit. "Eat up, lad! We have a big day of manual labor ahead of us!" After the prior evening's antics, RJ considered Connor an indentured servant.

As per Liz and RJ's landscape plans, there were two large cypress stumps to be dug out of the ground to prepare for a swimming pool. As Johnson and Connor chopped and dug and sweated, Johnson queried Connor about the evening before. Connor claimed that he remembered going to Blackbeard's, but didn't remember much after that. RJ wasn't buying that and kept after Connor. Connor was sweating sweet formaldehyde post-booze fumes from every pore.

"So you don't remember getting into a beef with the bouncers?"

"Nope."

"You don't remember badging them?"

"Uh-uhh."

"And you don't remember flashing your gun at them, and them telling you that they were calling the cops?"

"They said I did that? I don't think I did anything like that."

"How would you know? You remember nothing, right? I guess you don't remember groping that girl either?" Johnson was just making shit up now.

"I didn't do that!"

"Well, how would you know? You remember nothing. You know what? You're in deep shit."

"I don't feel so good."

"Shut up, shitbird, and keep digging."

Later that evening, after Connor escaped to his spartan rented room at the local air base, Johnson and Golden talked on the phone. So far RJ had received no page from Cap City PD, but there was always the chance that Blackbeard's had pushed it and a complaint was working through the system. They agreed to meet in the office early on Monday morning to check for messages from the PD. The sergeant from Blackbeard's had Johnson's business card, but not the identity of Connor. They would do whatever damage control possible, but the pair were due in St. Louis later that day to plan and execute a bunch of search warrants on west St. Louis drug dealers. The DEA task force there was asking for assistance from everyone that had a tactical team.

Monday morning arrived, and no one from Capital City PD had called. Maybe that was a good sign. Golden took a half hour to discuss Connor's career trajectory with him; the discussion began, "Shut up and listen!" Golden laid it out. Neither he nor Johnson were going to Hubble about the incident, despite the bind this put them in. However, all bets were off if Capital City PD came looking for Connor. Connor, tail between his legs, was restricted to the office for the duration of time that Golden and Johnson would be down in St. Louis on the drug raids.

On the drive to St. Louis, Golden and Johnson discussed what to do with the little knot head, providing Capital City PD didn't contact Customs about him.

And then Max announced, "I have a plan!"

For the balance of the ride the pair perfected the details for teaching the wayward trainee a lesson and getting a pound of his scrawny flesh for causing them a Friday evening of high anxiety. And for putting their asses on the line with Wally Hubble. They didn't need any help from a rookie in that department.

The plan would go down in the annals of law enforcement as one of the greatest practical jokes ever. Or could have.

First, they would contact Capital City PD detective Dusty Rhodes, their friend and former lab task force compadre. They would ask Dusty to research the call log and determine the disposition of the incident at Blackbeard's.

If there was nothing official going on, they could execute part two of the plan. They would have Rhodes call over to the Customs office and leave a message for RJ: "Call me as soon as possible." Then later, Golden would call into the office and check up on Connor. Make sure he was assembling, reading, and memorizing his manuals, and then have him check to see if there were any messages for Golden or Johnson. When Connor saw the "call Capital City PD ASAP" message he would shit. Oh, how delightful!

When the pair checked in at the St. Louis Field Office, they found an empty office and called into their pal at Capital City PD. Rhodes had been reassigned back to his normal investigative duties in homicide and was at his desk for a change.

"Rhodes, homicide."

"Hey, Dusty. Max and Ron here."

Dusty listened to their plan, then put them on hold while he had dispatch go back through the call log to get him an incident number and disposition. Being a homicide dick got you quick results. Moments later he was back on the line with Max and Ron. "Looks like your word to the sergeant that night paid off. They cleared the scene a few minutes later. Sarge put the disposition as 'disturbance call with the bouncers, suspect gone on arrival of units. All units 10-8.' I'm sure they had plenty of other in-progress calls on a Friday night. So when do you want me to call your office?"

Johnson and Golden mulled this over for a minute before asking Dusty to call after 5 p.m. where he would likely get the answering service. If one of the secretaries or agents took the call during working hours, they might take it on themselves to locate RJ, thus cutting young Connor out of the discovery loop.

Cackling to themselves, Johnson and Golden joined their SRT compadres and began making a plan to take down the armed and fortified dwelling of a West St. Louis drug dealer named Jimmie Jones. Jimmie Jones was a common name for a criminal, and that fact created the case that would later go down in Customs lore as "the case of the wrong negro." Surveillance in all black neighborhoods was difficult for white cops. The best way to get eyes on target was to make a few cruises by concealed in back of a ratty old surveillance van driven by a black agent from the local field office. RJ and Max spent the rest of the day in the back of the van doing drive-bys, snapping photos, and making detailed sketches of the target.

It was about 5:45 when the first emergency page hit Johnson's pager. RJ could tell it was from Connor as he had appended his badge number to the office number. The series of 911s after Connor's badge number signified emergency, emergency, emergency. The trap had sprung.

Two minutes later Golden's pager went off with an identical page. Mere moments later Dusty Rhodes paged. How delicious!

By the time Johnson and Golden returned to the field office, their pagers had blown up with frantic pages from Connor. It satisfied the pair that the anxiety level was sufficiently painful. They did not call Connor back.

Instead they called Rhodes, and he reported that not only had he made the call to the Customs office, but as luck would have it, Connor had answered the call and he tried to spill his guts about the drunken evening at Blackbeard's to Rhodes. Rhodes, being a long-time undercover operator, picked up the thread and told Connor that he needed to speak with Agent Johnson before proceeding…leaving Connor to twist in the wind.

Johnson and Golden spent the next two weeks raising and lowering Connor's anxiety level. First it was a good thing that the Capital City PD investigator is long-time buddy Dusty Rhodes, and then it's a bad thing. An interview date was set for Max and Connor to go over to the PD, and then the interview got canceled twice. For Connor's benefit, RJ and Max acted out hushed conversations about Detective Rhodes who they made out to be a crooked cop. What did Rhodes want from them? They batted the trainee around like a pair of cats with a fatigued mouse.

On a Friday afternoon, Johnson grabbed Connor for the trip over to Capital City PD Investigations. Per RJ and Max's plan, Connor was caught off balance by the unscheduled trip to the PD and he voiced his concern that Golden might not be a part of the interview. Max Golden allegedly had a good relationship with the questionable Detective Rhodes. RJ was dismissive and told Connor, "Golden ain't around and it's time to get this done."

At the PD, one could only wonder what Connor was thinking when Johnson led him through the frosted glass door labeled "Homicide."

After checking in with the receptionist, Detective Rhodes came out to get Connor and sequestered him in an interview room.

At this point Johnson and Rhodes went back to the detective squad area and met up with Golden and Liz, already there awaiting Connor's "delivery" to Detective Rhodes. Liz had, after all, spent a frantic Friday night searching for the little delinquent, and she wanted to see justice served too. Rhodes took them to the video room and turned on the video feed from the interview room. "You want to make a tape of this?" Johnson and Golden emphatically nodded their heads.

The homicide dicks that worked with Rhodes were all in the know about the wayward rookie agent and the practical, yet educational joke that was being pulled on him. Four of them also crowded into the video room to watch the show. The anticipation was electric!

Rhodes was the consummate interviewer. His old down-home cowboy appearance and Oklahoma drawl was very disarming, and a surprising number of murderers had confessed their homicidal tale to him over the years. Young Connor did not understand that he was about to be questioned by a maestro.

On the video monitor, Connor fidgeted and looked about, seemingly oblivious to the possibility that he was being watched. He straightened up when he heard Rhodes opening the door. Rhodes was all business as he set a large case binder, evidence envelopes, and his coffee cup on the steel table that separated him from Connor. The thick binder implied that there was already a mountain of information related to the case.

He led Connor through a bunch of softball questions about where he grew up, his childhood, getting hired by Customs, how long he had been there and so forth. Then he circled back on college life and Connor's drinking habits while there. Soon Chip Connor was blabbing about Penn State fraternity parties and out of control drinking. Then Rhodes brought it around to drunken liaisons with girls during those wild parties. He asked Connor if he had ever been a little rough with girls when the drinks were flowing. Connor denied any bad behavior with women. Rhodes changed tack again and asked about the night at Blackbeard's, thumbing to various sections of his binder, always softly pounding away. Connor quickly admitted to being very drunk and to the run-in with the bouncers at Blackbeard's where he had displayed his badge and flashed his gun.

In what could have been a risky moment, Rhodes took Connor's badge and gun as proof of the confrontation, and placed them in evidence envelopes. Then Rhodes dropped the hammer. "So, Chip, you might be wondering what you're doing here in homicide, but I think you know." Rhodes opened the binder to a crime scene photo of a young woman sprawled out on the ground, clothes torn off, a bullet wound in the center of her naked chest. He spun the binder around for Connor to see. "What we need to talk about is this dead girl in the alley behind Blackbeard's. She was shot with a 9mm, the same caliber gun as the one I now have in this envelope."

A collective gasp is expelled by everyone watching the video monitor. If possible, the tension went even higher among the onlooking investigators! A staged knock on the outside of the interview door called Rhodes out of the tiny room. He was careful to take the "evidence" with him on his way out. On the video monitor the gathered cops watched as Connor, who had held up well so far, collapsed on the steel table in front of him. The observers heard his muffled voice. "I'm so fucked, I'm so fucked..." Johnson and Golden had intimated to him that Rhodes was perhaps a corrupt cop and could be dealt with. Connor must have wondered what had happened to that plan. Unknown to him, it was about to be played out perfectly.

Prior to that big day at the police department, Golden, Johnson, and Liz had hit ATMs for all the cash they could remove in a single day. Golden collected the cash and had it converted to crisp $100 bills.

Outside the interview room door, Rhodes and Golden acted out an argument for Connor's benefit. Rhodes opened the door, and Golden barged into the interview room right behind Rhodes, demanding to know what was going on. Golden proclaimed that he and Rhodes had a "deal."

Rhodes shrugged his shoulders and said, "I told you how much. I didn't hear from you, so here we are."

Golden fired back, "I got your fucking money!" and counted out a grand in hundreds. He grabbed Connor by the elbow and seized the evidence envelopes from Rhodes with his other hand. "We're out of here!"

Golden led Connor out of the homicide offices to the lobby. Connor was vapor locking, gasping for air. His face was a mass of splotches. Connor whined to Max Golden, "Did you just do what I think you did?"

Max raised an eyebrow. "Of course. I told you I could handle Rhodes. By the way, you owe me a thousand bucks." Connor nodded his head dumbly.

Moments later, they were joined by RJ, Liz, Rhodes, and all the homicide dicks who had watched the prank. It was quite a sight as they all stood there in the ornate 100-year-old lobby that served the various investigative divisions of Capital City PD. A bunch of grizzled murder investigators with something to smile about for a change. Liz, RJ, and Max with great big grins. It finally dawned on Connor that he had been the subject of a joke, that he was not going to jail, and he was not going to lose his job. His legs buckled, and Golden had to grab him to keep him upright.

Dusty Rhodes squared off to Connor and solemnly admonished him, "Your training agents went to a lot of trouble to teach you a lesson. You got your nuts crushed back in that interview room, and you deserved it. They could have just told your boss what you did at Blackbeard's and you would have been fired, but they didn't. Everybody standing here has done something stupid during their career. Every single one of us, but we all caught a break and we're all still here. This was your break, son. Don't count on another one."

Rhodes handed Connor the video cassette as a souvenir and assured him that no one outside of the homicide guys would ever know about what had happened there that day. He handed an envelope with the $1,000 of flash money back to Max. With that, Rhodes smiled and shook Connor's hand and wished him good luck in his career. All the homicide detectives did the same before wandering back to their desks.

Connor, despite his immature moments, understood that a bunch of veteran cops had taken the time to scare the crap out of him, and to teach him some lessons about the responsibilities of his job. For some reason, he felt that he was now part of that fraternity. He verbalized to Golden, Johnson, and Liz that he appreciated the fact that they had just scared the shit out of him versus doing the easy thing, which would have been reporting the incident to RAC Hubble. Johnson and Golden had just risked their veteran asses to keep his narrow rookie ass from being fired. He knew it, and he thanked them.

Detective Rhodes was wrong about no one ever finding out about the Blackbeard incident and the joke that followed. In the months ahead, the practical joke would become grossly misunderstood.

Kramden had been so mesmerized with the tale he had forgotten to move. His bum hip threatened to lock up. He got to his feet and groaned. "Jesus, you fuckers were evil! I'm surprised the rook didn't have a heart attack right there at the PD. How 'bout a refill anyone...while I'm up."

RJ *looked at his watch and puffed on his cigar. Quinn pointed to his drink, but* RJ *declined the refill. He had a story to tell and didn't know how much time it would take in the telling.* RJ *was moving toward the heart of what had separated Max from his Night Police comrades. The boys gathered at Solly's that night all knew the what,* RJ *was trying to supply the why. Max could still show, and he wanted to get to the end before Max's arrival.*

CHAPTER 27

The Forecast Calls for Pain

Soon enough, Connor headed back to FLETC to finish the second half of his training; the 10 weeks of Customs-specific training where he would learn about the nuances of Customs laws, drugs, smuggling, and undercover work.

As Golden and Johnson had hoped, when Connor returned to FLETC, he was a model student. Connor's progress pleased Golden and Johnson, and they congratulated themselves for giving the lad focus.

Connor became pals with Freddy Spanos, another trainee from Connor's own field division, and the two competed for the coveted "Top New Agent" award handed out for the academy student with the best academic, PT, and shooting scores. Somewhere along the way at FLETC, Connor heard that other agencies gave their top students "Choice of Office," and he conflated this to his own situation with Customs. That by coming out number 1 or 2, they should have allowed him to go to an office in New Jersey. Things continued to deteriorate with Cynthia.

Connor returned to Capital City on a Friday in late July. He picked up his G-ride and headed back to the BOQ at the Air Force base.

Monday morning was filled with administrative work for Golden and Johnson. Johnson was preparing for two weeks of Navy "Fork & Spoon" school, his indoctrination course for a commission in the Navy Reserve. Max got up to speed on RJ's cases as he would cover for RJ over a two-week absence.

Connor was filling out a massive travel voucher to cover the 10 weeks of FLETC/Customs academy. He needed to recover the money ASAP because in contravention to all the rules, he had been using his government travel card to fly up to New Jersey on the weekends to see Cynthia. Connor had also used up the $2,000 in investigative funds that Customs had provided him. He had to figure a way to replenish those funds as soon as possible. Chip Connor was in a financial mess. Between sessions at the IBM Selectric typewriter, Connor bugged Golden and Johnson about getting Customs to let him have his "Choice of Office."

The more tolerant Johnson finally snapped at Connor, "Christ, Chip! Do your fucking probation here in the Midwest, and then ask for a transfer. It's fucking New Jersey! Nobody wants fucking New Jersey! How hard is that?"

RJ may have been kinder if he had known that Connor had less than 24 hours to live.

The following morning Johnson had his best court suit on, and he had shined his shoes to a high gloss. He was to be sworn in that morning at the Navy Recruiting Office. After the ceremony and paperwork, Johnson met Max and Connor at their favorite Mexican restaurant, Raul's. Johnson and Golden were downing celebratory margaritas on the rocks.

Connor was matching them drink for drink with melancholy beers. Connor sulked over being stuck in the boring center of the country, and Johnson's new military commission seemed to have ripped the scab off of his failed Army Ranger career.

After a four margarita lunch, the agents agreed to fuck off the rest of the day. Johnson was going home to lose the suit, and Golden and Connor were going back to the Customs office to wrap up. The trio agreed to regroup at the gym for a workout and a foreshortened workday.

Back at the Customs office there was a public reception area with pictures of Bush Senior and the Secretary of the Treasury. On the other side of the door and bulletproof glass a secretary's desk, word processor, etc. There was the steady drone of office life. Phones ringing. Conversations in offices, the Xerox machine thrashed away.

Amid this, a single gunshot shattered the office hum!

It altered the lives of all 12 persons present in the office for all time. The body of 24-year-old Special Agent Chip Connor lay dead on the floor, the through and through wound to his skull was pumping blood out onto the carpeted floor.

Special Agent Max Golden called 911 and in a quaking voice reported, "My partner has just been shot. Please send somebody fast!"

In the stunned silence after the gunshot, as if in slow motion, a knot of agents formed at the doorway of the office. Some had their guns drawn. The crumpled body on the floor stopped them from entering, that and one look at Agent Golden seated behind his desk, in shock.

Someone kneeled by the body to start first aid, but the steady voice of Agent Gus Knox stopped them. "Leave him be. He's gone."

Gus was the oldest agent in the office and in his many lives he had been a combat medic in Vietnam and later an ambulance attendant while he worked his way through college. If Gus said the guy was gone, he was gone.

Johnson was just headed out of the front door of his house in sweats with a gym bag in hand when the kitchen phone rang. It was Agent Romanowski calling from the office. "Ron, you need to get back here quick. Chip is dead."

Johnson told Romo to knock it off and join them all at the gym. Romanowski could not convince Johnson that anything had happened to Connor. Romo got Golden on the phone with Johnson. Within a second of hearing Golden's voice Johnson knew that something bad had happened. "I'm on my way!"

RAC Hubble was in the office at the time of the shooting. He had always been a worthless slug, and this day was no different.

Hubble devolved into a whimpering slob. "Oh, God, I told them boys not to play with guns," as though he was already building a defense to what had happened. "They will put a stamp on my ass and transfer me to DC," he moaned.

Gus Knox took charge of the scene.

The two secretaries were near hysteria when Gus intercepted them in the passageway. He led them back to their desks up front and calmly told them, "I'm going to need some help from you girls. Don't fall apart on me. There will be a lot of people here in a few minutes—paramedics, firemen, policemen. I need you here to open both doors for them. Chrissy, you open doors. Linda, try to keep a log going of who comes and goes. That will be hard, but try."

Later no one could remember who picked up the five-shot Smith and Wesson, opened its cylinder, and placed it on Agent Golden's desk.

As Gus had predicted, the relative quiet of shocked aftermath transformed into a tidal wave of first responders. Firemen in their rustling turnout gear and walkie-talkies, paramedics with a rolling gurney, oxygen bottles, and finally some uniformed policemen. There were a few minutes of chaos as firemen and paramedics came to the same conclusion that Gus had formed several minutes earlier. Special Agent Chip Connor was deceased. It was now a dead body that had died by violent means and was the purview of the police. Customs could have had the investigation because it was the death of a federal agent, but in reality the local cops had more expertise.

A police sergeant was now on scene along with four patrolmen. The sergeant quickly put out a "no further assistance needed" to stop the onslaught of cops responding to a reported shooting at a federal law enforcement office. As it was, 15 patrol cars choked the block around the office building. At first glance the gunshot looked to be self-inflicted, but the one agent who had witnessed the shooting was a basket case and unable to provide much help.

Sergeant Ricci used a landline in the Customs office to call dispatch to deliver an update and to request the on-call homicide detective. It was not up to a street cop, even an experienced sergeant like Ricci to determine cause of death.

Detective Dusty Rhodes was the on-call, and he had just cleared the county courthouse when his pager went off. During the short drive over to the federal office he was filled with a bad feeling that caused his tormented stomach to knot up even more. He knew most of the agents in that office, and was close friends with two of them, Special Agents Max Golden and Ron Johnson.

Rhodes met the sergeant in the secretarial area of the Customs office and learned what he could, then he went to the office where two patrolmen stood guard at the doorway. They nodded to Rhodes as he moved between them to take in the scene. He recognized the rookie agent on the floor. The last time he had seen him alive, shaken but visibly relieved, had been in the detective's office lobby during the denouement of what had been a great practical joke and an object lesson for the rookie. That was just a few months ago.

Rhodes got on the phone and called over to his boss in homicide. "Hey, Skipper. Yeah, I'm here. I got to ask you to send somebody else over on this one."

"How come? Uniforms on scene said that it looked like a suicide."

"Not necessarily, boss, and I know the deceased and the potential shooter, so I'm out of this one. Better get a crew here to interview everyone in the office. It looks complicated. You'll want the best evidence people you can get."

RJ made a red lights and siren run from his home to the office. All the police and fire rigs double parked around the building confirmed the horrible truth.

After badging his way past the uniformed cops, Johnson made it into the inner office. Before he could make it to Golden, homicide detective Dusty Rhodes intercepted him and shoved him into an empty office. Rhodes grabbed Johnson by his suit lapels and whispered to him, "You need to tell Max to shut up! And you need to get him an attorney ASAP! He is in trouble here!"

With that, he led Johnson to another office cleared out for the purpose of sequestering Golden. Max was a mess, but he rose and threw his arms around his buddy, clutching him and sobbing.

Agent Romanowski came in a few minutes later and Johnson gave him an urgent task. "Call any local cop you know and get the name and a number for their Fraternal Order of Police attorney. We're not FOP, but I'll figure out the money! Max needs an attorney and damn fast."

Moments later the Capital City PD homicide lieutenant and Detective Rhodes motioned Johnson to leave the room. Out in the hall the lieutenant explained that they needed to take Golden to the PD to question him. After some back-and-forth Johnson and Rhodes convinced the lieutenant to let Johnson drive Golden over to the PD.

As he led Golden out of the office, Johnson got one last look at Connor's lifeless body, eyes sightless, a huge pool of blood surrounding his head.

Once in the car Johnson asked Golden what the fuck had happened.

Max laid out the scenario for RJ. When he and Connor returned to the office, Connor had started up again about "Office of Choice" and needing to be near Cynthia. Connor disparaged the Midwest in general and the people there in particular. He whined that he had no friends, and he didn't want to make friends with a bunch of hillbillies. Max was trying to finish some last-minute paperwork so they could make their early exit from the office, but Connor continued his whining. Max reached his boiling point and yelled, "If your life is so bad, why don't you just kill yourself?"

Angry and frustrated with Connor, Max unloaded his five-shot backup gun save one round, spun the cylinder and pointed it at Connor's head. According to Max, Connor dared Max to pull the trigger. When Max didn't, Connor reached up and tried to pull the trigger. They struggled for a minute, and the gun went off.

Johnson took it all in and told his buddy, "Okay, pal, I got it, but you need to shut up now and not say anything until you have an attorney. We're trying like hell to get you one. You got that? Can you do that?"

In RJ's mind it was a tragic perfect storm. A clash of two dynamic personalities. Only Connor and Max could have engaged in such a deadly dance. It could not have happened with any other pair of agents. Max Golden with his many domestic pressures, unhappy with being back in the field office. Chip Connor who didn't give a fuck about anything except getting home to New Jersey. Connor could, however, gain some status by standing up to Golden's challenge.

At Capital City PD Homicide, Golden was placed in an interview room by the homicide lieutenant, ironically the same one where the practical joke on Connor had been videotaped just a couple of months before. None of the homicide detectives were smiling now. Now the rookie was dead and the agent in the locked interview room may have been the shooter. They all felt sick inside.

Golden held his mud with the homicide lieutenant and one of the other senior homicide dicks. He told them he wanted to help, but figured he should at least consult a lawyer first. Johnson and Rhodes watched it all from the video feed room. The same room where they had videotaped the practical joke on Connor.

Johnson had called Romo back at the Customs office and verified that the local FOP attorney was on his way to the homicide office. Johnson so informed the lieutenant and was rewarded with a sour look.

The FOP attorney arrived about 40 minutes later and gave Golden the same advice that his partner had. "Shut up."

The attorney spent some time with the lieutenant, and Johnson overheard the lieutenant state that they were booking Golden on unspecified homicide charges.

A few minutes later Johnson and the attorney huddled. "Your partner made some pretty damaging admissions to the uniform cops before they brought him here. He doesn't need me right now. He won't be talking to the detectives tonight, but he will need a criminal defense attorney soon."

Johnson had a few minutes alone with Max and told him he would find a criminal defense guy for him. He told him to hang tough until they could get him bailed. Golden asked Johnson to explain things as best as possible to his wife.

Back at the Customs office, it was night time, and a lot had happened. The police and the coroner were gone and Chip's body had been removed. An industrial cleanup crew in chemical suits ran their machines over the carpet in the office that Golden and the old-timer Gus had shared. Another team worked on the blood-spattered wall.

The Special Agent in Charge from St. Louis had come down and was there in the Customs office managing the myriad of things that had to be done after the death of an agent. He was one of the good guys, and his compassion was real. The SAC asked Johnson what had transpired over at the PD. Johnson explained to the SAC that Max had been booked after meeting with a lawyer. RJ, not fully comprehending the dynamics, asked the SAC if Golden could come back to work if the PD figured out that the whole thing was an accident or a suicide on Connor's part. The SAC seemed to understand where Johnson was coming from, but shook his head from side to side saying, "Ron, Max will never come back to Customs."

Johnson had one last shit job to do before the evening was over and that was to go see Golden's wife. Johnson had to work through some language issues and the emotions when he delivered the bad news to Akiko. They ended up holding on to each other and crying in the Goldens' living room. Johnson assured her he would keep her posted and that the next step was to find Max a good attorney and get him bailed out.

The next morning Dusty Rhodes got a hold of Johnson and told him to contact Clive Barnes. RJ knew Barnes as an accomplished defense attorney who had defended several high-profile clients in federal court. Nobody enjoyed being cross-examined by Clive Barnes, but he wasn't a crook like so many of the high-profile narco attorneys were. Johnson, not wanting to mope around the Customs office with the other mopers, made the short drive to Barnes' office.

It was one of the smartest things he ever did. Rhodes had teed Barnes up for Johnson, and when he arrived Barnes had cleared his calendar. He turned out to be one of the good guys. A former Army Staff Sergeant with a 12-month 'Nam tour to his credit. He did his Army time after graduating from college, refusing a commission. He wanted to do his two years as a draftee and go home. And eventually to law school.

Barnes was a take-charge kind of guy and informed Johnson that he was on the case and that they needed to get Golden out of the county jail as soon as possible. "My name isn't worth a damn in this town if I can't get a bail bondsman to post bail for Max on my word."

From that moment on, Johnson felt that his partner was in the best of hands.

On Thursday Golden was released, based upon a hasty habeas corpus writ filed by Barnes. He hadn't needed a bail bondsman at all. The prosecutor didn't know what charge he wanted to file on Golden and therefore didn't fight it.

Max went home and finished burning his life down to the foundation. Golden informed his wife it was over. He told her about the year-long affair he had been having. While Akiko stood in the living room like a statue, Golden packed a few things. Later that day he moved into a cheap motel.

Just days after the shooting, Johnson had to report to Officer Candidate School back east. Horrible timing, but military orders were not negotiable. En route to the Navy school in Rhode Island, RJ stopped in New Jersey to attend a memorial for Chip Connor. There RJ met the family and Chip's old girlfriend Cynthia. The family was in shock, and surprisingly they didn't have many questions. They appreciated Johnson being there.

While RJ was learning how to be a proper Naval Officer, Customs Internal Affairs descended on the Cap City field office and they were looking for answers. Lesser agents spilled all they knew about Connor and the antics of Johnson and Golden. What they didn't know they were happy to guess at, whether related to Connor's death or not.

When Johnson returned from Officer Candidate School two weeks later, he was walking into a trap. Romanowski, only mid-twenties but wise beyond his years, grabbed up Johnson before the IA guys could start on him.

Romo told Johnson, "They know everything. They have everything. Fucking rats in this office made up what they didn't know. They're looking for a scapegoat big time. Connor is dead, Golden is going to jail. You are it!"

Johnson spent a week in interviews with IA. Romo was right, the IA bubbas were loaded for bear. All Johnson could do was try to debunk or deflect the allegations of wrongdoing. Chip Connor had shared many of the exploits of Johnson and Golden with friends and family, painting a picture of wild, flamboyant agents working on the edge of the law. It would have been easy to lay it all on Golden, but RJ couldn't.

Connor's FLETC buddy Spanos did a job nobody ever wants to do. He went through his late friend Connor's things before returning them to the family. Spanos was smart enough to look for things that could embarrass or disappoint the family. He discovered the unlabeled souvenir videotape of the Capital City PD prank and at first thought the unmarked tape might be porno. After playing it, he knew different.

Freddy Spanos didn't know what the tape meant, but he was one of the new breed of college student magically morphed into federal investigator. He was hurting over the death of his FLETC buddy Chip Connor, and the concept of never ratting to IA was not ingrained in him like it would have been to someone who had been a real cop. Spanos had heard all about Golden and Johnson from Connor. According to Connor, Golden and Johnson were super-agents who followed no rulebook. As Freddy viewed and reviewed the tape, he could only speculate about the circumstances of Connor's apparent arrest, and Golden barging into the interview to buy his release. None of it made any sense. Why would Connor have a videotape of such an event? Then Spanos did what no Night Policeman would ever do. He turned the tape over to IA. Now IA had video proof of some very questionable behavior.

Back in the Customs office, rumors swirled; Connor had committed suicide, there had been a game of Russian roulette, Max Golden was drunk and straight up shot Connor in the head. The truth was, nobody besides Max Golden and Chip Connor would ever know what happened that horrible day. Both Golden and Connor had gunshot residue on their hands, but that only supported the fact that they both had hands near the gun when it went off. It couldn't determine who pulled the trigger.

IA pulled Johnson in again and asked about the contents of the tape. Johnson tried to explain the practical joke, but IA didn't buy his explanation. They saw something more sinister and turned the tape over to the district attorney along with their theories. IA now had a lead to another mystery. Seeing Golden count the money out in the video underscored the fact that no one could find the $2,000 cash in investigative funds that Connor should have had in his possession. Was the missing money part of some intricate bribe scheme played out on the videotape? In fact,

Connor had spent the $2,000 of government funds during his weekend trips home to New Jersey from the academy.

From their interviews with the office toadies, Internal Affairs had a picture of Max Golden as a man living beyond his means. Had Golden somehow ended up with the kid's undercover money? Was Golden extorting money from the kid because he had bailed him out of some arrest scenario with the police?

Were the cops corrupt like the tape seemed to show? These dark suspicions seemed confirmed when the PD homicide dicks were lukewarm to the Customs IA guys when they turned over the videotape. In reality, their lack of enthusiasm was embarrassment on the part of the homicide detectives. How would they explain a homicide detective, a homicide suspect, and a homicide victim all together in a homicide interview room two months prior to the homicide? The district attorney failed to see any humor or redeeming intentions.

Johnson and Liz were set to get married on Saturday of that week. The date had been chosen more than a year earlier. By mid-week, RJ offered to Liz that she might want to reconsider. It was more than likely that Customs would fire him in the very near future.

The district attorney thought he now had on the tape all the motive he needed. Corruption and money. Their buddy Max was re-arrested. When he was originally booked on the night of the shooting, the DA was unsure of what to charge Max with and Max's attorney was able to get him out the next day. This time the charges were first-degree murder. Clive Barnes had to engage the bail bondsman to keep Golden out of pretrial confinement.

For a few moments, the air seemed to have been sucked out of the small room where the brothers gathered that night.

"The fucking videotape," Kramden gasped. "A tape of a fucking joke! Couldn't they see it was a fucking joke?"

Rimjob, who had plenty of experience with trouble, was uncharacteristically serious. "Bet the fucking homicide dicks shit when that tape surfaced."

RJ relit his dormant cigar. "Yeah, that took some explaining. It all added to the distrust between agencies. The DA's office was already worried about the PD, what with the homicide guys being involved with Connor and Golden. Customs IA started thinking the homicide dicks were corrupt after they saw Golden count out a grand to Rhodes on the videotape. The homicide guys being real cops, thought the Customs IA guys were douchebags. The upshot of the deal was the Customs IA gumshoes became the DA's investigative team."

RJ was still wondering why Golden hadn't arrived, yet thankful that he could finish the story in Golden's absence. He picked up the pace to get to the end…

CHAPTER 28

The Aftermath

It split the office down the middle in the months after the shooting. Some were happy to put the boots to Golden, either out of jealousy or anger over forcing them to confront violent death in the safe bubble of their office. Others saw it as a stupid tragedy. A perfect storm between Connor and Golden where no one won and everybody lost.

As part of his termination review, Johnson would read the statements of all of his fellow agents. It was nothing that he would expect from fellow cops, and the disappointment would last the rest of his days.

Only his informants held their mud. IA tracked down every single one of Johnson's informants and questioned them about any wrongdoing by Johnson or Golden. ZZ led off the parade, and was a stud, but to a man they all swore that Johnson had been nothing but professional. They all had the good sense not to mention the drinking, driving, fucking, fighting, and hell raising that went with undercover work.

RJ held on to his job despite a recommendation for termination by Internal Affairs. A sympathetic Special Agent in Charge, and former wild man himself, intervened for Johnson.

Attorney Barnes elected to go with a court trial, a judge but no jury. His theory was to own all the batshit crazy antics of Golden and Johnson. No jury would understand the outlandish behavior of those engaged in UC work and the bizarre things that went on daily while kicking down hundreds of meth labs. The bottom line of Barnes' defense strategy: Golden was an effective, sometimes wild, undercover narcotics agent, but he had not murdered Connor.

The prank video taken at Capital City PD was the centerpiece of the prosecution's case. They portrayed Max Golden as a rogue agent torturing his hapless trainee. The DA hammered away about Connor's missing agent cashier money, sowing the seeds of doubt about theft, extortion, or worse.

Johnson testified to help Golden by revealing the stupid and often immature behavior of Connor, and how, contrary to the prosecution's theory, Johnson and Golden had covered for the kid, and had tried to straighten him out. Tough love. Connor's family had enough time to become bitter and angry. They ass-eyed Johnson throughout the trial.

RJ's testimony for his buddy Max was not without cost. IA sat through the entire trial and learned of previously uncovered transgressions by Golden and Johnson. Golden was no longer an agent, and thus beyond the reach of IA; however, they made another case on Johnson based on his failure to report Connor's rule-violating behavior to RAC Hubble. Internal Affairs recommended firing Johnson again.

The judge bought Barnes' theory to a point, but as he addressed Max at the conclusion of the trial he stated that regardless of who pulled the trigger, it was Max's gun and Max had introduced the gun into the situation. The judge handed down a guilty verdict for a lesser charge of negligent homicide. Better than murder one, but not good for Golden.

Maxie was still out on bail, and he told RJ that he would run. He had his German passport, and he had the French Foreign Legion as an option. He didn't need to return to the United States. Ever.

Golden manned the fuck up, he didn't run. He seemed to know that he would have to atone for what he did, or never be able to face himself in the mirror again. The judge accommodated and sentenced Maxie to 10 years in prison for the death of Chip Connor.

The prison system wanted to place Max in Administrative Segregation, a relatively safe place for former cops and anyone else likely to get killed while in custody. Max refused it and chose to gut it out in general population. He knew there was no credit for good time if doing time in Administrative Segregation. He was a tough motherfucker.

RJ was done. "You guys know Maxie was released from prison 10 days ago. He did five years in general population. He has a five-year parole tail yet to deal with."

Quinn ran his hand through his wiry steel-gray hair, his eyes misty. "He's still our brother," he croaked.

Rimjob drained off his rye and nodded his support.

Kramden leaned toward RJ and put a hand on his shoulder. "Thanks for sharing that, my brother. I know that last bit wasn't easy. Anything we can we do to help Maxie? A job? I can get him into the union. Even if he—"

Tino appeared in the doorway, stopping Kramden mid-sentence. "Maxie called. Said to offer his regrets, but he had something important to do." Every man in the room focused on the words slipping from Tino's lips. "Something about getting right with the man?"

For once The Night Police fell silent.

RJ jumped up. "Aw, fuck!"

He dashed past Tino, vaulting the bar to get to the phone behind it. He punched in the number for the Seneca Hotel and barked at the clerk to be connected to Golden's room. The phone rang. And rang, and rang…

ACKNOWLEDGEMENTS

Writing a book was more of a challenge than we expected but it was also a hell of a lot more fun and rewarding than we might have imagined. The Night Police would never have happened without the love and support of our families and our brotherhood in law enforcement and the U.S. Coast Guard.

Thank you, to our families and friends:

Janet, Kelsey, Lamoyne, Michele & Jessica, the Trapper and Randella.

Pat & Suzy, Sgt. Baldini, Deano, Brooksie, Christie, Craig, the Guh-nome, Jerry, Glitz, D-White, Frank James, 1B & 2B, Cliff, Beverage & Evans, Kipper, Dudley, Head, Tommy & Milli, Rinna, TR Navin, Momma, Tomato & Mrs. Face, Walleye, Cookie, TK, Keech, Sharoni, T-stead, Big Bob, La Prevotte and Woodie.

A very special thanks to those committed early on and became our readers providing commentary, advice and counsel:

Brother Coast Guard officers; CDR Charlie, and CAPT Tom, SGT/LCDR Brett Linden, San Jose PD, retired, USCGR, retired.

Randy Berg Kirwan and LT Gil Berg, California Fish and Game, retired… from day one!

For Liz Spitzer who saved everything from day one and said "There must be a book!"

To CAPT Robert Hanley, USCGR, retired, thank you for taking that first plunge, guiding and encouraging us, suggesting this was worth doing.

And finally, thank you to Kali Roberts who helped us navigate the Social Media jungle.

ABOUT THE AUTHORS

Chris Berg

In 1977 Chris became the third generation of his family to sign on as a lawman. Serving as a patrol officer, evidence technician (long before CSI was a thing), and vice/intelligence detective it was his posting as an undercover narcotics agent that fit him best. He relished the life of hand to hand undercover drug "buys", clandestine lab investigations and the requisite counterfeit persona. Chris still revels in the adventures and friendships that come with being part of the police fraternity.

After retiring due to injury, Chris had a successful second career in corporate America and… it bored him to death. The high point of that life was traveling the world; Malaysia, Dubai, Beijing, Moscow, Rio, Hong Kong and much more. Still, that world was never a fit, not for an ex-Night Policeman.

Chris and his wife Janet now call northern California and Boston home. Their daughter Kelsey, currently in grad school, is likely the fourth generation of law enforcement in the family. Chris keeps up with his passions: baseball, fishing, and all things cooking and BBQ, not necessarily in that order.

Paul James Smith

Paul served community and country in a variety of pursuits from age 19 to age 59. After completely flunking out at San Diego State, a Marine Corps recruiter handily outsmarted him, and he fell for the old "aviation guarantee". This launched a long and checkered career of service as enlisted marine, a local lawman, Federal Agent, and reserve Coast Guard officer where his assignments included command of two expeditionary units, Commander, Maritime Security Force, Guantanamo Bay, and four wartime deployments to the Persian Gulf.

Paul's 31 years of cop experiences ran the gamut-Patrolman, Field Training Officer, SWAT, Detective, Federal Agent, Sniper and Sniper Instructor, and National Tactical Team Leader. The cases were varied too; seizing meth labs, busting outlaw motorcycle gangsters, and special operations at Ruby Ridge and Waco.

After retiring from active service, Paul and his wife Kay ran a gun shop in Alaska for a few years. He built custom rifles, and they collectively lost their minds to boredom. They now live at the edge of Puget Sound in the Pacific Northwest, he writes, she gardens, together they go Dungeness crabbing from their kayak. They are enjoying life to the fullest.

Find us at www.nightpolice.com and write us at thenightpolicenovels@gmail.com.